HUSH
LITTLE
GIRL

BOOKS BY LISA REGAN

Vanishing Girls
The Girl With No Name
Her Mother's Grave
Her Final Confession
The Bones She Buried
Her Silent Cry
Cold Heart Creek
Find Her Alive
Save Her Soul
Breathe Your Last

HUSH
LITTLE
GIRL

LISA REGAN

Bookouture

Published by Bookouture in 2021

An imprint of Storyfire Ltd.
Carmelite House
50 Victoria Embankment
London EC4Y 0DZ

www.bookouture.com

ISBN: 978-1-80019-138-9
eBook ISBN: 978-1-80019-137-2

In loving memory of Dr. Chris Justofin, who saved my life, and for Dr. Katherine Dahlsgaard, who saved the life of someone I love.

PROLOGUE

Neither Josie nor Noah had time to brace for impact. The deer shot out of the trees to their left, a blur of faded brown. Its body met the front end of Noah's new Chevrolet with perfectly imperfect timing. The hood of the car smashed inward like an aluminum soda can. Noah had no time to brake. Both their bodies launched forward. The seatbelt snapped taut across Josie's body and her head whipped forward and back, leaving her disoriented. Blinking away the mind fog, she looked ahead to see a tendril of smoke rising from the compacted hood of the car. Noah's voice floated over to her from the driver's seat. "Josie? You okay? Josie?"

She turned her head toward him, flinching at the pain that streaked from the base of her skull down her neck. Blood trickled from a small cut on Noah's forehead. Reaching toward him, she said, "You're bleeding."

He wiped the sleeve of his jacket across his head. "I'm fine," he said. "Are you?"

Josie's mind started to kick back into gear, catching up with her body. Other than her neck, everything felt okay. "I'm getting out," she said.

She undid her seatbelt and tried to open the door, but it was stuck.

Noah said, "The frame bent. You'll have to get out my side."

He unlatched his seatbelt and got out, extending a hand inside the car to help pull Josie clear. It was late January, and the weather had been miserable for days. Gray clouds hung low and heavy over the city of Denton, occasionally gracing them with a dusting of snow. On the shoulder of the road, Josie pulled her coat tighter around her and looked up and down the winding mountain road. All they could see were trees and a ribbon of asphalt stretching miles in either direction.

Noah said, "We're at least three miles from Harper's Peak."

"More like five," Josie told him. She pointed in the direction they'd been headed—back into the city. "Two more miles into town."

The city of Denton was nestled in a valley in Central Pennsylvania along the banks of the Susquehanna River. Most of its thirty thousand residents lived in the main area of town where neighborhoods were grouped closely together. However, in its entirety, the city spanned twenty-five square miles and encompassed the rural areas all around it. Lonely, winding roads like the one they were on snaked outward from the city proper and into the mountains in every direction.

Josie and Noah walked toward the front of the car where the deer lay on its side, unmoving. There was no visible injury, but Josie knew the impact had likely been enough to kill it. She took a few steps closer, noting that it had no antlers and its abdomen was swollen. "Good God," she said. "I hope this isn't a mommy deer."

Noah drew up closer behind her and placed a hand on her shoulder. "Don't get too close," he said. "If she's still alive and springs up, she could hurt you."

Josie made no move to walk away. Instead, she stared at the doe, a sadness swirling around her insides, stirring up old feelings best left dormant.

"Josie," Noah said. "It was an accident."

"I know," she said. It certainly wasn't the first time either of them had hit a deer on the road. In Central Pennsylvania, accidents like this were a given. She wasn't sure why this one bothered her so much.

"Do you think it's bad luck?" she blurted, as icy rain began to spit from the sky.

Noah said, "What do you mean?"

She turned to him. Blood gathered in a fat bead along the cut on his forehead and slid down toward his right eye. Again, he swiped at it with his sleeve.

Josie fished a crumpled tissue from her jeans pocket. She slid her free hand around to the back of his head, threading her fingers through his thick, brown hair, and pressed the tissue to his forehead with the other hand, keeping pressure on it. His breath came out in a puff, the cold air making it visible. She said, "We're on our way home from finalizing our wedding plans, and we hit a deer. Maybe a deer about to have a fawn."

Noah put his hands on her shoulders and smiled at her. "We've had all the bad luck that two people can have already, don't you think?"

Josie lifted the tissue and saw the bleeding had stopped. Dropping her arms, she looked into his hazel eyes. They had known each other for over seven years, dated for three years, and in that time, hell had been visited upon them both many times over. Maybe he was right.

He took the tissue from her and kissed her forehead. "Don't read anything into this. With all the times we've been back and forth to Harper's Peak in the last three months, it would be weird if we *didn't* hit something." Again, he glanced up and down the empty road. "I didn't see any residences or businesses or anything on the way back from Harper's Peak, though. No one we could ask for help."

Josie took her cell phone from her pocket and tried calling one of her team. Both of them worked for the Denton Police Department, Noah as a lieutenant and Josie as a detective. Josie knew that the other detectives on the force, Gretchen Palmer and Finn Mettner, would come help them at a moment's notice. "I can't get any service," she said. "Let me see your phone."

He handed it to her. "Try making a hot spot."

Josie tried making hot spots with both their phones but got nothing. No internet, no service at all. She walked back and forth along the road, holding the phones in the air, trying to get a signal, but there was nothing. They were in a dead zone.

Noah held out his hand for his phone and Josie returned it. "You stay with the car. I'll walk toward town and keep trying to get a signal. If I get any bars, I'll call Gretchen or Mettner. If I don't, I'll stop at the first house I see and ask to use the landline," he said.

"I'll go with you," said Josie.

"It's cold," he said. "It's starting to sleet. Stay in the car where you'll be dry and somewhat warm. I can cover two miles in no time."

Under her coat, her body shivered. The icy rain had turned heavy and wet. Each drop that splattered into her black hair plastered her locks to her head. She looked at the car, longing to get back in. "Do you feel dizzy?" she asked him. "Light-headed?"

Noah laughed softly. "I'm not concussed, if that's what you're worried about. Get in the car. I'll be as quick as I can."

Josie kissed him before climbing back into the driver's seat. It wasn't much warmer inside the car now that the engine was off—and now that it had been totaled—but it was wonderfully dry. She watched Noah jog down the road until the sleet against the window blurred him into a dark speck. Then he disappeared.

Again, she tried to get service on her phone, but there was nothing. A few minutes after Noah vanished from the horizon, she heard a noise that made her insides quiver. Josie climbed out of the car and went back to the deer. It lifted its head from the ground and emitted a high-pitched mewling that went right through Josie's bones.

Agony.

"Shit," she said, looking around. Everything in her wanted to respond to the sound of the animal's pain with action. If it were a person, she'd be on the ground rendering aid or at least comfort, but that wasn't possible. There was no choice but to stand by and listen to the poor doe's last noises. They were both helpless—animal and woman. Josie hated that feeling more than any other feeling in the world.

By the time she registered the sound of a vehicle approaching behind her, she could barely swallow over the lump in her throat. Turning, she saw an old, white pickup pulling up behind Noah's car. Its engine idled loudly. At the back of the inside of the truck cab, affixed to a gun rack, was a shotgun. The driver put the four-way emergency blinkers on and hopped out, leaving the gun behind. A woman in her early fifties walked toward Josie. She was taller than Josie and curvy, wearing faded jeans, heavy boots, and a thick rain jacket. Her long, curly brown hair was threaded with gray. Brow furrowed, she said, "You okay, miss?"

Josie motioned toward the deer and explained what had happened.

The woman extended a hand and Josie shook it. "Lorelei Mitchell," she said.

"Josie Quinn."

Josie waited for a spark of recognition. She was semi-famous in Denton for having solved some cases that were so shocking, they'd gained national news coverage. Also, her twin sister was a famous journalist. But Lorelei Mitchell only said, "How long ago did your fiancé walk off?"

Josie took her phone out to check the time but realized she didn't know. She'd been too upset about the deer to keep track of how long it had been. She felt as though she'd been standing alone on the road with the keening animal for hours, but it was probably less than five minutes. "I'm not sure," she told Lorelei. "Maybe ten, fifteen minutes?"

Lorelei pointed to her truck. "Why don't you hop in? My place is back less than a half a mile. I get cell service there, believe it or not. I've also got a landline you can use to call for help."

"We didn't see any houses," Josie pointed out.

Lorelei smiled. "I know. The driveway's hidden. I like my privacy."

"Thank you," Josie said. "But if it's all the same to you, I'd rather wait for my fiancé."

"I don't normally recommend that women get into vehicles with strangers, but I promise you'll be safe with me," Lorelei added.

Josie smiled tightly. "I appreciate that, but I can wait."

Lorelei was quiet long enough for the deer's cries to fill Josie's ears again. She went back to her truck. Again, Josie's attention was drawn to the gun, although she didn't know why. But Lorelei didn't even glance at the gun. Instead, she returned with a photo in her hand. An actual photograph on glossy paper. She handed it to Josie. "Those are my girls. They're eight and twelve. They're waiting back at the house for me. It's just us. Hence all the privacy. Got to keep them safe. Come with me. You can meet them, make some calls, and wait in a nice warm, dry house until help comes. I'll even feed you."

The deer's cries had slowed somewhat but they were still loud and piercing. Josie tore her gaze away from its tortured eyes, wanting to look at anything else but the dying animal. She stared at the photograph. Both girls had shoulder-length brown hair. The younger girl's hair was poker-straight, but the older girl's was curly like Lorelei's. "The youngest is Emily," Lorelei said. "The older one is Holly."

In the photo, Holly had one arm wrapped protectively around Emily's shoulder. Emily gave a toothy grin. Holly's smile was closed-lipped but no less infectious. They wore matching T-shirts with a drawing of a sloth and underneath, the words: *My Spirit Animal*. Josie gave a little laugh.

"Cute, aren't they?" Lorelei said with a grin.

Josie was about to hand the photo back when she noticed Holly's eyelashes. They were completely white.

Lorelei took a step closer and pointed at Holly's face. "You're looking at her eyelashes, right?" she said. "It's okay. Everyone notices. She has poliosis."

Josie could barely hear over the deer. She looked up at Lorelei. "What?"

"Poliosis. It's a genetic thing. Harmless. Just the absence of melanin in your hair or eyelashes. She hates it, but I think it makes her look striking."

Josie gave her the photo. "I'm sorry. I can't—I can't concentrate. Yes, let's go back to the house."

"Get in," Lorelei told her.

Josie climbed into the truck and strapped herself in. Lorelei got in and turned the truck around, doing a three-point turn in the middle of the road. They could still hear the suffering deer. Before she pulled away, she put the truck back in park and said, "Hold on."

Lorelei turned her body, reaching into the back seat and riffling around. Before Josie could ask any questions, she was out of the truck, her shotgun in her hand. Josie twisted in her seat, noticing two boxes of ammunition on the floor in the back. One box was open and a shell was missing. Her fingers punched at the seatbelt release button so she could get out and go after Lorelei.

A gunshot boomed, echoing all around them. The keening stopped. Josie sat completely frozen in her seat. Seconds later, Lorelei got back into the truck. Securing the shotgun to the rack behind their heads, she offered Josie a smile. "I'll call the game commission when we get to my place."

"You shot her," Josie said.

"She was suffering, and no one was going to save her. No one could save her."

Josie stared at her, open-mouthed.

Lorelei put the truck in drive and pulled back onto the road. "You can't stop it, you know."

"Suffering?" Josie said.

Lorelei laughed. "Well, that, too, yes, but I meant death. You can't stop death."

CHAPTER ONE

Three Months Later

Josie stared at herself in the full-sized, freestanding mirror, barely recognizing the woman who stared back. She had chosen a simple, strapless wedding dress with a long, lacy train that she could sweep up into a bustle. Her mother Shannon had said it looked like something a Grecian goddess would wear. Josie liked the simplicity and elegance of it, as well as the mobility it allowed her. As a detective for the city of Denton, Pennsylvania, Josie was used to wearing khaki pants and polo shirts. Work never seemed to slow down, and she rarely got to dress up other than for funerals. Pushing that thought out of her mind, she ran her hands down over her hips. This was a happy day.

She turned her head from side to side. Her twin sister, Trinity Payne, a famous journalist who lived in New York City, had brought both a make-up artist and a hair stylist to Denton to work on Josie as well as the members of Josie's bridal party, which consisted of Trinity, Josie's friend, Misty Derossi, and Josie's friend and colleague, Detective Gretchen Palmer. The make-up artist and hairdresser had done a remarkable job. Josie's black locks had been pulled up and twisted into a chignon. Her skin glowed. Even the thin scar that ran down the right side of her face from her ear to beneath her chin, was almost invisible. The photographer that Trinity had also chosen flitted around her, taking pictures from every angle.

A hand squeezed her shoulder and Trinity's face appeared behind her in the mirror. "You look amazing. Noah is going to lose it when he sees you coming down the aisle."

"I look like you on a normal day," Josie observed.

Trinity laughed and waved a dismissive hand. "Oh please," she said.

The photographer snapped several photos of the two of them. Trinity's black hair floated at her shoulders. The cobalt blue of the bridesmaid's dress Josie had chosen was a lovely contrast against Trinity's porcelain skin. As always, her make-up was impeccable.

From the corner of the suite, where she sat at a small, round table, Josie's grandmother, Lisette Matson, laughed. "Imagine, Josie. You could look like a movie star every day with a bit of make-up."

Trinity laughed and reached up to adjust a strand of Josie's hair. "I'm not a movie star, remember? I'm a journalist."

"Who's about to have her very own show on national network television," Lisette pointed out. "I'm happy for you, dear."

Josie turned and raised a brow at Lisette. "I wear make-up. Just not… industrial-strength make-up."

On the other side of the room, two heavy wooden chairs with crushed velvet cushions had been placed side by side for Misty and Gretchen to occupy while the hair stylist and make-up artist continued working their magic. Misty, her face upturned while the make-up artist brushed foundation along her jawline, said, "I ask her if I can do her make-up all the time, and she says no."

Josie said, "I certainly don't need this much make-up for work."

Beside Misty, Gretchen scowled as the hair stylist used her fingers to work mousse into Gretchen's short, spiky brown and gray hair. "That's true," she agreed.

"I need to sit down," Josie said. She padded over to the table and carefully sat across from Lisette. She reached out for a piece of fresh fruit from the bowl that the resort had provided, but Trinity dashed over and smacked her hand. "No. No eating with that dress on. Not until after the ceremony."

"You have to be kidding me," Josie said.

Trinity's flinty gaze bore down on her. "You know I'm not."

The heavy door to their suite opened and their mother, Shannon, swept in. She beamed at Josie. As she drew closer, studying Josie with obvious pride and awe, the photographer snapped more photos. "Look at you! Absolutely stunning." One of her fists opened to reveal a crumpled tissue which she pressed to her eyes.

"Mom," Trinity complained. "You're going to ruin your make-up."

"I can't help it," Shannon said. "Besides, if you think I'm bad, wait till you see your father. He's a mess." She placed her other hand on Josie's shoulder. "For thirty years, we thought this day was out of reach. Gone from us forever."

Josie patted her hand. "I know."

"Dammit," Trinity said. "I said no crying! No crying at this wedding."

Josie laughed and glanced at Lisette, who had a twinkle in her blue eyes. Josie had been born to Shannon and Christian Payne. When she and her sister were only three weeks old, a former housecleaner, Lila Jensen, set the Paynes' home on fire with the babies inside. Their nanny managed to rescue Trinity, but Lila stole away with Josie and passed her off as her own child for years. Both local authorities and the Paynes believed that Josie had perished in the fire. But Josie had been taken two hours away to Denton, where her vile abductor told Lisette's son, Eli Matson, that Josie was his daughter. He had no reason to disbelieve Lila and had raised Josie as his own until his death when Josie was only six years old. Josie had lived in terror, enduring one trauma after another at the hands of Lila, until Lisette got custody of her at age fourteen. From then until three years ago, when the truth finally came out and Josie was reunited with the Paynes, Josie and Lisette had only had each other.

Josie had married her high school sweetheart, Ray Quinn, just after college, but that wedding had been small with a limited number of guests, and the only family members in attendance had been Lisette and Ray's mother. No one had walked Josie down the aisle to Ray, and that had suited her just fine at the time. Her life to that point had hardly been normal, and she had endured all of her hardships largely on her own. It had made sense to her that she alone should walk down the aisle to her groom. Now, her biological father was in her life. They'd formed a bond over the years, and she was thrilled to have him there to walk her down the aisle to Noah Fraley.

"How are things on the groom's side of the hall?" Misty asked before any of them could dissolve into happy tears.

Shannon waved the tissue in the air. "Oh, you know, it's a mad house over there. Only Noah is completely ready, and Harris is chasing the dog around the suite."

"Dammit," Misty said, pushing the make-up artist away. "I'll go over there and tell him to settle down."

"I'll go with you," said the photographer, following Misty out of the bridal suite.

Harris was Misty's four-year-old son. After Josie and Ray broke up, Ray had fallen hard for Misty, but he had died before their son was born. Oddly enough, Josie and Misty had become very good friends in the wake of Ray's death. Harris, together with Josie and Noah's Boston Terrier, Trout, was supposed to be on ring-bearer duty.

"I don't know why you two insisted on having the dog in the ceremony," Trinity said, not for the first time.

Shannon said, "Trinity, really. It's Josie's wedding. She can do whatever she wants—and she should."

Trinity folded her arms across her chest. "Well, as her unofficial wedding planner, I objected strenuously to having the dog in the ceremony."

Josie laughed. "Unofficial? Really? I can count on one hand the number of decisions I got to make about this wedding." She turned to Shannon and Lisette. "She even booked the band!"

Trinity said, "It's the Walton-Marquette Project, out of Chester County. You remember them, right, Mom?"

Shannon nodded. "We saw them at the Winter MusicFest. They're fabulous. Everyone will love them, Josie."

Josie waved a hand. "I know they will. Honestly, I'm grateful for all your help, Trin. But having Trout in our wedding is non-negotiable. It will be adorable, and the owners, Celeste and Adam, were fine with us doing it and having Trout here all weekend."

Lisette said, "I can't imagine a better wedding venue, Josie. This place is amazing."

Josie stood and walked over to the large windows that overlooked the northeast edge of Harper's Peak's grounds. They were empty save for two men striding across the expansive lawn below. One wore a maroon polo shirt and pressed khakis, the uniform of resort staff. The other man wore a light-colored suit, but Josie recognized him as Tom Booth, the resort's managing director. When Josie first met him, she thought he was just Celeste Harper's assistant since he was usually found at her side with an iPad in his hands, tapping away at the screen while she barked instructions. As he hurried across the lawn, she saw the iPad tucked beneath one of his arms.

The Harper's Peak property had originally been a homestead settled by the Harper family in the early 1800s. It encompassed hundreds of acres of land spanning two mountaintops. Initially, there was an old stone house which now served as the personal residence for the resort's present-day owners, Celeste Harper and her husband, Adam Long. There was also a tiny white one-room church that sat on one of the mountain peaks. The original Harper settlers had used it as a schoolhouse as well as their place of worship. Now it hosted wedding ceremonies.

Subsequent generations of the Harper family had added additional buildings to their estate. First, the Harper family built the large bed and breakfast which now served as a sought-after location for wedding parties to assemble and prepare for the ceremony and reception. It had been named Griffin Hall after Celeste's father, Griffin Harper. Then, years later, a larger hotel and resort was built beside it. The grounds of Harper's Peak were breathtaking with their carefully manicured gardens and mountain overlooks. Josie would have chosen the resort for their wedding based on the photos of the venue alone. Her heart fluttered imagining that in just a couple of short hours, she'd be standing in the tiny church on one of the overlooks staring into the hazel eyes of her new husband, Noah.

A door slammed in the hallway. Seconds later, Misty and the photographer entered the bridal suite. With a tight smile, Misty said, "Things are settled over there. It wasn't too bad."

She sat back down in her chair and let the make-up artist finish up. Beside her, Gretchen waved off the hair stylist so she could check an alert on her phone. The photographer said, "Shall we get some photos of you with your mother and grandmother?"

"Sure," said Josie.

Lisette stood up and grabbed her walker, shuffling over toward Josie. "Shall we take them in front of the window?" she asked.

The photographer smiled. "Sure, let's try that."

Gretchen stood up. "I'll be right back."

Josie heard the door to the groom's suite across the hall slam again as Gretchen left the room.

"What's going on?" Josie said.

Trinity said, "What?"

Josie said, "Something's going on."

Lisette said, "You're getting married, dear. That's what's going on."

Everyone laughed. Except Misty. Josie stared at her. "Misty?"

She said nothing. From the corner of her eye, Josie saw motion outside. Turning back to the window, she watched as Gretchen and their colleague—and one of Noah's groomsmen—Detective Finn Mettner strode across the grounds, headed in the same direction as the staff members. Tracing her mental map of Harper's Peak, Josie tried to figure out where they might be going. In that direction was the church where they were about to be married. Celeste and Adam had arranged for a pre-wedding gathering downstairs where guests could mingle, have hors d'oeuvres and drinks before the ceremony. They'd be transported to the church in a resort car roughly a half hour before the proceedings began. It made sense that the staff might be heading out there to open the church and get things ready, but why were Mettner and Gretchen headed that way? There was an urgency in the way they walked that set Josie's teeth on edge.

Shannon said, "Nothing is going on, Josie."

Josie pointed out the window. "Where is everyone going? I just saw Tom and another staff member, Gretchen, and Mett—" she stopped speaking as their Chief of Police emerged from the first floor of the building and went after the two detectives. "And Chief Chitwood just went that way. Toward the church."

Trinity touched Josie's elbow, trying to gently turn her attention back to the photographer. "They're probably just setting up. Celeste told me the church is locked except for weddings."

Josie looked into her sister's striking blue eyes. "You don't need two detectives and the Chief of Police to set up for a wedding." She turned back to Misty. "What's going on?"

All eyes went to Misty, who wore a grimace. "It's nothing to do with the wedding, Josie."

Josie held her skirt in both hands and shuffled over to Misty, looking down into her face. "Tell me."

Softly, Misty said, "He told me not to."

"Who?"

"Mett. He said not to ruin your day."

"Misty."

Tears glistened in the corners of Misty's eyes. She choked out the words, "They found a body."

Behind Josie, the other women gasped.

Shannon said, "What? Where?"

"I don't know," Misty said.

Josie moved toward the door, but Trinity rushed across the room and blocked her way. "Josie, this is your wedding day. You're not a detective today, you're a bride. I know how dedicated you are to your work, but you are allowed to take time off to tend to your personal life. You're marrying Noah today. Make that your priority. You've got very capable colleagues to handle whatever is happening out there."

Josie stared at her sister, feeling herself relent.

Shannon walked over and again, touched Josie's shoulder. "Misty said they found a body. It doesn't mean there was any kind of foul play. It could be someone who had a medical event—a heart attack or something—and passed."

"Right," Josie said. "You're right." She smiled. "Let's take those photos."

But as she walked back to the window, she saw Officer Hummel, dressed in a suit since he was one of their wedding guests, stalking off in the direction everyone else had gone. Hummel was the head of Denton PD's Evidence Response Team. "Misty," Josie said. "Did they say anything else about the body? Anything at all?"

Misty gave a long sigh.

Trinity said, "Don't."

Misty said, "She's going to find out eventually, whether it's now or after the wedding."

"Then let her find out after, Misty."

"I don't lie to Josie," Misty announced. "Mett told me out in the hallway before he left. It was a child, Josie. A young girl."

Josie felt as though someone had punched her in the gut. One hand rested over her stomach. "What else? What else did Mett tell you?"

"Nothing else," Misty said. "That's it."

Lisette said, "Josie, I know this is terrible. It's a horrible, horrible thing. No one knows that better than me, but this is your wedding day."

"Please," Shannon said. "You've got over fifty guests downstairs, and Noah. Sweet, wonderful Noah. This is his day, too."

Lisette added, "You don't have to fight all the fights, Josie. Not every case is your burden to bear."

Josie knew this was true.

But a child, said a voice in her head.

Misty stood up and walked over. "They're right, Josie. I know it's difficult to go on and have a happy day after hearing about something so awful, but you have to try. You deserve to have a beautiful day. There are others on your team who can handle this just as well as you would."

Josie knew this was true as well. Her colleagues were the very best in the business. Of course, with her and Noah getting married, that left Gretchen and Mettner to do the work. Josie walked over to the dresser where a clutch purse rested with her personal items inside. Taking out her phone, she said, "I'm just going to call Gretchen."

"Josie!" Trinity objected, but the phone was already ringing.

Gretchen answered on the fourth ring. "Boss," she said. "I might have to forfeit my place as a bridesmaid."

"I understand," Josie said. "What've you got?"

They dropped easily into work speak, Gretchen rattling off details in the tone she used on every case. "Young girl, twelve or thirteen, possibly. Laid out at the base of the church steps like she's sleeping. No obvious signs of trauma."

"So you don't know if it's a homicide," Josie said.

There was a second of hesitation. "Let's just say it's suspicious."

"You think she was a guest here?" Josie asked.

"Not sure, but it will be easy to figure out. If any guests are looking for a missing twelve- or thirteen-year-old with white eyelashes, we'll know they're looking for this girl."

Josie felt a cold shock go through her. "What did you say?"

"Her eyelashes. They're white. It's the strangest thing. But it's a pretty distinct feature, so…"

Josie had stopped listening. The hand that held her phone dropped to her side. Her phone fell onto the carpet.

Trinity walked over and tugged at Josie's elbow. "Come on, now. Let Gretchen handle this. You know she's more than qualified."

Josie heard Lorelei Mitchell's voice in her head. *Poliosis. It's a genetic thing. Harmless. Just the absence of melanin in your hair or eyelashes. She hates it, but I think it makes her look striking.*

"I have to go," said Josie. This time, when Trinity tried to block her way, Josie pushed her aside and strode toward the door. She was only vaguely aware of the chorus of protests at her back. The door to the groom's suite opened only a second after Josie emerged. Out stepped Noah, looking so handsome in his tuxedo that it momentarily took her breath away.

"Josie," he said.

They stared at one another. In a dim corner of her mind, Josie realized it was bad luck for the groom to see the bride before the ceremony. But the bad luck had begun long before this moment, hadn't it? When the young girl in front of the church died.

Noah's eyes traveled the length of her body and then back up to her face. His jaw hung open for a second. Then he closed his mouth and swallowed. "Wow," he said, voice husky. "You look… amazing."

"So do you," she breathed.

For a moment, she considered going back to the bridal suite, taking all the requisite photos, and then heading downstairs to the wedding hall as if nothing outside was amiss. She could walk arm-in-arm with her biological father down the aisle toward this man. This lovely, incredible, kind, decent human being that she loved with her whole heart. They could say their vows and dance into the night, their partnership strengthened by their promise to one another. No one would blame her. In fact, Josie knew everyone who had come for this event would be very upset with her if she didn't do that.

Noah said, "Misty told you about the body."

Josie nodded.

"What did she say? They wouldn't tell me anything other than that they found a body."

"She said it was a little girl, Noah. They found her outside the church."

His face took on an expression of sadness.

Josie said, "I saw Hummel heading in that direction. They wouldn't need an Evidence Response officer unless…"

"It was a murder," he finished.

"Suspicious," Josie corrected. "I talked to Gretchen." She relayed what Gretchen had told her about the girl's eyelashes.

"You met her," Noah said.

Josie nodded. "The day we hit the deer and her mother took me back to her house while you went for help. Her name was Holly."

Silence fell between them. Josie looked down at her dress, immaculate white. How could she tell him? If a child had been murdered in the grounds of the resort where they were planning to marry, on their wedding day, Josie wasn't sure she could go through with it. It wasn't just any child, it was a girl she had met only three months earlier. A sweet, quiet girl with a shy smile but a fierceness about her, particularly in the way she had hovered protectively over her little sister. A deep ache opened in Josie's chest and flooded her body.

She sensed more than saw Noah take two long strides toward her. Then his hand appeared, palm open, inviting. She placed her own hand in his and looked up at him.

"Let's go," he said.

CHAPTER TWO

In the lobby, Celeste Harper waited, her tall, thin frame draped in a regal maroon gown that flowed to her ankles. Dark curls cascaded to her bare shoulders. Beside her stood her husband, Adam Long, dressed in his customary chef's garb. He held his white hat in both hands. His eyes didn't seem to know where to look. Although he wasn't that much older than his wife, his hair had already turned bright white and he hadn't bothered to regularly dye it. "Makes me look more distinguished," he had joked during one of the many meetings Josie and Noah had had with him, Celeste, and Tom to plan their nuptials. Celeste was heir and owner of the resort, and Adam was the head chef. They were usually pleasant and generous with their smiles, but as Josie and Noah descended the grand central staircase hand-in-hand, Josie saw that Adam's skin was ashen. Celeste held her cell phone to one ear while she pressed her other hand against her forehead. She paced back and forth near the lobby's front desk, whispering angrily into her phone.

Adam saw them first and offered a weak smile. Before he could speak, Celeste ended her call, tucked her cell phone into a hidden pocket of her dress and held up both hands, signaling for them to stop. "Please," she said. "I don't know what you've heard, but everything is going to be fine. We've got this under control."

Adam didn't look convinced. His fingers worried the stitching of his hat.

Josie said, "We understand the body of a child has been found at the church."

Celeste frowned, her brow furrowing. "Sadly, yes. But the police are handling it. I assure you, you need not concern yourself with such a terrible thing on your wedding day."

Josie said, "We are the police."

Celeste smiled. "I know you are. I only meant that other members of your department are already there. You have no need to worry. It's being handled by your colleagues as we speak."

Noah said, "Yes, we need to get over there and speak with them."

Adam said, "Oh, I don't think—I mean, this is your wedding day. It would be terrible to see that."

Celeste nodded along with him. "It's horribly tragic. We're not suggesting otherwise, but you shouldn't let it derail your entire wedding."

Josie said, "If she was found outside the church, and there was foul play, our Evidence Response Team is going to need a couple of hours, at least, to process the scene. That means our ceremony can't take place there anyway. We're just going to take a walk to the church to talk with our colleagues."

The skin around Celeste's eyes tightened. "Now? Like that? You're both already dressed for the ceremony, which we can move. It doesn't have to be at the church. There are plenty of other lovely areas at the resort we can offer."

"Yes," said Adam. "We can adjust everything as needed. Your guests are already in the pre-wedding area. They seem to be having a wonderful time. I wouldn't recommend—"

Josie tugged at Noah's hand, moving around Adam and Celeste. "We'll be back," she said.

Outside, the spring air was a balmy seventy degrees. A light breeze blew across the grounds as they took the pathway from the entrance of Griffin Hall to the church. Josie's heels clacked and her gown swished against the asphalt. They strode in silence toward the church on Griffin's overlook. As they neared, they saw two hotel workers and Tom Booth seated on a stone bench to their right.

One staff member had his face in his hands. The man in the middle wept silently, swiping at his eyes with the back of his hand. Tom stared straight ahead, eyes vacant, a cigarette between his lips. His iPad lay abandoned on the seat beside him. Up ahead, between two hedgerows, stood Sawyer Hayes, one of Denton city's Emergency Services workers. Today, he was dressed sharply in a navy suit. His black hair was slicked away from his face, making him look more striking and polished than Josie had ever seen him. He was a guest at their wedding, even though Noah had grown to dislike him. They had only invited him because he was Lisette's grandson. Her only living blood relative.

The woman who eventually went on to kidnap Josie as an infant, Lila Jensen, had been in a relationship with Lisette's son, Eli Matson. They broke up for a little over a year and during that time, Eli struck up a relationship with a different woman. That woman became pregnant with Sawyer. Before she could tell Eli about the pregnancy, Lila was back in his life, passing Josie off as his baby, and threatening anyone who might come between them. Sawyer's mother never spoke to Eli again and had only told Sawyer about his true parentage on her deathbed two years earlier. He sought Lisette out and their DNA tests were a match. Things between him and Josie had always been prickly, but she'd done her best to treat him like family, for Lisette's sake, at least.

Now his blue eyes locked on her, traveling up and down her body. Ignoring Noah, he said, "You're choosing *this* over your own wedding?"

"Hey," Noah said. "Watch it."

Josie held up a hand to indicate they should both stop speaking. "I've got information that the team needs, Sawyer."

"Of course you do," he muttered.

"What are *you* doing here?" Noah challenged.

For the first time, Sawyer looked at him. "When word first came in to Griffin Hall, Tom said the girl was unresponsive. I came up to see if I could help, but when I got here it was pretty clear that she was already gone."

"Then you're no longer needed here," Noah told him. He moved closer to Josie, putting a hand on her lower back and pressing her forward past Sawyer. "Excuse us."

Wordlessly, Sawyer turned and started walking back toward Griffin Hall. Just beyond where he'd been standing was a uniformed Denton police officer with a clipboard. His eyes went wide with shock as they approached.

"Detective Quinn, Lieutenant Fraley, what are you—this isn't—this is a crime scene."

Josie glanced at his nametag. "Brennan, we're aware that you've got a crime scene here. We'd like to have a look at it."

He looked them both up and down. "Like… that?"

Josie and Noah looked at one another and then back at Brennan. Noah said, "It's my understanding that Detectives Mettner and Palmer, Chief Chitwood, and Officer Hummel are already on the scene."

"Yeah."

"They were guests at our wedding," Josie said. "They're not dressed much differently than us."

"Log us in," Noah said, motioning to the clipboard.

Shaking his head, Brennan wrote their names on the clipboard and let them pass. Josie and Noah walked further down the path until they reached a long strip of crime scene tape that had been tied to the various azalea bushes and other flowers that surrounded the open area in front of the church. Standing at the edge of the tape were Gretchen, Mettner, and Chief Chitwood. Mettner talked tersely into his cell phone. Beyond the tape was Officer Hummel, now wearing a Tyvek suit over his wedding clothes. With him was Officer Jenny Chan. She hadn't been a guest at the wedding, so Josie knew that Hummel must have called her to bring the crime scene equipment. Chan took photos while Hummel sketched out the scene in a notebook.

There was a set of stone steps that led to the front doors of the church. On the grass in front of the bottom step lay Holly Mitchell. She was dressed in a pair of pajamas: purple cotton, with yellow stars all over them. Only her feet were bare. She was indeed "laid out" as Gretchen had described—in the same way a person was generally positioned in a casket. Her legs were straight, her arms tucked at her sides and folded over her chest, some object beneath her hands. Her eyes were closed, and her brown hair fanned out around her head. Small flowers dotted her long locks. Josie noted white bloodroot, yellow buttercups, blue violets, and purple dead-nettle—all wildflowers that could be found anywhere in Pennsylvania this time of year.

"Someone arranged her body," she muttered.

Chitwood, Gretchen, and Mettner—now off the phone—turned and looked at her.

"Boss," Mettner said. "You shouldn't be here." He looked past her at Noah. "You either."

"I know who this girl is," Josie explained.

Chitwood folded his arms over his thin chest. "How in the hell do you know this girl, Quinn?"

Josie explained how Lorelei had picked her up from the side of the road three months earlier; how she'd gone back to Lorelei's house until Noah came to get her, and how she had met Lorelei's daughters.

"We're going to need to talk with her mother right away," said Gretchen.

"Who found her?" Noah asked.

"Member of the staff," said Mettner. "He came out here to unlock the church doors and make sure everything was tidy and in order for the ceremony. He was pretty shaken. We'll get a statement from him later."

"Was the church locked?" Noah asked.

Mettner nodded. "Yes. No one was inside. No sign of a break-in. Whoever left her here had no interest in going inside."

"But they left her here so she'd be found," Josie said. "Was the person who found her the one who called 911?"

Gretchen said, "No, it was Celeste. The guy who found the body called the front desk. Two of his co-workers came out and then reported back to Celeste. She immediately called 911. Dispatch called Mett. Pretty much everyone necessary to secure and process this scene is at your wedding. So here we are."

From behind them came the sound of heels clacking along the path. They all turned to see Dr. Anya Feist, the Medical Examiner, approaching. She was wearing a pale pink A-line dress that came to her knees, complemented by pale pink stilettos. Her silver-blonde hair cascaded to her shoulders and shimmered in the sunlight. Josie and her team usually only ever saw the doctor in scrubs or a Tyvek suit. She looked like a different woman. Still, she had the same grim smile she usually greeted them with at crime scenes. She stopped short and stared at Josie and Noah. With a sigh and a shake of her head, she said, "Mettner just called me to come out here. You two should have had a destination wedding." She turned to Mettner. "What've you got?"

He told her what little they knew.

She pointed to a rolling suitcase that Officer Chan often brought to crime scenes, which had been left a few feet away but outside the crime scene tape. "I'll get suited up."

She slid her heels off and walked over to the suitcase, pulling out a Tyvek suit, booties, a skull cap and gloves. The suit was an awkward fit over her dress, but she made it work. She waited for Hummel and Chan to finish their photos and sketches and then slipped under the tape. Josie's gaze jumped back and forth from the case to the body. In her wedding dress there was no way she would be able to get into one of the Tyvek suits, and she wasn't about to contaminate the scene. She would have to wait for Dr. Feist's assessment.

The mood was somber and the day eerily silent, as if even the birds were too sad to sing. Dr. Feist knelt beside Holly Mitchell's head and used a gloved finger to lift the girl's eyelids, one after the other. "Petechiae in the sclera of the eyes."

Josie knew this meant that there were pinpoint red spots in the whites of the girl's eyes indicating that she had been deprived of oxygen at some point before her death. The spots appeared when the small capillaries in the eyes hemorrhaged. It usually indicated death by asphyxiation or strangulation.

Dr. Feist leaned down, taking a closer look at the girl's neck. "Bruising," she noted. "Not from any kind of ligature, though. This bruising is irregular, more indicative of strangulation. Based on the pattern, it looks like maybe the person began to strangle her, stopped, and then finished the job later. Hummel, make sure you bag her hands in case there's skin under her nails."

Gently, Dr. Feist probed the girl's hands, trying to dislodge them from whatever object they held against her body. The hands didn't budge. "She's still in full rigor," Dr. Feist said.

Mettner said, "Does that mean she's been dead only a couple of hours?"

Dr. Feist glanced up at him. "Rigor can take effect anywhere between one and six hours after death, Detective Mettner. The average is two to four hours. Rigor can last up to seventy-two hours. If you're looking for time of death, I'll have a better idea when I get her on the table. I'll need to take her internal temperature and do some calculations, but it's very likely she's been dead for several hours."

"You think this is where she died?" asked Mettner.

Dr. Feist frowned. "Hard to say. I don't see any signs of a struggle. No marks in the grass, no broken tree branches. Then again, she's not streaked with dirt or anything to indicate that she's been dragged along the ground. Other than the hemorrhaging in her eyes and the bruising on her throat, it looks like she just laid down and went to sleep. Poor girl."

Mettner tapped away at the note-taking app on his phone.

Gretchen said, "We're going to have to talk to everyone who is or was here today. I'll call in more back-up for that."

"What's that she's got in her hands?" Josie asked.

Dr. Feist nodded toward Hummel and then moved out of his way so that he could kneel beside the girl. "It's some kind of crude… doll, I think. Chan, what do you think?"

Chan walked over and peered down. "That's weird," she said. "I think you're right, though. It's meant to be a doll."

"I can't get close in this dress," Josie said. "Can one of you take a photo and text it to Mett so I can see?"

Chan and Hummel froze, looking at Josie momentarily before turning their gazes toward Chief Chitwood. Josie looked at him as well. He shook his head, wisps of his white hair floating over his balding scalp. With a sigh, he said, "Quinn, Fraley, you're supposed to be getting married today." He looked at his wristwatch. "In about an hour, by my calculations. Why don't you let us take care of this?"

Josie motioned toward Holly Mitchell. "I met that girl. I met her mother and her sister. I can't walk away from this."

Gretchen said, "Boss, no one is asking you to walk away. We're only asking you to wait until after your wedding to get involved."

Mettner said, "Walking out on your wedding is kind of shitty, boss."

"Hey," said Noah. "Watch it, Mett. It's my wedding, too."

Mettner shrugged, unfazed. "It's still shitty."

Josie said, "Our wedding venue is a crime scene."

Noah stepped forward, toward Mettner. "If you don't understand why we need to be here, to be involved, then you really don't know us at all."

Josie loved Noah even more than she already did for including himself in that statement. His unflinching and unwavering support, along with his uncanny ability to understand her, were exactly the reasons she was marrying him. She stepped up and slid her hand into his. "Just let me check on Holly's mother. She lives nearby."

The Chief said, "We'll send someone. You two get back to your wedding."

Josie said, "You won't be able to find it unless one of us takes you."

"You two don't have to do everything, you know. Mettner and Gretchen are perfectly capable of handling this while the two of you get married. This is a huge resort. They could find somewhere else to have the ceremony. Your guests are already here. The band. The kitchen staff are cooking up a storm. You're going to lose a lot of money if you don't get back to the hotel and get married."

Josie glanced toward the body again and blinked back tears. She felt Noah's hand squeeze hers. Could they get married an hour after the body of a child was found at their wedding venue? At the doorstep to the church in which they were going to exchange vows? She knew the answer to that question, but she knew their colleagues and family would fight them every step of the way. She said, "One of you come with us to Lorelei Mitchell's house so she can be notified."

Gretchen said, "Then you'll come back here and get married?"

"Yes," said Josie and Noah in unison. The gentle pressure of Noah's hand told her that he was lying, too.

CHAPTER THREE

Josie and Noah piled into Gretchen's car while Gretchen stood just outside the driver's side door and used her cell phone to call in more units. Noah sat in the front seat and Josie positioned herself across the entire back seat. Her dress was easy to move around in, but the bustle took up a lot of room. She had desperately wanted to change into comfortable clothes, but going back to the hotel and facing everyone would have taken far too long. There would be too many people for them to convince that what they were doing was acceptable. Josie couldn't think of a single person, except perhaps her grandmother, Lisette, who would think that walking out on their own wedding to assist in solving a murder was okay. Once the time for the wedding had passed and Josie and Noah were still unmarried, their guests were far less likely to object to them changing clothes.

"You okay?" Noah asked.

Josie looked up to see him turned toward her, staring. "Yeah, you?"

He smiled. "Of course. I'm with you."

"The wedding—" Josie started.

"Can wait. We'll work it out. Let's just check on Lorelei and go from there."

Josie leaned forward and kissed him. He reached up and cupped her cheek, his warm palm lingering there. His hazel eyes darkened. "You had a bad feeling the day we hit the deer. I didn't listen."

Josie leaned into his hand. "I wanted to believe it was true—that we'd had our fill of bad luck. Noah, Lorelei was fiercely protective of her kids. I know I only spent a little over an hour with them, but it was obvious. I can't see her letting either of them out of her sight."

What she didn't say was that she was afraid of what they'd find at Lorelei's home.

Before he could respond, Gretchen rapped against the driver's side window. Both of them looked at her. With one hand she spoke into her cell phone, but with the other she signaled toward Griffin Hall. Trinity strode toward the vehicle, a look of fury flashing across her face. Jogging to catch up with her was her boyfriend, Drake Nally. He was an FBI agent with the New York City field office. Josie had worked with him on a case in the past. While he wouldn't be able to lend any help with local murders, Josie hoped he'd be able to calm Trinity down. But Josie knew that was a tall order, given that Trinity was a force to be reckoned with.

Noah must have sensed Josie's thoughts. He said, "This isn't good." He opened the passenger's side door. "You go with Gretchen. I'll run interference."

Gretchen hung up and got into the car as Noah jogged over to Trinity and Drake. Josie watched him put his hands up and block her way as she tried to step around him. Drake circled her and stood shoulder to shoulder with Noah, keeping her at bay.

As they pulled away from Griffin Hall and down the long, winding drive that led from Harper's Peak to the road at the base of the mountain, Gretchen said, "You two aren't getting married today, are you?"

"No," Josie said.

Gretchen sighed. "No one is going to be happy about this, you know."

"We know," said Josie. "Make a left."

Gretchen turned left onto the road. "When I say no one is going to be happy about this, I mean your families are going to be pissed. You know that, right?"

Josie said, "Would you want the memory of your wedding day to be one in which a child was murdered at the venue?"

"Good point," said Gretchen. She held up her phone. "Take it. Hummel texted me a photo of that... thing Holly was holding."

Josie grabbed the phone and swiped until she found the text message from Hummel. The item looked like a doll that a very young child might make. A pinecone made up the body. Two acorns had been affixed to it to look like bulging eyes. Tiny twigs had been tucked into the folds of the pinecone to make a nose, mouth, and then arms and legs. Had it not been found on the body of a dead girl, it might be comical. Instead, it only roiled the acid in Josie's stomach. It didn't look like anything a twelve-year-old girl would make or have with her. Obviously, whoever had staged her body on the overlook had purposely left it with her, but who had made it? Why had they left it?

"Creepy, right?" Gretchen said.

Josie leaned forward and dropped the phone onto the front seat. "Yeah," she said. "It's up here on the left."

Gretchen slowed the vehicle. "What's up here on the left? There's nothing out here."

"There is," Josie insisted. "Pull onto the shoulder. Over there."

Gretchen stopped the car in the middle of the deserted road. "Have you lost your mind?"

"Just pull over!" Josie exclaimed.

With a shake of her head, Gretchen pulled the car onto the grassy shoulder of the road. Josie leaned forward between the seats again and pointed toward their left. "There," she said. "There are two sycamore trees, about a car's length apart. Pull through those trees and you'll see a driveway."

Gretchen did as Josie asked and maneuvered her vehicle between the two trees. Ahead, two metal posts came into view. A chain ran from one to the other and hanging from it was a sign that read: "No Trespassing."

Gretchen said, "These people live here? This is how you get to their house?"

Josie said, "Lorelei said she liked her privacy."

At the time, Josie had found it a little bit odd, but she certainly hadn't thought there was anything sinister behind Lorelei's insistence on privacy. She was a woman living alone with two young girls.

Gretchen stared ahead at the chain. "She liked her privacy, or she was hiding from something? Or someone?"

Josie saw a barely perceptible shiver ripple through Gretchen's frame. She knew a thing or two about hiding from dangerous people.

"I'm not sure now," Josie admitted. "Nothing seemed amiss when I was here. Lorelei just said she liked to live 'off the grid' as much as possible."

"Like a doomsday prepper?" Gretchen asked.

"No, not like that," Josie said. "She wasn't building a bunker or anything. It was more like she grew a lot of her own food. There's a big garden and greenhouse behind the house. You'll see. She told me she homeschooled her kids. Also she said she didn't allow electronics in the house."

"No electronics. Even television?"

"Not till they got older, she said. She had a laptop, but the girls weren't allowed access to it. I was able to get cell service when she brought me here. I think because it's close to Harper's Peak."

"I would say that whole set-up sounds weird, but that's how I grew up. Not the homeschooling, but the lack of technology. I mean, we had TV and landlines, but that was it."

The longer they spoke, the greater the uneasiness building in Josie's stomach grew. Had Holly snuck out of the house? If so, why? Had she gone to meet someone? How many people did she have access to while she was being homeschooled? Did Lorelei even know she was gone? Josie said, "You want me to get the chain?"

Gretchen raised a brow. "In that dress? No. Hang on."

She got out and unhooked the chain, setting it to one side so that their vehicle could pass.

"The house is about a quarter mile up this drive," Josie said once Gretchen was back in the car. The drive was merely two ruts in the mud made by the wheels of Lorelei Mitchell's pickup truck. The house came into view. It was a charming, two-story stone home with a peaked roof made of red tin and a spacious front porch. A small wooden log normally used for garden edging had been sunk into the ground to mark the separation of the dirt driveway and the front yard. Paving stones led the way to the porch steps. Gretchen parked beside the truck and turned the engine off. "Seeing as you're dressed like that, why don't I try the door and you wait here," she told Josie.

"Sure," Josie said.

Gretchen gave her a dubious look but got out and headed toward Lorelei's front door. Josie wriggled out of the back seat and stood next to the car. Her white heels sank into the dirt. She took a deep breath, adjusting her dress. It was nearing late afternoon, and the sun shone brightly through the trees overhead. A heady floral scent wafted through the air. Josie had no doubt it came from the tightly packed flowerbed in front of the porch. She listened to Gretchen knock and call out Lorelei's name.

No response.

The feeling of uneasiness turning Josie's stomach went into overdrive. She glanced at the truck. The shotgun was no longer hanging from the cab window. But it wouldn't be if Lorelei was home, Josie remembered. In January when they'd arrived at this very spot, she had watched Lorelei climb into the rear of the truck's cab and lift the small back seats to reveal a gun safe tucked beneath them. It was so cleverly disguised, it merely looked like it was part of the black metal base of the seats. Lorelei had used a key from her keychain to unlock it, slide her shotgun and boxes of ammunition inside, and secure it again before turning the seats back down. Josie would never have known it was there.

Gretchen knocked harder this time, and Josie heard a loud creak. "The door's open," said Gretchen. She moved closer to the open door and tried calling Lorelei again.

Josie hobbled over to the truck and peered inside. On the headrest of the driver's seat was a bloody handprint.

"Shit," Josie said. Hitching her dress up, she scrambled toward the other side of the truck. Another bloody handprint marred the truck's door handle. While the rest of the front looked undisturbed, the back seat was a different story. The seats were up and the lid of the gun safe was mangled. From where Josie stood, it looked as though someone had used a heavy object to smash in the lock mechanism and then pry open the safe. Lorelei's shotgun was gone.

Josie turned, her feet already trying to run toward Gretchen, but her heels got stuck again. She fell forward, catching herself with her palms. Slipping her feet out of her shoes, she left them behind and clambered up the front porch steps. "Gretchen," she called. "Something's wrong. Something's really wrong."

CHAPTER FOUR

Gretchen went back to her vehicle and retrieved her phone from the front seat. Josie moved close enough to look over her shoulder and see that she was texting both Mettner and the Chief to request back-up and the Evidence Response Team. Tucking the phone into her bra, she leaned back into the car and took a gun from her clutch purse. Handing it to Josie, she said, "This is my service weapon. You'll use this one."

Taking the Glock, barrel pointed downward, Josie said, "You brought this to my wedding?"

Gretchen grimaced. "I bring it everywhere. It's nothing personal. Come on."

She led Josie around to the trunk of the car and popped it open. She pushed aside a few emergency supplies—ponchos, first aid kit, jump starter, and flashlight—to reveal a small metal rectangular-shaped box with a silver lock on it. Josie knew at once it was where Gretchen kept her personal gun. Metal jangled in Gretchen's hand as she searched for the key. Once she found it, she opened the box and pulled out a Ruger Security-9 together with a full magazine. She palmed the magazine into the gun and chambered a round with expert precision. Keeping the barrel of her gun toward the ground, she said, "What are we talking about here? What kind of weapon did this woman have?"

"A Winchester 1200," Josie answered.

Gretchen's mouth pressed into a thin line. Then she said, "Okay. You've been in this house before. You'll take the lead."

Josie nodded.

They could have stayed outside and waited for back-up, but so far what they knew was that one of the home's residents had been murdered; there were two bloody handprints at the scene, and one missing shotgun. The front door had been left open. If Lorelei or Emily were still inside and one or both of them were injured, waiting for back-up could be the difference between life and death. Josie and Gretchen had to go in and make sure that no one in the house needed aid. Neither of them stated the other obvious issue: the killer could potentially still be inside.

Josie said, "Take off those heels."

Without hesitation, Gretchen kicked off her taupe heels and followed Josie up the front steps. They positioned themselves on opposite sides of the door, elbows tucked against their bodies, pistols pulled in close to their torsos but at the ready.

"I'm going left," Josie said.

Gretchen nodded. She would go right. Reaching forward, Gretchen pushed the door open, and Josie stepped through it smoothly and quickly, immediately moving left while Gretchen went right. Her feet, snug in sheer pantyhose, moved lightly and silently along the left side of the room. Her eyes followed the barrel of her gun, her mind cataloguing things in rapid-fire fashion. Old yellow couch and loveseat. Beanbag chairs.

Gretchen swept the other side of the room, moving in sync with Josie until they met at a doorway to what Josie knew was a dining room. A rushing started in her ears. Her heart raced. Gretchen fell slightly behind her, waiting on Josie's lead. In law enforcement, doorways were known as the fatal funnel because when you were clearing a structure, they became a choke-point where officers were most vulnerable and most likely to die. Josie took a second to try to slow down the adrenaline shooting through her veins. "Right," she said quietly to Gretchen.

Gretchen squeezed her shoulder, indicating she understood the plan. Josie moved into the dining room first, moving to the right while Gretchen moved to the left, eyes and gun barrels panning each corner of the room for any threats. Again, Josie's mind quickly catalogued what she saw. Dark wooden table taking up most of the room. Four chairs. Two tucked in, one pulled slightly out, and the last knocked on its side. Markers, sketch pads, and a coloring book scattered across the table and the floor. A bowl of cereal overturned on the hardwood floor. Droplets of dried blood leading to the next choke-point. This doorway was narrower.

Again, Gretchen moved in tandem with Josie, staying a slight step behind her. "Left," Josie said as she moved into the kitchen. Gretchen went the opposite way, her eyes and gun barrel focused on the corners that Josie was not covering.

The kitchen was as she remembered it. Countertops and cabinets lining the walls. A large island counter in the center. Decorated in gray with red accents. Large windows at the back of the house overlooking the back porch and garden. Dried herbs hanging upside-down over the sink. There were also things that hadn't been there before. Broken glass shimmered on the tile floor. The refrigerator door dented inward. A smear of blood with two brown, curly hairs stuck to one of the corners of the countertop. Below that, a cascade of dried blood running down the side of the counter and splattering across the floor. Josie's eyes kept searching, following her gun.

"Back door," she said tersely, indicating that it had been left ajar. "Footprints."

Josie counted three of them—two that looked to be from large, likely male, sneakers, and one smaller barefoot print, all in crimson.

"Body," Gretchen said.

Keeping her weapon ready, Josie took a wide arc across the room to the other side of the island, avoiding the blood as best she could, and drew up beside Gretchen. "Shit," she breathed.

Barefoot and clad in a pair of distressed jeans and a white peasant blouse, Lorelei lay face-up on the floor. Her arms were thrown wide, a smattering of bullet holes in her chest. Whoever had shot her had used the buckshot at close range. Josie looked around, noting the spent shotgun shell on the floor near Lorelei's feet. A pool of congealed blood spread beneath her body, some of it having soaked into her unruly brown and gray curls. A gash had opened up on one side of her forehead, along her hairline. The blood was now dry and flaky. Her face was frozen in a look of shock and horror that threatened to derail Josie's emotions.

"Emily," Josie choked out. "Let's go."

Gretchen stayed in position while Josie took a quick glance out the back door. No discernible threats. Josie skirted the body, not wanting to disturb the crime scene any more than they already had, and went back to the living room. Josie's heartbeat sped up again as they climbed the steps, pistols pointed upward. She had to concentrate on not tripping over her dress. On level ground, it swished lightly over the floor, but stairs were another matter. Josie stayed in the lead, Gretchen behind her, her own gun angled away from Josie's line of fire. Their bodies were nearly touching, and Josie felt comfort knowing that Gretchen, who had twenty years on the job, had her back.

Over the sound of her own breathing and pounding heart, Josie heard a thud. Both of them froze near the top of the steps. Josie wanted to run, to rush ahead to see if someone was still in the house, if Emily was alive, but she quelled the urge. In these situations, smooth and steady was safest. In a quiet voice meant only for Gretchen, Josie said, "Right, hallway," indicating that at the top of the stairs was a hallway—another dangerous narrow point for officers clearing a house—and that she would take the right side.

Again, Gretchen's hand squeezed Josie's bare shoulder, signaling for her to proceed. Josie reached the landing and turned right, registering a dim, carpeted hallway. Gretchen lagged a step behind, taking the left wall.

"Open door," Josie said, as they came to the first door in the hall. They cleared any open doors first. This one was the bathroom. Empty. No blood. No signs of struggle. The next door was open as well. This one was Lorelei's bedroom. As they cleared it, Josie took in the details: king-sized bed with messy blankets, one wall of closet space, one wall of windows. A small dresser with a mirror on top. Clean squares along the edges of the mirror told Josie several items had previously been tucked in there. Photographs, most likely. As they moved out of the room, Josie saw the torn corner of a color photograph still stuck under the edge of one side of the mirror. She didn't have time to think about who had taken them.

They moved back into the hallway, clearing each one of the remaining rooms. One was extremely large, decorated in various shades of purple with a twin bed on each side. Next to each bed was a small white desk and dresser. One side of the room held a few dolls, toys, and stuffed animals while the other held mostly books and art supplies. Emily and Holly, Josie thought. They'd shared a room. Beside what Josie guessed was Holly's desk, a large swath of the wall had been painted with chalkboard paint and framed with wood trim. A plastic cup on the floor held various colored chalks. From a small string affixed to one side of the wood trim hung an eraser. The wall itself was decorated in colorful drawings. Josie could easily tell which had been drawn by Holly and which had been drawn by her younger, less practiced sister. Dogs, frogs, horses, stick figures, happy faces, hearts, and rainbows told the story of two happy girls—completely at odds with the two crime scenes Josie had seen so far today.

The last room in the house was painted a bland tan color. It, too, had a section painted as a chalkboard, but there were no drawings, no chalk, and no eraser. A bare twin mattress lay in the center of the floor. The closet had no door. It was barren. On one wall was a poster of a man rock-climbing above the word 'Perseverance', and on the wall opposite, what looked like an angry child's drawing. A face with jagged, torn features had been drawn in black marker and then scribbled over with blue and red. Neither of the remaining bedrooms showed any signs of struggle or violence.

"Nothing," Gretchen said as they stood in that final room.

They lowered their weapons. Josie stepped back into the hallway and called out Emily's name. Gretchen followed suit. No response.

"Attic?" Gretchen asked.

They searched the rooms upstairs until they found a small, pull-down door in the ceiling of Lorelei's bedroom closet. Gretchen climbed up the rickety wooden steps until her head disappeared into darkness. "It's just a crawl space. I don't see anything."

Josie asked, "Do we need a flashlight?"

Gretchen labored back down to the floor and pushed a hand through her hair. "No. Right at the top there's a quarter-inch-thick coating of dust, undisturbed. No one's been up there in a while."

"You heard the noise when we were on the steps, though, right?" Josie said.

"Yeah," said Gretchen.

They'd checked every room, every closet, every place a human could possibly hide and found no one. Yet, Josie couldn't shake the feeling they weren't alone.

Gretchen said, "They're living out here in the middle of the woods. Could have been an animal on the roof or something?"

Josie didn't feel reassured but nodded in agreement. "Let's see if there's a basement. Then we'll check the greenhouse."

Retracing their steps downstairs, they continued to call out for Emily, but still received no response. They found the basement door in the dining room, and cleared the musty space the same way as they had the rest of the house but found nothing other than a washer and dryer and a cabinet full of jarred food.

Back in the living room, Gretchen wiped sweat from her brow. "Emily's not here, boss."

"Neither is the gun," Josie noted, feeling a tightness in her chest. "Which means that whoever shot Lorelei still has it and may have Emily as well."

They moved back outside and walked down the steps. The air felt good against Josie's skin. "Let's check the greenhouse."

Wordlessly, Gretchen followed Josie to the back of the house. An expansive back porch stood several feet above a fenced-in vegetable garden. The gate hung open. Josie lifted her weapon as she passed through it, her feet sinking into the soft dirt of the garden. Walking between two rows of fledgling plants, she headed toward the greenhouse with Gretchen in tow. Around them, the only noise they could hear was birdsong.

"You smell that?" Gretchen said.

"Fire," replied Josie.

The greenhouse door was closed but not locked. The smell of a recent fire stung Josie's nostrils as she swung the door open and stepped inside. It was at least ten degrees warmer inside the structure. Two of the tables inside had been overturned, soil and seeds strewn everywhere. Josie and Gretchen picked their way through the detritus until they came to the far end of the greenhouse. Overhead, the roof vents were propped open. On the ground near the louvre vent were several large terracotta planters filled with ashes, small pieces of paper, and what looked like remnants of both a laptop and cell phone.

Documents of some kind and Lorelei's electronics, Josie guessed. What the hell was going on here?

Gretchen said, "We have to go back to the road so we can signal the others. They'll never find the driveway."

Josie said, "You go. I'll stay here and call the Chief to let him know we need search teams. Let's go back to the car and get your phone."

Gretchen shook her head. "Boss, I can't leave you here alone."

"I can handle myself. The others should be here any second. You go flag them down."

With a sigh, Gretchen turned and trudged out of the greenhouse. Josie followed her until they reached her car. Gretchen climbed in behind the wheel. Fishing her phone from the console, she handed it to Josie. "Stay alert."

Josie nodded and watched Gretchen make a three-point turn before heading back to the road. Alone in the large clearing, Josie held the gun at her side with one hand and with the other, dialed Chief Chitwood's number.

"Palmer," he answered brusquely. "I've got extra officers and ERT headed your way. Dr. Feist said she'd go with them too in case there's a body. They should all be there now, actually. Where's Quinn? Things here are getting a little tense. We've got a groom, over fifty confused guests, and no bride."

"It's me, Chief," Josie said.

"Dammit, Quinn," he responded. "I don't think I'm going to like what you have to say."

"No," Josie agreed. "You won't. Not one bit."

CHAPTER FIVE

Gretchen returned with three patrol vehicles in tow. Josie stationed one of the uniformed officers at the front of the house and one at the back to make sure that the scene inside the house and the greenhouse wouldn't be disturbed. The other patrol officers were sent off to search the woods around the house for Emily or any sign of the killer. Josie itched to get out there and join the search but in her wedding dress, it wasn't practical. Besides, Chief Chitwood had contacted the Alcott County Sheriff to ask for assistance from their K-9 unit, and Josie wanted to be there when the search and rescue dog arrived. Hummel was still busy at the Harper's Peak scene, so he had dispatched Officer Chan and two other members of the ERT to process the Mitchell house. They arrived shortly after the patrol vehicles and got to work, followed five minutes later by Dr. Feist.

As everyone set to work, Josie and Gretchen waited outside near Gretchen's car. The clearing around Lorelei's house was remarkably quiet. The only noises were the calls of birds flitting through the trees overhead and the light breeze drifting through the leaves. It was so peaceful here, so beautiful. Insulated. What the hell had happened? How had violence found Lorelei and her children? Why? What about the items burned in the greenhouse? Had Lorelei done it, or had her killer? What didn't they want anyone to know?

Gretchen said, "We need to ask for an Amber Alert for Emily."

"Yes," Josie said. "Someone's going to have to fill out the NCIC form and then we can call it in. I'll call the station, see who's at the front desk. I can guide them through it."

"We have no photos of this girl," Gretchen remarked. "I didn't see any in the house, did you?"

Josie shook her head. "No, but Lorelei kept one in her truck. I'll see if the ERT can find it when they process the truck. For now, let me call and get this process started."

Gretchen said, "I'll ask one of them to come out and check inside the truck for the photo now."

Josie nodded and dialed the front desk at the Denton Police headquarters. Their normal desk sergeant, Dan Lamay was at Josie's wedding, so another officer was filling in for him. Josie walked him through the process of inputting all of Emily's known information into the National Crime Information Center database. Gretchen returned midway through to tell her that the ERT officer hadn't found any photos in the truck. It was up to Josie to provide a description from having met the girl three months ago. She had to estimate the height and weight: roughly four feet tall, approximately fifty to fifty-five pounds. What she knew for sure was that Emily had straight, shoulder-length brown hair and hazel eyes. In fact, when they'd first met, Emily's eyes had reminded Josie of Noah's. She finished that call and then dialed the state police to finalize the process of getting the Amber Alert issued. Several minutes after hanging up, the cell phones of everyone on the scene began to buzz and chirp as the alert went out statewide.

Josie felt only slightly better.

Gretchen said, "Mett is still at Harper's Peak handling statements from the staff, so I'll be the lead here. What can you tell me about Lorelei Mitchell and her kids?"

Josie shrugged. "Not much more than I already told you. I was only here for about two hours. My cell phone worked here, so I called Noah and Mett. Lorelei gave me coffee. The girls came into the kitchen from the garden. We all sat at the dining room table together. Lorelei had just made banana bread. The girls seemed excited to meet me."

Gretchen panned the area. "Being homeschooled out here? I guess they don't get too many visitors."

Josie remembered how young Emily had peppered her with questions and had even gone so far as to ask about Josie's scar. A flush had crept up Lorelei's face as she scolded Emily for being intrusive. Holly had simply laughed and put an arm across Emily's shoulders. "I didn't get to ask Lorelei many questions because I was talking with the girls," said Josie.

"What about their father?"

"Lorelei said it was just them. None of them brought up the subject, and there didn't seem to be any evidence of a male presence in the house."

Gretchen said, "This intense need for privacy makes me wonder if this was a domestic issue."

It hadn't occurred to Josie back in January, but now she wondered if Lorelei had escaped from an abusive relationship and was hiding out here in the woods. If that was the case, the girls' father would be their prime suspect in Holly and Lorelei's murders and Emily's disappearance.

Gretchen said, "We're going to have to find out who their father is when we get back to the station. Do you know what she did for a living?"

Josie shook her head. "No, I don't know anything about her beyond what I've told you." In most murder investigations, they started with the victim's inner circle and moved outward, but it appeared that Lorelei Mitchell had no inner circle. Again, Josie thought of domestic violence survivors. Often their abusers systematically isolated them from most or all of their family and friends. Is that what had happened here? By the time Lorelei escaped the relationship with her daughters, did they have no support network? How long had they been out here, Josie wondered? Who did they depend on or look to in emergencies?

Josie mentally retraced their steps through the house earlier. There had been a stunning lack of personal effects. No photographs—or if there had been, they'd been taken and possibly destroyed in the greenhouse. Josie and Noah's house was filled with photos of their loved ones. Their fridge was covered in drawings from Harris and Noah's niece as well as invitations they received for birthday parties, weddings, barbecues, and all kinds of social events. Josie hadn't seen any of that in the Mitchell household. She also hadn't seen any filing cabinet or desk of any kind. Most people had something in place to hold their important documents like birth certificates, banking information, social security cards and such, even if it was just a box. Lorelei had probably hidden these types of personal effects. If the killer hadn't taken them, they'd probably be able to find them. "When the ERT is done, we'll see what kinds of personal effects and documents we can find," Josie added.

Officer Chan emerged from the house, clad in Tyvek from head to toe and carrying evidence bags. She deposited them into her vehicle and picked up a camera and sketch pad. "I'm going to start in the greenhouse now," she told them. "The house will be done soon and you two can have a look around if you'd like."

Josie and Gretchen nodded and watched her walk off. Josie had no idea how much time had passed, but the sun had dropped lower in the sky. She probably should have been walking down the aisle by now, or maybe she and Noah would have already been wed. She nudged Gretchen in the ribs. "Can I use your phone to call Noah?"

"Of course."

Josie found Noah in Gretchen's contact list and hit the call icon. He answered after four rings. "Gretchen? What's going on?"

"It's me," Josie said.

"Josie," he said. "I heard about Lorelei. I'm so sorry. They just took Holly Mitchell to the morgue. Any word on Emily?"

"Not yet," she said. "The Sheriff is sending a K-9 unit. How are things there?"

Noah laughed. "All of our guests are still here but getting very restless. Celeste is furious, as is Tom, but Adam is being very accommodating. He had already started the food for the reception. He suggested just having the reception since everyone is already here. Let the band play, feed everyone, and we can reschedule our actual wedding to another time."

"That sounds good," Josie said. She looked down at her feet. Her pantyhose were dark with grime and dirt. A few pieces of grass clung to her ankles. The bottom of her dress was now stained brown as well. "Noah, I'm sorry."

"Josie," he said. "A child was murdered at our wedding venue. Her mother was killed as well, and now her younger sister is missing. Do you think I want to get married like this?"

"No," Josie said. "I know you don't. I just needed to hear it."

"I love you," he said. "Call me after the K-9 unit does their search."

Josie felt hot, uncharacteristic tears sting the backs of her eyes as she handed the phone back to Gretchen. She couldn't even identify the emotions threatening to overwhelm her or separate them from one another. Devastation at the fate of Lorelei and her daughters. Worry for Emily Mitchell. Sadness that her wedding was off for the moment. Gratitude that her would-be husband was on exactly the same page as her about the day. She felt overwhelmed by her love for him.

"You're lucky," Gretchen said. "Noah's a good person."

Unable to speak without letting loose her tears, Josie nodded.

"So you get married on a different day. It's not the end of the world."

Before Josie could respond, Dr. Feist appeared on the front porch. She walked down the steps and over to her small pickup truck where she began peeling off her crime scene garb. Her skin was paler than usual, and her hair was in disarray from the skull cap. Beneath the Tyvek suit, her pink dress was rumpled. Josie and Gretchen hurried over to her.

"My guess is the cause of death was exsanguination."

Gretchen said, "She bled out from the gunshot wounds."

Dr. Feist nodded. "But she had a pretty good head injury as well."

Josie thought of the blood and hair on the corner of the kitchen island.

Gretchen said, "Any idea on the time of death?"

"She's in full rigor, just like Holly Mitchell. I can't really pinpoint it without getting her on the table."

Josie thought of the spilled cereal in the dining area. "Is it possible they were both killed this morning?"

"Absolutely," Dr. Feist said. "I'll know more once I do the autopsy. I'll perform Holly's first, then Lorelei's." She looked directly at Josie. "I assume you're not getting married today."

"No, not today. We'll reschedule."

Dr. Feist shook her head sadly. "Destination wedding. Seriously. Think about it. I'm going to go home to change into some scrubs, and then I'll head over to the morgue. I'll let you know if I see anything that might help you find whoever did this."

"Thank you," Josie said.

They watched Dr. Feist pull away, then waited some more. The other ERT officers finished processing the inside of the house and moved to the greenhouse to help Chan. An ambulance carried Lorelei's body away. Gretchen's phone chirped intermittently with texts from Mettner, who was still interviewing staff members at Harper's Peak. Finally, they heard the sound of another vehicle bouncing along the drive. An Alcott County Sheriff's SUV came into view. Josie immediately recognized Deputy Maureen Sandoval. They'd worked together before. Sandoval smiled as she stepped out of the vehicle. Crow's feet crinkled at the corners of her eyes. Josie estimated her to be in her mid-fifties. She wore boots, khaki pants, and a navy polo shirt with the sheriff's insignia on it. Her gray-brown hair was pulled back into a tight ponytail.

Looking both Josie and Gretchen up and down, Sandoval said, "Don't think I've ever seen a bride and her bridesmaid at a crime scene before. This is a first."

Gretchen managed a smile. "Yeah, it's a first for us, too."

From the back of the SUV, they heard a bark. Josie said, "Have you got Rini with you?"

"Sure do, and she's ready to work." Sandoval walked slowly to the back of the SUV and popped the hatch, revealing a large dog cage. Inside, Rini, a four-year-old German Shepherd, sat up straight. Her tongue lolled. Eager, soulful brown eyes looked from Sandoval to Josie and Gretchen and then back. "Just a minute, girl," said Sandoval, turning to Josie and Gretchen. "What've you got?"

Josie brought her up to speed.

"I'm gonna need something with Emily's scent on it. Maybe something she wore? That would probably be easiest since you've got access to the house."

"I'll look," said Gretchen.

While Gretchen went into the house to find an item for Rini to scent, Sandoval took the dog from the truck and hooked a leash to her collar. "Down," she commanded and Rini, with a slight whine, lay on the grass, waiting for further instructions.

Gretchen returned with a crumpled pink T-shirt. "This was in the hamper on what we believe is Emily's side of the room." She held it up, and Josie could see that it was definitely Emily's size. Too small for Holly.

"That'll do," said Sandoval. She gave Rini a command that brought her to standing and guided her over so that she could sniff the shirt in Gretchen's hand. As Rini's nose pressed into the fabric, Sandoval slipped a harness onto the dog, all the while murmuring that Rini was a good girl. Then, once Sandoval was satisfied that Rini had gotten the scent, she said, "Now it's time to work, Rini."

The dog took off in the direction of the truck, her nose alternating between the ground and the air just above her head. She circled the truck twice, jumped at the passenger's side door twice, and gave up, heading around toward the back of the house. Josie and Gretchen followed. Rini worked the perimeter of the garden, then slipped through the garden gate. She went up to the greenhouse doors but then turned and headed back toward the house. She loped up the steps to the back porch. The patrol officer there looked to Josie and Gretchen for permission to let her continue her search.

"It's okay," Josie said.

With a nod, he let Rini and Sandoval into the house. Josie and Gretchen followed. By the time they reached the kitchen, they could hear Rini's paws pounding up the stairs. Avoiding Lorelei's blood on one side of the island countertop and broken glass on the other in their stockinged feet, they, too, went upstairs. They had just reached the top of the steps when they heard Rini barking.

Josie picked up her pace, finding Rini and Sandoval in the girls' room. Rini sat in the center of the room, barking. Once Sandoval saw them, she gave Rini another command and the dog quieted and lay down.

Josie knew that search-and-rescue dogs gave indicators when they found what they were looking for. She also knew that Rini would always give an active indicator when making a live find—meaning that she would bark when she found a live person.

Except Emily wasn't there.

CHAPTER SIX

They tore the room apart, moving every piece of furniture, taking the beds apart, but found nothing. Sandoval took Rini back outside and repeated the exercise twice more. Twice more the dog ended up in Emily and Holly's room, giving her active indicator that she had found Emily.

"With all due respect to Rini," Gretchen said, standing in the bedroom with dog and handler for the third time. "She's just wrong. I mean, this is Emily's bedroom. Of course it's going to smell like her."

Sandoval seemed just as confused as Josie and Gretchen. "That doesn't matter. People shed scent all day long. Rini would be able to find it. She's never missed a live find before. I'm not sure—something's not right. Let me—how about if I call a colleague? Maybe we can get another dog out here to do the same search and see what happens?"

Josie couldn't help but think that every second that went by was another second that Emily was getting further and further out of reach. But they had no choice. There were already searchers in the woods. The Amber Alert had gone out. She'd never known search-and-rescue dogs to get things wrong. Sometimes the scent stopped for reasons beyond their control, but they were extremely reliable. She looked down at Rini's earnest face. The dog knew she was right. What was Josie missing?

She moved around the perimeter of the room once more, this time looking for places where the carpet might be loose, but found nothing. If there was some hidden compartment in the floorboards, Josie didn't see how one would get to it.

Looking back at Gretchen and Sandoval, she asked, "Is it possible she's… in the wall?"

Gretchen raised a brow. "Boss, how would an eight-year-old get into a wall? If someone put her in a wall, we'd know it. Holly and Lorelei Mitchell weren't dead long enough for someone to patch and paint a wall. Plus, why leave Lorelei's body in the kitchen, Holly's at Harper's Peak but then go to the trouble of hiding Emily—alive? We've torn this place up. She's not here. Come on. We'll wait for the other dog and see what happens. I'll call dispatch and request more searchers."

Glumly, Josie followed them out of the room. As they got to the bottom of the steps, she thought she heard another thud, the same as she and Gretchen had heard earlier, but neither Gretchen nor Sandoval heard it. Outside, both Gretchen and Sandoval made phone calls while Josie stared at the house. Behind it, the sun had begun to set, leaving the sky awash in orange and red. If they were going to be there into the night, they'd need to turn on some lights.

Josie went back inside, flicking light switches as she went, and noticing more strange details. The beanbag chairs in the living room and lack of a coffee table or end tables. The wall art was stretched canvas, not glass. In one corner were two plastic sets of drawers. Josie opened a couple of them to see that they contained arts and crafts supplies. Paper, crayons, markers, glitter, glue, tape, felt pieces, ribbon, paint, sponges caked with dried paint. No brushes and no scissors. In the dining room the tables and chairs were made of oak but there was nothing else in the room. No centerpiece on the table. No sideboard or hutch. The overturned cereal bowl and spoon were plastic. Moving into the kitchen, Josie opened and closed drawers, noting that all the utensils were plastic. Also, there were no knives. Anywhere in the kitchen. Not even butter knives.

She opened the cabinets, finding plastic dinnerware but ceramic dinnerware as well. The coffee mugs were ceramic. In one of the upper cabinets, she found several orange pill bottles. All of the drugs had been prescribed to Lorelei. Josie committed them to memory: methylphenidate, risperidone, aripiprazole, olanzapine, alprazolam. Josie didn't recognize all of them, but from some of her previous cases, she knew at least two of the drugs were anti-psychotics, often prescribed for schizophrenia or bipolar disorder, among other things. Had Lorelei been struggling with either of those—or some other mental health issue? Josie checked the bottles again to see they had all been prescribed by a Dr. Vincent Buckley. She made a mental note to track down the doctor to find out what he knew about Lorelei and her children. They could likely get a warrant for Lorelei's medical chart as well.

She went back up the stairs and found Lorelei's room. Searching the closet, she found no personal effects or documents of any kind. However, all of her clothes were folded and placed in plastic storage cubes. No hangers. Josie searched the single nightstand drawer but found nothing of interest. Standing next to the king-sized bed, she turned in a circle, marveling at how bare the room seemed. Something on the back of the door caught her eye. She took a few steps toward it and saw there was a lock on the door. Not just any kind of lock but a deadbolt. Who put a deadbolt lock on the inside of their bedroom door?

Josie went back into the hallway and checked the other bedroom doors. Emily and Holly's room also had a deadbolt lock on the inside of their door. The last bedroom had no lock.

"What the hell?" she muttered to herself as she returned to Lorelei's room. Her eyes panned the room again, landing on the bed once more. The mattress sat on what appeared to be a solid metal frame. It took several tries for Josie to dislodge the mattress and push it partially off the frame. In the middle of the metal frame was a small, sliding metal door.

Josie ran down the steps as fast as her wedding dress would allow. "Chan!" she hollered as she burst onto the back porch, overlooking the garden and greenhouse. "Chan!"

Officer Chan was just leaving the greenhouse. She stopped in the center of the garden and stared at Josie. "You got something?"

"I think so."

A few minutes later, Josie and Gretchen stood in the doorway of Lorelei's bedroom as Chan used gloved hands to pull items from the hollow core of the bedframe, narrating as she went. "Three boxes of ammunition for a Winchester 1200 shotgun. A large plastic sewing kit. A small plastic bin filled with… knives of various sizes. A smaller plastic container with three pair of scissors in it." Using a flashlight, she searched the compartment one last time. "That's it."

"Nothing else?" Josie said.

"Sorry," Chan said. "Just all this weird stuff. Want me to log it in as evidence?"

"No," Gretchen said. "I don't think you need to. Thanks."

She gave them a mock salute before leaving them alone in the room. Josie said, "She knew she was in danger."

"Yes," Gretchen agreed.

Josie opened her mouth to speak again but a sound froze her in place. Another thud, this one louder, closer. They looked at one another, eyes wide. "She's here," Josie said quietly.

"She can't be," Gretchen replied. "We searched every nook and cranny of this place."

"Rini scented her here, in this house, in her own room."

"Boss, the dog could be wrong."

"You heard Sandoval. Rini's never been wrong before."

With a sigh, Gretchen said, "What are we missing?"

Again, they walked through the house, calling out Emily's name, telling her it was safe to come out from her hiding place. In the rooms that were carpeted, they checked for loose seams, and in the rooms that weren't, they checked for loose floorboards. They looked behind furniture and inside closets to see if there were any secret compartments they had missed.

Nothing.

Back outside, Sandoval and Rini waited by her SUV for another dog and handler to arrive. Josie stared at the house, thinking of the day that Lorelei had brought her here. If Lorelei believed she was in so much danger, why would she bring a stranger to her home? Had she known she was in danger when Josie was her guest, or had something happened in the three months since they'd met? Something to make her hide all the sharp items in her home in a secret compartment under her mattress, and put deadbolt locks on the insides of the occupied bedroom doors?

Josie thought back to that day in January. Everything downstairs had been the same. She just hadn't realized at the time that Lorelei had effectively rid her home of harmful objects like knives and scissors or even glass from wall art that could be shattered and used to hurt someone. Josie hadn't had any reason to think that Lorelei and her daughters were in danger, or even that they were afraid. In fact, Lorelei had left both girls home alone that day. Would she have left them alone if she was so afraid someone was going to injure them?

"Boss?" Gretchen said.

Josie looked away from the front door and back at Gretchen, suddenly realizing she had taken several steps back toward the house. Her stockinged feet were at the base of the steps. Where they had been the day she trailed Lorelei into the house. Josie visualized that cold, nasty day once more. By the time they reached the house, the sleet was coming down harder. Josie's boots squished in the layer of wet snow accumulating on each step as she followed Lorelei to the front door.

"It sticks sometimes," Lorelei had said as she struggled to turn the key in the lock. Laughing, she had put her full weight into it, and in doing so, fell forward a bit, her shoulder hitting the doorbell. Josie remembered hearing the muted chime from inside. She'd done it twice before the door opened.

But what if it hadn't been an accident? What if it had been purposeful?

Josie's fingers reached out, lingering over the doorbell.

Behind her, Gretchen padded up the steps. "Boss?" she said again.

Josie pressed the bell, hearing the chime from inside, louder now, because the front door was slightly ajar. She counted off three seconds and rang it again. Then she stepped inside, again picturing Lorelei. She'd been talking to Josie as she walked through the living room, telling Josie how she grew much of her own food out back even in winter, as she was lucky enough to have a greenhouse. In the dining room, one of the chairs was against the wall rather than tucked beneath the table. Lorelei had dragged it across the room, putting it back in place, but making a horrific noise as its feet scraped across the tile floor. At the time, Josie had absently wondered why she didn't just pick it up, but Lorelei was talking about how she homeschooled her girls and Josie didn't want to be rude, so she focused on Lorelei's words.

Now, Josie picked up one of the chairs, put it against the wall where she'd seen it the first time she visited. Then she dragged it across the room, causing a sound akin to a shriek. In the doorway, Gretchen winced.

"Let me call the girls," Lorelei had said then, returning to the living room. At the bottom of the steps, she had called their names. When she didn't get any response, she banged on the wall three times.

Gretchen moved out of her way as Josie went to the bottom of the steps. She didn't call for Emily. Instead, she banged on the wall three times, in approximately the same place Lorelei had.

Then she listened.

Gretchen said, "You want to tell me what's happening right now, boss?"

Josie didn't take her eyes off the top of the steps. "She was signaling them," she told Gretchen. "The day I was here with them. She had left them here alone. When we got here, she did all these things that I didn't even realize were significant at the time. They must have been hiding and she was giving them an all-clear. Doorbell twice, chair scraping over the floor, three bangs on the wall."

"Was that it?"

"Shit."

Josie followed in Lorelei's footsteps, heading halfway up the stairs. Lorelei had stopped on the fifth or sixth step and stomped on it four times. Turning back to Josie, she'd smiled. "This old carpet," she'd said. "Keeps getting loose."

But now Josie saw there was no loose area of carpet. It was part of the signal. Without boots or shoes of any kind, it would be difficult to make a lot of noise. Josie hitched up her dress and lifted one foot as far as she could, bringing it down hard four times on the step.

She waited. A rustling came from somewhere on the second floor. Then a quiet creak, followed by more rustling, another creak, and the sound of small feet scuttering along the hallway. Josie's heart seemed to stop for a split second.

Emily Mitchell appeared at the top of the steps. Her brown hair was messy and matted. Wrinkles covered her blue pajamas. She was missing a sock. Clutched in her arms was a stuffed dog with long, floppy ears.

Josie's heart thundered back to life. She'd spent the last several hours trying not to think about what might be happening to this little girl at the hands of a ruthless killer. Seeing her alive, safe, and unharmed sent a surge of relief through Josie's veins.

"Hi, Emily," she said.

CHAPTER SEVEN

Emily stared at Josie warily, unmoving. Josie climbed another step. How long had the girl been hiding? How many hours? She had to be starving, exhausted, and terrified. Josie smiled. "I'm so glad you came out," she said. "We're here to help you."

Emily's grip on the stuffed dog tightened as Josie climbed the final few steps, kneeling on the landing so she was face to face with her. "It's safe now, Emily."

Her hazel eyes widened as she took in Josie's dress. "Did I die?" she whispered.

For the umpteenth time that day, Josie felt her heart might break apart in her chest. "No," she reassured her. "You are very much alive."

"Are you an angel?"

Josie laughed. "No. I'm a police officer."

Emily still didn't move, but Josie took it as a good sign that she wasn't recoiling. She whispered, "You look like an angel."

Josie looked down at her dress and smiled once more. "Thank you. I was supposed to get married today. That's why I look like this. But I am really a police officer, and I came here to get you and make sure you stay safe. There are a bunch more police officers downstairs and outside, waiting for us."

Emily didn't respond.

Josie said, "I was here before, you know? A few months ago. I had coffee and banana bread with you and your mom and sister."

One of Emily's eyebrows raised ever so slightly.

Josie massaged the right side of her face, feeling the thin scar beneath her fingers as she rubbed the make-up away. She turned her head so Emily could get a clear view. "Remember this? You asked me about it."

Emily's face changed instantly, a look of recognition and excitement flashing across it. Then it quickly died. "Where's Mama and Holly?"

Josie glanced at the bottom of the steps to see Gretchen standing there. What could Josie say? What should she say? She didn't know how much Emily knew or what she had seen. Telling her the truth would be emotionally catastrophic, but Josie couldn't see the advantage in lying. In her experience, adults sometimes had this natural instinct to lie to children about bad things, thinking they were somehow shielding or protecting them, when often, children took things better than adults. Josie's own childhood had been filled with trauma, abuse, and uncertainty, and yet, the truth, no matter how difficult it was to hear, had always made life simpler to navigate.

Josie said, "I'm very sorry, Emily, but they're not with us anymore."

"They're dead," Emily said. It wasn't a question, and there was no hint of hopefulness in her tone that perhaps Josie would oppose this statement. She knew.

"I'm so sorry, Emily."

"Mama said the bad things might happen," Emily said. "She was right."

"What bad things?" Josie asked.

"Mama said I never had to talk about them if I didn't want to."

"Okay," Josie said, not wanting to press the issue. The girl's psyche was surely very fragile at this point, and Josie wasn't about to say or do anything that might cause more damage. Instead, she said, "You were so smart by hiding, and you were so disciplined staying in your hiding spot until I gave you the signal to come out."

Emily nodded. "Holly taught me."

Josie exchanged a brief glance with Gretchen. She was one of the most stoic detectives Josie had ever met, but Josie could see the strain in her face. What the hell had been going on in this house that Emily's older sister had taught her to hide when bad things happened?

"Did Holly hide with you today at all?" Josie asked.

Emily shook her head. "No. She couldn't hide today. I went by myself."

"That was very good," Josie assured her. "I'm glad you did. Can you show me where your hiding place is?"

Emily's lips pursed momentarily as she regarded Josie. Then she leaned in and in a hushed tone, said, "Do you have a gun?"

"I do," Josie said. "I don't have it right this second, but yes, I own a gun. Are you worried about that?"

With one hand, Emily stroked the top of her stuffed dog's head. "I'm worried you won't be ready for the bad things, like Mama and Holly."

The breath seemed to rush out of Josie's body all at once. She took a beat to make sure her composure didn't crack. "It's my job to be ready for the bad things, Emily. I promise that I will do everything I can to keep you safe, and so will all the other police officers here today. Okay?"

Emily reached out and touched Josie's face, her small fingers, as light as a butterfly's touch, tracing Josie's scar. "You didn't tell me what this was from," she said. "But now I know. It was from the bad things, wasn't it?"

Josie swallowed over the growing lump in her throat. "Yes," she croaked. "It was."

"You're still here."

"Yes."

Emily turned and started walking down the hallway. "Come on. I'll show you our hiding place."

CHAPTER EIGHT

Josie heard Gretchen climb the stairs behind her as she followed Emily to the girls' bedroom. What had they missed? Emily walked over to the section of wall that formed a chalkboard and wrapped her fingers around the string holding the eraser. She tugged at it, hard and fast, and the trim surrounding the chalkboard paint popped out of the wall, swinging like a door. Across the room, Gretchen gasped.

Josie looked at the other side of the trim to see that the hinges had been painted purple to blend in with the wall. One would have had to look very closely to notice anything off about it. Josie touched the inside of the makeshift hatch. Whoever had built it had been pretty creative. It was made of drywall and wood. Plus, it wasn't in the shape of a door. The bottom of it was at Emily's knee level which meant she had to climb in and out of it, almost as if it were a window. Josie poked her head inside, but it was dark.

"Just a minute," said Emily. Tucking her stuffed dog beneath her armpit, she deftly climbed inside the large hole in the wall. A few seconds later, a light snapped on. Josie leaned her upper body inside once more. The space was the size of a large closet, the walls unpainted drywall. Josie tried to visualize what was on the other side—Lorelei's closet. Had her closet originally been a walk-in closet? Had she or someone else walled it off to make a hiding place?

"We don't have plugs in here," Emily said. She pointed to a small battery-powered lamp on the floor in the corner of the space. There were two sleeping bags, each one with a pillow. A pile of books sat between the two bags. Next to those was a pile of flashlights and book lights. In another corner was a camping toilet with a roll of toilet paper beside it. The smell of urine wafted toward Josie. Another scent, this one rancid, filled Josie's nostrils. Her eyes searched the tiny space until she saw its source: a half-eaten column of string cheese, a browned apple core, and a banana peel. Next to that was a half-eaten cup of yogurt with a plastic spoon poking out of it. Josie pointed to the food. "Did you bring that with you today?"

"No, I put it in here the last time we had to hide."

"When was that?" Josie asked, wondering how long the food had been there and if Emily was going to get food poisoning from having eaten it.

"I don't know," she answered. "But when I tried to eat the food, it didn't taste very good."

"How does your belly feel? Do you feel sick?"

Emily shrugged. "I don't know." She walked over and stood on top of the blue sleeping bag. "This one's mine."

Josie nodded and held out a hand, waving Emily back out into the bedroom. "Okay, very good, Emily. You can come back out. Thank you for showing me."

Emily climbed back out and stood staring up at Josie. "I hide in other places, too, but that's our special hiding place."

"Why is it special?" Josie asked.

"'Cause only me and Holly and Mama know where it is. No one ever found us there. Not ever. I also hide in the cabinets in the kitchen sometimes, and behind the beanbag chairs in the living room and under the dining room table."

"Why do you have to hide so much?" Josie asked her.

Matter-of-factly, she said, "I already told you."

"Because of the bad things."

She nodded.

"Okay." Josie pointed toward Emily's dresser. "I'm going to need you to pack a few things. Some clothes, and anything else you want to bring with you. Maybe some books or plushies? Also, you'll need two socks and a pair of shoes. Can you find those things for me?"

Emily shrugged again. "Sure."

Josie and Gretchen watched as she walked over to her dresser and began taking clothes out, lining each folded item up on the bed. When she finished, she reached under the bed and pulled out a duffel bag. Gretchen walked over to Josie's side and muttered, "We're going to have to call child services."

"I know," Josie said. "But I think we should take her to the hospital first and have her evaluated. We need to try to locate Lorelei's next of kin as well."

Gretchen waved her phone in the air. "I'll be in the hall making some calls."

Josie nodded. Once Gretchen was out of the room, Josie walked over to Emily, who had made four piles of clothes on her bed. Each pile had a shirt, pants, underwear, and socks. Under her breath, Emily counted the piles. "One, two, three, four. One, two, three, four."

"Can I help you?" Josie asked.

Emily paused and without looking at her, shook her head. With a frown, she started counting again. "One, two, three, four." She repeated the process six times and then she began to pack the piles into the duffel bag. When she finished, Josie walked over to the dresser and selected a pair of socks from her top dresser drawer. Emily pulled them on and then retrieved a pair of sneakers from under her bed. Once those were on, Josie helped her zip up her overfull duffel bag.

"Wait!" Emily said when Josie went to pick up the bag. "I need to bring my other things."

"What other things?"

Emily walked over to her desk and pointed to a pile of random items arranged into a circle. There was a small gray stone roughly the size of a quarter, a tiny pink sequin, a bird feather, an unused birthday candle, and a bright red bottle cap that had come from a gallon of milk. Emily began counting them, her small finger hovering over each object as she did. "One, two, three, four, five."

She repeated the count six times. Then she looked up at Josie. "Now I can put them in my bag."

Perplexed, Josie watched as Emily carefully put each item into one of the side pockets of the duffel bag. "I'm ready," she told Josie.

Josie had a lot of questions, but her immediate priority was to get Emily out of the house. It was still a crime scene. "Emily, what's going to happen now is that I'm going to take you to the hospital, okay? Because bad things happened here today, we'd like the doctors to talk to you, okay?"

Emily nodded.

"Then you might have to go stay with someone—a stranger, but someone who will keep you safe—until we find a place for you to live permanently. Do you understand?"

"You mean a foster home."

Surprised, Josie said, "Yes, exactly. How do you know about foster homes?"

"I'm not supposed to say."

"Who told you not to say?" Josie asked.

"My mom," Emily replied.

Again, Josie was wary of pushing the girl too hard. On top of that, there were legal implications of any conversations that Josie had with the girl without a guardian or parent present. To get a proper statement from her, Josie would need to wait until they'd either located next of kin or until Emily had been taken into the care of the Commonwealth of Pennsylvania. Still, Josie had no idea how long it would be before she could get such a statement, and it was clear that there was a killer on the loose—a killer who had no issues murdering children. Changing subjects, Josie asked, "Do you hide in the wall a lot?"

Emily shrugged. "Sometimes."

"Can you tell me who you're hiding from when you go in there?"

Slowly, Emily brought her index finger up and pressed it against her lips in the universal symbol for hush.

Josie managed a smile, trying to put her at ease. "You can tell me, Emily. Nothing bad will happen to you now, and you don't need to hide anymore. It's really important that I know who you and Holly hid from when you went into that little room."

"I can't," Emily whispered.

"Why not?"

"Because if I say, bad things will keep happening."

Josie felt a chill slither down her neck. She worked hard to keep her smile in place. "Okay," she told Emily. "Let's get you out of here."

Josie guided her outside to Gretchen's car and strapped her into the back seat. Gretchen had called off the search and the Amber Alert. The patrol officers had gone, as had Deputy Sandoval and Rini. Everyone on the ERT had gone except for Officer Jenny Chan, who was packing up evidence bags in the back of her SUV. Josie left Gretchen standing by the driver's side of her car, on the phone to the hospital, and walked over to Chan. "Anything interesting from the greenhouse?"

Chan peeled off her Tyvek suit and booties, crumpled them up and tossed them into the back seat. "Afraid not. A whole lot of ashes. A destroyed laptop and phone. I can have a tech expert look at them, but I think they're too damaged to get anything from them. You'd be better off just getting a warrant for her phone records. I also found some bits of what look like color photographs, but none that have anything identifying in them. Scraps from what look like documents of some kind. Hard to say. There are some scraps with the ends of words on them, but without context, I'm not sure they mean anything. Sorry."

Josie shook her head. "It's not your fault. I appreciate you being here."

Chan pulled off her skull cap and shook out her long, dark hair. "Sorry about your wedding."

Josie gave a wan smile. "We can get married another day. Hey, did you find anything of interest inside the truck?"

"No, I'm sorry. Nothing in the truck except Lorelei's vehicle registration and insurance card."

Josie thanked her, watched her pack up the rest of the vehicle and start down the driveway. It was almost dark now. The sounds of the night started to rise all around them: frogs peeping and trilling; cicadas rattling; crickets chirping.

Josie turned back and began walking toward Gretchen's car. Gretchen was now on the phone with Chief Chitwood. Josie could tell by her tone and the way she kept saying, "Yes, sir." She had put her heels back on as she paced beside the vehicle, occasionally pausing to wrench one of the spikes from the soft ground. From the back seat window, Emily stared at Josie, looking frozen, her eyes so wide that Josie felt a little shiver pass through her. Josie stopped in place, feeling as though Emily was trying to communicate something to her. Then, slowly, Emily's head swiveled toward the front steps of the house. Josie's gaze followed hers.

A cry escaped Josie's throat before she could clamp her hand over her mouth. Gretchen stopped dead in her tracks.

There, on the top step, was a pinecone doll.

Josie spun in a circle, looking all around them. There was nothing. No one. She strode over to the car. The movement seemed to reanimate Gretchen. She dove into the open window of the driver's side door and grabbed her gun. Josie said, "Lock her inside the car."

"We have to get her out of here, boss."

"Call for back-up."

A whirring sound made them both turn to the back seat window. Emily had used the button to lower it. She said, "He's already gone."

"Who?" Josie said. "Who's already gone? Who was here, Emily? Who left that doll? You saw him, didn't you?"

Emily gave a solemn nod. Gretchen said, "Who was it? Who was just here?"

She lifted her finger to her lips again. Hush.

"Emily," Josie said, trying to keep the frustration and desperation out of her voice. "It's very important that you tell us who left that doll."

No response.

"Was it your father?" Gretchen asked.

"I don't have a daddy," she said.

"Then who was it, Emily?" Josie asked. "You can tell us. We're the police. We need to know who he is so we can arrest him. We think he's the one who hurt your mom and Holly. Please, Emily, tell us whatever you know."

She shook her head and lowered her eyes.

Gretchen lowered her voice so only Josie could hear. "Maybe she doesn't want to tell us while we're at the house. We need to get her out of here."

Josie nodded. "Call for back-up. As soon as they get here, we leave with Emily."

While Gretchen made yet another phone call, Josie slid into the back seat beside Emily. They watched Gretchen finish her call, one hand pressing the phone to her ear while the other held her pistol out, panning the area in front of the car.

The pinecone doll stared at them, it's freakish, googly eyes now sinister and menacing. Josie felt Emily's warm hand on her arm. She looked over at her.

Emily said, "It means he's sorry."

CHAPTER NINE

Outside one of the glass-partitioned rooms in Denton Memorial's Emergency Department, Josie paced. A nurse and doctor were inside the room with Emily. They had pulled the curtains across the glass when they went inside so Josie couldn't tell where they were in terms of their exam. Gretchen had gone home to change before heading back to Lorelei Mitchell's house to help with the search for whoever had left the creepy pinecone doll. Chan was going to meet her back out there to process the doll. Then Mettner was going to meet with Gretchen at Lorelei's house to compare notes. A social worker from the county's health and human services department was due at the hospital any minute. Josie still wore her wedding dress, and every person who walked past her stared. She wished she had thought to bring her own phone. She could have called Noah and asked him to bring her a change of clothes.

A woman in a black pantsuit strode down the hall toward Josie. Soft brown curls floated around her face. Over one shoulder was slung a messenger bag. In her hand was a paper coffee cup. She stopped when she got to Josie and gave a wry smile. "I'm looking for an eight-year-old girl found at a murder scene. I was told to stop when I saw the lady in the wedding dress."

Josie laughed and extended a hand. "Detective Josie Quinn. Excuse the dress. Are you from child services?"

The woman shook Josie's hand and then produced her credentials. "Yes. Marcie Riebe."

Josie pointed toward the glass enclosure. "The medical staff are examining her now."

Marcie looked up and down the hall. She spotted a linen bin and wheeled it over to where Josie stood. She took a small laptop out of her messenger bag and set it on top of the bin. Next to it, she set her coffee. After a few clicks and some fast typing, she looked up at Josie and said, "Why don't you tell me what happened?"

Josie told Marcie everything they knew. She tapped away furiously at her keyboard, pausing occasionally to fire off questions. When Josie was finished, she said, "The first thing we need to do is try to locate her next of kin. I'd like to keep her with family if at all possible, especially given the trauma she's been through."

"I agree," Josie said. "My team will get to work on it as soon as possible. Right now, they're still out in the field."

Before Marcie could say more, the doctor emerged from Emily's room. Josie knew him from many trips to the Emergency Department related to cases she was working. Dr. Ahmed Nashat was smart, sensitive, and no-nonsense. Josie made the introductions between him and Marcie. He gave them both a pained smile. "She appears to be in excellent health. Well nourished, no signs of any injuries or physical trauma. No signs at all of long-term abuse. She is alert and oriented. On exam, she is around the fiftieth percentile for milestones for her age. She's bright and articulate, although she does refuse to answer some questions. I'm a little concerned about the psychological trauma she's had today. I've called for a psych consult. The only issue at this point is that she does appear to have a case of food poisoning. She threw up twice while we were in with her."

Josie sighed. "I was worried about that." She told them about the spoiled food they'd found in Emily's hiding place.

Dr. Nashat nodded. "That would do it. If it's okay with you, Ms. Riebe, I'd like to keep her for at least a few hours, perhaps overnight, to make sure she's stable."

"That will be fine," said Marcie.

Josie asked, "Doctor, does Emily already have a medical chart here?"

He shook his head. "No, I'm afraid not. She's not in our system." He looked at Marcie. "Registration will probably be reliant on you to provide financial details."

"Great," said Marcie with a tight smile. "If you don't mind, I'd like to go in and speak with her now."

"Of course," said Dr. Nashat. "Just one more thing. We asked her if she knew of anyone we could call—family or friends—and she said, 'Pax is a friend.'"

"Pax?" Josie repeated.

"Yes. P-A-X. That's what she said. When we asked who he was, she said that he was a friend her mother helped. She also said that his dad didn't like him coming to their house. We asked her if she had seen him today. She said no."

Marcie smiled. "I'll see if I can get more information from her about this Pax person."

"Thank you," Josie said. "As soon as I talk with my team, we'll see if we can locate him and his father."

Marcie disappeared into the room and the doctor moved on to other patients, leaving Josie alone in the hallway once more. Moments later, the sound of heavy footsteps on tile drew her attention. She looked up to see Noah striding down the hall. Her relief was so profound, she thought she might buckle. He had changed into regular clothes: jeans, a black T-shirt under a light jacket, and boots. In his hands he carried a burgundy-colored cloth tote bag that said, "Harper's Peak" on it in elaborate script.

His smile made her knees go weak. "You brought a change of clothes for me," she said.

He stopped before her and kissed her lips. "And your phone, your weapon, and I went by the house to get your laptop."

"Thank you."

"The band is still playing at Harper's Peak," he told her. "Misty and Harris took Trout home with them. Your grandmother, parents, brother, Trinity and Drake are staying the night at the hotel. So are my sister and brother. Celeste and Tom weren't thrilled about any of this, but Adam was very accommodating."

Josie laughed. "So everyone's having our wedding without us."

"This time," he said.

"Have you heard anything?" Josie asked, taking the bag from him.

"No one on the staff at Harper's Peak remembers ever seeing Holly Mitchell before—alive or dead. They've got no cameras out in the gardens or at the overlooks. They do have cameras in all the parking lots. I went through all the footage, but didn't see anyone getting a body out of their car. I looked at the footage from cameras overlooking the staff parking lots and cameras at the exteriors of all the buildings, thinking maybe Holly came there alive with someone, was killed in one of the buildings and then carried to the overlook, but there's nothing on any of the footage to suggest that."

Josie said, "There was clearly a confrontation of some kind at the house. I think she was probably killed there."

"Me too," Noah said. "But we have to cover all the bases so we don't miss anything. Celeste has Tom hard at work getting our team access to everyone on the premises. Mett was questioning guests when I left. He was hoping maybe one of the guests saw the killer on the grounds but didn't realize it at the time. He wasn't having much luck, though. It looks like no one saw anything. We think whoever brought her body there came through the woods."

"Lorelei's house is a couple of miles from Harper's Peak. That's a long trek."

Noah said, "Unless Holly escaped the house and the killer caught up with her in the woods, murdered her, and carried her to the church."

Josie thought about the pinecone doll and how Emily had said that it meant "he" was sorry. Had the killer not meant to kill Holly? Or was he just sorry that he had? Was that the significance of the doll placed on her body? Did the church itself have some significance? "Her body was staged at the church," she told Noah. "It has meaning. He didn't move Lorelei's body."

"When Gretchen called Mett, she said you two had discussed the possibility that this was a domestic situation. If that was the case, he probably wasn't sorry he killed Lorelei. It would make more sense that perhaps he chased Holly into the woods. Maybe he never intended to kill her, but he'd gone too far and felt remorse for her death."

"He left her somewhere beautiful," Josie added. "Somewhere she would be found."

"And he left her body in a dignified way."

"True," said Josie.

"Mett got a few more people to come in and search the woods near Harper's Peak. Chief approved the overtime."

"That's great," Josie said. She held up the bag. "I need to get changed. Then I want to see what I can find out about Lorelei's background. But I need help getting out of this dress."

CHAPTER TEN

Twenty minutes later they emerged from an unused room in the basement of the hospital. Josie's skin was flushed. She looked over at Noah to see that his was as well. She could still feel his mouth on her throat and his hands on her hips as the wedding dress fell to the floor and Noah kicked it aside. She couldn't remember them being so hungry for one another, not even at the beginning of their relationship, but she had needed him the same way she used to need several shots of Wild Turkey whenever life's darkest moments threatened to overtake her. It was clear from the second his fingers brushed over the buttons of her dress that Noah had needed her just as badly. As they stepped into the empty hallway with its jaundiced walls and grimy tile floor, Josie tucked loose strands of hair behind her ears and adjusted the gun holster at her waist. She slung the bag with the laptop over her shoulder and looked back at Noah, who held her wedding dress over one arm. Strands of his thick, brown hair jutted out wildly. Josie reached up to smooth them down, still feeling remnants of the wild electricity crackling between them.

Softly, Noah said, "Maybe we should almost get married more often."

Before Josie could respond, another voice came from down the hall. "Hey, lovebirds. I've been looking for you—either of you, actually."

They turned to see Dr. Feist standing outside the doors to the city morgue, dressed in her signature blue scrubs and skull cap. She waved them over. "I called Mett and Gretchen, both of whom are otherwise engaged. They both said one of you should be available to hear autopsy results." She stared at them, a slow smile curving her lips. "Or did I interrupt something?"

Noah held out the wedding dress. "Josie had to get changed."

Dr. Feist raised a brow. "Sure. Whatever. Come on. You can leave that in my office for safekeeping until you're ready to take it home."

They followed her down the hall and into the exam room. It was windowless, its walls pale gray cinderblock. In the center of the room were two stainless steel autopsy tables with light fixtures overhead. As always, the combination of chemicals and decomposition made for a stomach-turning odor. No matter how many times Josie smelled it, she never got used to it. Dr. Feist took the dress from Noah and disappeared into her office in the adjoining room. Before them, both examination tables were occupied. The bodies were covered with sheets, but Josie knew the larger one was Lorelei and the smaller one was Holly. Dr. Feist returned with a laptop and opened it up while standing at the stainless steel countertop that ran along the back wall of the room. She pulled up a set of x-rays and then turned back to Josie and Noah.

"Whose exam would you like to hear about first?"

Josie swallowed. "Lorelei's."

Dr. Feist gave a solemn nod. "I was able to confirm her identity using her driver's license which the ERT took from her home. I found no evidence of sexual assault. Her cause of death was, as I predicted, exsanguination. She bled out from a gunshot wound to the chest. I extracted a number of shotgun pellets from her abdomen and chest cavity. There was massive internal damage, but I believe the worst of the damage came from one pellet that punched through her left lung, causing a sucking chest wound, and another pellet that went right through her heart. Basically, her left lung and heart were shredded. All the heavy scientific language will be in my final report. In addition to that, she had quite a nasty head injury. However, it appears to have happened probably within minutes of her death, as I would have expected to see swelling in the brain or a subdural hematoma, but that didn't have time to materialize."

"Time of death?" Josie asked.

"Given her body temperature and the temperature of the house, I'd say she died sometime between six a.m. and ten a.m. There was coffee and some oatmeal in her stomach, so it appears she'd just had breakfast. There are some incidental findings I think you should be aware of. They have nothing to do with her death, but may impact your case."

She walked over to the table with the larger form on it and peeled back the sheet to just above Lorelei's breasts. Brushing aside Lorelei's curls, Dr. Feist indicated the skin along the side of her neck and down to her trapezius muscles. Josie leaned in and immediately saw at least a half-dozen silver-white lines, each one about an inch long. "Stab wounds," she said.

"Yes," said Dr. Feist. "Very old ones. These healed a very long time ago. Many more are on her upper back and neck. I counted thirty-four in all. Most were relatively superficial, meaning they didn't penetrate beneath the fascia. Two of them, however, nicked the left collarbone and another penetrated the back of her neck deeply enough to nick the bone of her spinal column, taking a small chip out of it, but not damaging any of the nerves or vessels around it. She was extraordinarily lucky."

Noah said, "You're saying someone stabbed her thirty-four times in her upper back and neck?"

"Yes," said Dr. Feist. "My guess is that she was attacked from behind. Probably a blitz attack—lightning fast and relentless."

"My God," said Josie. "Is there any way to tell how old they are?"

Dr. Feist shook her head. "I can't say for certain. Several years is my guess."

A moment of silence unfurled around them as they considered what Lorelei had survived at some point in her life. As if of their own will, Josie's fingers brushed over the scar on her face. When she saw Dr. Feist watching her, she lowered her hand.

"What about Holly?" asked Noah.

Dr. Feist grimaced. "Her case is a little more complicated. Have you ever heard of 'talk and die' syndrome?"

Josie and Noah shook their heads in unison.

"That's shorthand neurologists use when they're talking about a closed head injury, usually an epidural hematoma, which is when blood accumulates between the dura—the covering of the brain—and the skull. With a 'talk and die' injury, the person usually sustains a head injury without a skull fracture. They usually appear just fine for minutes, even hours. They're laughing, walking, talking—"

"Until they die," Noah filled in.

"Right. The decline happens extremely rapidly. The accumulation of blood can cause pressure and swelling in your brain. It can even cause your brain to shift inside your skull. That's what I saw on examination with Holly Mitchell. She had a very large epidural hematoma that put intense pressure on her brain and caused it to swell and shift. That is her cause of death."

Josie said, "Is it possible to tell how long it was between the time she sustained the head injury and when she died?"

Dr. Feist frowned. "Unfortunately, no. As I said, with 'talk and die' syndrome, a person could seem fine for five minutes or for several hours before death. Given her body temperature as well as the outdoor temperatures, she probably died between eight a.m. and noon."

Noah asked, "Is there any way to tell what injured her?"

Dr. Feist said, "I'm afraid not. The injury was over her left ear, behind the temple. Either someone struck her, or she sustained some sort of fall, although she would have had to land at exactly the right angle with exactly the right amount of force to sustain this type of injury."

"But you don't think she fell," Josie said. "Earlier, at the scene, you said she had bruising around her neck and petechiae in her eyes."

"Yes," said Dr. Feist. "If you would have a look…" she trailed off, staring at them both, waiting for them to consent to seeing Holly's body once more.

Josie nodded and followed Dr. Feist over to Holly's body. Noah trailed them. With great care, Dr. Feist pulled the sheet down and tucked it over Holly's shoulders. Her eyes were closed, her white eyelashes stark beneath the overhead light. "Poliosis," said Dr. Feist, following Josie's gaze.

"Yes," Josie said. "Lorelei said she had it."

"It's usually seen in the form of a white forelock or a white patch of hair somewhere on the head, but sometimes results in white eyelashes. It's simply a lack of melanin in the hair roots. On its own, without a co-occurring medical condition, it's entirely harmless."

"Is it genetic?" Noah asked.

Dr. Feist nodded. "Usually, yes."

Josie said, "Did she have a co-occurring condition?"

"I found no evidence of any medical conditions on exam."

Their eyes returned to Holly's face. Dr. Feist had arranged her hair so that they couldn't see where she'd used the bone saw to cut into Holly's skull. She wasn't the first child victim they'd ever seen, and she would certainly not be the last, but it never got easier to stand over the body of a young person who had had so much life ahead of them. Josie made a silent vow to find who had done this to Holly and make sure they never hurt anyone ever again.

Dr. Feist snapped on a pair of latex gloves and pointed to several dark, finger-sized bruises scattered over Holly's throat and neck. "She had significant soft tissue injuries to her throat and neck, but nothing that would have killed her."

"Someone tried strangling her and then changed their mind and hit her on the head?" Noah asked.

"Or someone tried to strangle her, she put up a fight, and they ultimately hit her on the head."

Josie said, "But you said she was alive for some time after her head injury."

"Yes," said Dr. Feist. "She had to have been."

"Would she have been down for any length of time so that the killer might think she was dead?" Noah asked.

"Perhaps. Or the killer was with her until her decline and death and then staged her body. There are a few other things you should be aware of." Dr. Feist lifted a side of the sheet to expose one of Holly's delicate hands. "We did get a great deal of skin from beneath her fingernails. Hummel has sent it to the state police lab for DNA analysis. She managed to scratch up her attacker pretty well."

Josie felt a small spiral of excitement. They could now check any suspects for scratches, and if they found a suspect, they'd have DNA to match him against, although it would take weeks, if not months, to get a DNA profile back.

"Also, the bottoms of her feet are freshly scraped up," Dr. Feist went on, moving to the bottom of the table and uncovering Holly's bare feet. Josie and Noah crowded around for a closer look. There were several fresh lacerations crisscrossing the soles of her feet.

Dr. Feist said, "When they brought her in, her feet were covered in dirt and mud, and I dug some pine needles out of one of the cuts in her feet."

"She was in the forest," Josie said. "Before she died."

"I believe so," said Dr. Feist.

"She got out of the house," said Noah.

"She might have even witnessed Lorelei's murder," Josie agreed. "Or maybe she knew what might happen. She told Emily to hide, and then at some point she had a confrontation with the killer—either while she was still at the house or after she made it into the woods."

"Or," Noah said, "the killer attacked her and tried to strangle her, but she escaped into the woods and then he tracked her down and gave her a head injury sufficient to kill her."

"Regardless of the order of things," Dr. Feist said, "the manner of death is homicide."

"Any signs of sexual assault?" Josie asked.

"No. None at all, but there is one more thing you should be aware of. I believe that this girl was the victim of ongoing physical abuse."

Josie's head snapped toward Dr. Feist. "Really? What makes you say that?"

Dr. Feist went back to Holly's head and used her index finger to beckon them closer. Once they were beside her, she gently brushed the hair away from Holly's left ear.

"Jesus," said Noah.

The ear was grossly deformed. The outer part of the ear was swollen, bulbous, and lumpy. "Cauliflower ear," Josie muttered.

"Right," said Dr. Feist. "Blood clots form beneath the skin. The skin pulls away from the cartilage, and fibrous tissue forms. That's the least scientific version. It forms as a result of repeated trauma to the outer ear. Either this kid was a pro wrestler or someone was routinely hitting her around the head. This isn't something that happens with one strike. It develops over time."

"My God," Josie said. She thought of the medications in Lorelei's kitchen cabinets. While violence wasn't a hallmark of either schizophrenia or bipolar disorder, it wasn't out of the question that a person suffering from either of those illnesses could become violent. However, Josie still couldn't quite believe that Lorelei was abusive. She had been killed today, too. She'd built a secret hiding place for her girls between the walls of the bedrooms. She kept sharp objects in a secret cubby under her mattress. Had there been someone else living with them?

"There are also a few other indicators of chronic physical abuse," Dr. Feist went on. She walked over to her laptop and motioned them over. Several clicks later, x-ray images of a rib cage lit the screen. "Here, here, and here you can see healed posterior rib fractures. They're quite old, but as I said, they're posterior, which is almost always indicative of abuse."

"What's the mechanism of injury?" Noah asked.

"Usually, these posterior rib fractures occur from pressure—an adult or bigger person squeezing the child and shaking them or putting a great deal of pressure on their body from front to back. This is very unusual to see in children as a result of some kind of accident. These fractures likely happened when she was much younger, but between these and her cauliflower ear, it appears as though she sustained prolonged abuse during her life."

Josie felt as though someone had lowered lead weights onto her shoulders. Her mind kept returning to the day she'd met Lorelei and her girls. Nothing at all about them had sent up any red flags. How had Josie missed it? What was she missing now?

"What about her medical records?" Noah asked. "If she lived in Denton, she would have sought treatment here, most likely."

"And Lorelei would have had to put down an emergency contact," Josie added.

Dr. Feist said, "I don't have access to those records. You'd have to get a warrant and serve it on health information management."

"Come on," Josie said to Noah. "We'll get warrants for both their medical records. But first, we need to find out everything we can about Lorelei Mitchell."

CHAPTER ELEVEN

Josie and Noah stopped in to check on Emily before they left. She had fallen asleep, arms wrapped around her stuffed dog. Her cheeks were bright red, and her mouth hung open. Strings of brown hair were matted to the sides of her face. Josie felt a profound sadness looking at her. At only eight years old, her entire life had been turned upside-down and her future was uncertain. Yet she'd been so brave and stoic through all of it. Josie felt Noah's palm warm on her shoulder. In a chair at the side of the bed, Marcie tapped away at her laptop. When she saw them, she stood and came to the door. "She finally fell asleep. She's pretty sick, though. Dr. Nashat will keep her overnight. That should give you some time to search for next of kin. Otherwise, she goes into the system."

"Did she tell you anything?" Josie asked.

Marcie shook her head. "Nothing more than she told you."

"What about her friend Pax? Did you ask her about him?"

"I did. She would only say that his dad doesn't like her mom very much, but that Pax is a friend. I asked her what kinds of things they do together, and she said he brings her fruit, and they play games. I asked if he ever hurt her or anyone in her family, and she said no. I asked her when she last saw him and she didn't know. She was, however, certain that she had not seen him today."

"Did she know his last name?" Noah asked. "Or where he lives?"

"She said he would ride his mountain bike to their house. That's all. But she's only eight. It's not unusual that she wouldn't know details adults take for granted, like his last name."

Josie sighed. "We'll see what we can turn up."

*

It was late by the time the entire team was assembled at the station-house. Their police headquarters was housed in an old, three-story stone building that was on the city's historic register. It had been converted from the town hall into the police station over sixty-five years ago, and with its double casement arched windows and old bell tower at one end, it resembled a castle. On the second floor was what they called the great room—an open area filled with desks and filing cabinets where the detectives worked and uniformed officers did their paperwork. The Chief's office was across from the bullpen. Josie, Noah, Gretchen, and Mettner all had their own permanent desks which were pushed up against one another, forming a large rectangle. They all sat at their desks now, waiting for the Chief to arrive. Gretchen typed reports. Josie entered Lorelei's name and other vital information into a series of databases, trying to find any information she could. Beside her, Noah prepared a warrant for Lorelei's and Holly's medical records. Mett scrolled through notes he'd made in his phone.

The only other permanent desk now belonged to their press liaison, Amber Watts. Mettner had brought her to the wedding as his date, and now, perched on the edge of her desk with a tablet in hand, she still wore a low-cut, pale pastel green dress that hugged her svelte figure. Her thick auburn curls cascaded down her back. It wasn't lost on Josie that every few seconds Mettner's eyes drifted away from this phone screen toward Amber.

Noah leaned over and whispered in Josie's ear, "Do you think Mett was really upset about us walking out on our wedding, or upset that we ruined his romantic night with Watts?"

She laughed quietly. Mettner had been smitten with Amber from the day she walked into the stationhouse, but he'd never been quite this obvious about it. Josie wondered if the wedding was their first date or if they'd already been out together.

"Detectives!" hollered Chief Chitwood as he emerged from the stairwell. In his hands he carried a cardboard box filled with food that Josie immediately recognized from the menu offered at their wedding reception. Chitwood placed it in the center of their desks. "Adam Long sent that. It was left over from the reception."

All four of them dove in, and for the first time that day, Josie realized how hungry she was. She hadn't eaten in many hours. Chitwood gave them a few minutes to eat before he launched into the briefing. "Any of you talk to Dr. Feist?" he asked. "Either of the autopsies done yet?"

Josie said, "We did. Both are finished."

She and Noah told the team everything they'd learned from the medical examiner. There was a long moment of uneasy silence as they all took in the savagery of the attacks on Lorelei and her daughter. Then Chitwood turned to Mettner. "What've you got, Mett?"

Mettner picked up his phone, scrolling. "Not a hell of a lot," he said. "None of the Harper's Peak staff or the guests we interviewed saw a damn thing. We found nothing on the CCTV footage from any of the buildings or parking lots. None of the staff recalled ever seeing Holly before, and we think with her white eyelashes, anyone would have remembered her. We believe she must have been brought onto the grounds through the woods. Search teams didn't find anything. There were a couple of paths that led away from Harper's Peak through the woods, but none of them led to the Mitchell household. If she was brought in a car, whoever did it managed not to get captured on camera or be seen by the staff or guests. The last time anyone was at the church was the evening before, around seven p.m., when Tom Booth went to the church to open it and get it ready for today's ceremony. We know from the autopsy that she died today, though, so the killer left her there sometime this morning or early afternoon."

Gretchen said, "We've gotten a warrant for Lorelei's cell phone records. If we can get those, maybe we can see who she last called or texted."

Mettner sighed. "Unfortunately, those are going to take almost a week to come back. Three days at the most, the carrier said."

Noah said, "The DNA under Holly's nails will take even longer than that to come back. Weeks, maybe even months."

"Then we need to work with what we know until we get them," Josie said. "What else have you got?"

Mettner said, "The ERT wasn't able to get any prints from Holly's body or that creepy pinecone thing that was left with her."

Gretchen said, "Chan couldn't get prints from the other stick man that was left at the Mitchell house."

Mettner lifted his chin in Josie's direction. "Any idea what the meaning is behind those?"

Josie stopped scrolling through the search results on her computer concerning Lorelei Mitchell and met Mettner's eyes. "Clearly they're dolls of some sort. Emily said that they mean 'he's sorry', so my guess is that the killer made one for Holly as a symbol of his remorse, and that the one he left at the house was intended for Emily."

"But he didn't kill Emily," Noah said.

"No, but he killed her family. Plus, Emily obviously knows who this person is, even though she won't tell us."

Mettner sighed and swiped a hand down his face. "You're telling me we could go get this killer now if this kid would just tell us who he is?"

"It's not that simple, Mett," Noah said.

"It sounds like it is," Mettner shot back. "I know she's been traumatized, and she is afraid, but if the case is that easy to crack, someone should be over at the hospital right now trying to get this information out of her."

Josie said, "The social worker is there with her now. The attending physician ordered a psych consult. A psychologist might have better luck coaxing the information out of her. I know it's frustrating, Mett, but going after an eight-year-old girl who just lost everyone she loved in a brutal double murder is not going to help things. We need to work with what we've got."

"Which is nothing," Mettner said, tossing his phone onto the desk. Amber sidled over and put her hand on his shoulder. "I'm sorry," he mumbled. A shudder ran through him. "Seeing that poor girl. It got to me."

Sometimes Josie forgot that Mett didn't have as many years on the job as the rest of them—or as many heartbreaking cases under his belt.

Gretchen said, "It gets to all of us, Mett. If it didn't, I'd be worried about you."

From lowered lashes, he looked at each one of them. "You never show it."

Josie said, "I've been known to lose my shit now and then."

Mettner scoffed. "Please. You never lose your shit."

"Not true," Gretchen said. "The boss cried up a tree during the floods last year."

Mettner raised a skeptical brow at Gretchen.

"It's true," Josie confirmed. "I'll say this, though: a tree is a pretty good place to come undone. No one can really see you."

The room erupted into laughter. Even Chitwood gave a less severe frown.

Gretchen got the conversation back on track. "All right. Let's talk about what we have, because we have a few things to run with. We got prints from the house, for one thing. We were able to match Lorelei's, Holly's, and Emily's. We've got four other sets of prints that are unidentified."

The Chief said, "Any of them turn up in AFIS?"

The Automated Fingerprint Identification System only held records of fingerprints from people who had either been arrested or convicted of a crime.

Gretchen held her pen straight in the air. "As a matter of fact, yes. One of the sets belongs to Reed Bryan, age fifty-eight. He was arrested and charged with aggravated assault nine years ago. Looks like a domestic issue. Wife dropped the charges."

"Really?" said Noah. "Where does Reed live?"

"He's got a farm south of Denton, but he also owns Bryan's Farm Fresh Produce which has a market about three miles away from Lorelei's house."

"I know that place," Josie said. "You have to pass it to get to both Lorelei's house and to Harper's Peak."

Chitwood said, "How many prints did they find in the house from this guy?"

Gretchen flipped a page in her notebook. "Two sets. One on the front door and one on the doorway into the kitchen. Nothing upstairs."

"But not the truck," Chitwood said.

"No, sir. The only clear prints we got from the truck were from Lorelei and her kids. Chan couldn't get anything from the other set—the handprints—because of the smeared blood."

"It's after midnight now. Let's leave it till the morning then. If he was the killer, I'd expect his prints to be all over the place. First thing tomorrow, someone's got to talk to him. What else did Chan get from the house, Palmer?"

Gretchen looked at her notes again. "First, let's start inside the house. Lorelei Mitchell's blood type is A positive. The blood found on the kitchen island countertop and floor was A positive. The drops of blood from the dining room into the kitchen were O positive."

"Someone else bled at the scene," Josie said.

"But not Holly," said Noah. "She didn't have any open wounds or lacerations of any kind."

"It had to be the killer then," Mettner said.

"I agree," said Gretchen. "The blood found on the outside and inside of the truck was also O positive."

Chitwood said, "Do we know Reed Bryan's blood type?"

"No, sir," Gretchen said.

"We can't say for sure whether Reed's prints were found on the truck," Josie said, "Although whoever left the handprints on the truck did so in his own blood."

"We can ask Reed Bryan his blood type and whether or not he's got any recent injuries when we question him," Gretchen said. "If he's cooperative. If he doesn't have a rock-solid alibi. Also, Chan was able to get impressions of the footprints near the back door. Actually, there were some on the back porch as well. One was from a men's size ten boot. Hummel's asked the state police to run the impression through the footwear database to see if he can get a match on the brand, but that's going to take some time. The other impression was from a bare foot. Chan estimated the shoe size is probably a woman's six."

Noah said, "That could be from Holly. She wasn't wearing any shoes and her feet were torn up—Dr. Feist says likely from running through the forest."

Gretchen said, "I'll ask Chan to send the impression over to Dr. Feist for a comparison."

Josie said, "It was early morning. They were having breakfast. The killer showed up. There was some kind of confrontation that took place in the kitchen."

Noah said, "That's probably when Lorelei got hit in the head. The killer was injured somehow. He went out to her truck and got the gun."

"At some point during all of this, Holly tells Emily to hide," Gretchen interjected.

Noah nodded. "He shoots Lorelei."

Josie said, "Holly runs out the back door to get away, and he goes after her."

"He took the gun with him," said Gretchen. "It's nowhere to be found."

Mettner said, "But he didn't shoot Holly. He tried to strangle her and then ultimately caused some kind of head injury—at least, that's what Dr. Feist told you at the hospital, right?"

"Right," Josie replied. "It's possible that he attacked Holly while they were still inside the house and she got away. Dr. Feist said she was alive for at least some period of time after she sustained the head injury. She might have gotten away when he went to get the gun. Then after he killed Lorelei he went after her, but by the time he found her, she was dead from the head injury."

Chitwood said, "Congratulations! You're all geniuses. You figured out what happened in that house. How does this get us closer to finding the killer? Come on! I can't have a child-killer running around this city. The cat's already out of the bag because of the Amber Alert. The press is already sniffing around. Right, Watts?"

Amber nodded. "I've been getting calls all evening. We had to release Emily Mitchell's name with the Amber Alert, but I'm trying to keep both Lorelei and Holly out of the press so far, for the sake of Emily's privacy."

Chitwood said, "Have any of you taken a look at Lorelei Mitchell's close associates?"

Josie pointed to her computer screen. "I've been searching databases for the last hour. All her close associates are dead."

"What do you mean?" asked Chitwood.

"I've been searching for any personal information I can find since I got here," Josie said. "Her only listed family is her mother, who is deceased. In fact, her mother died when she was nine years old. There's no indication here of what happened to her."

"She probably went into foster care," Gretchen said. "Maybe that's why Emily knew what it was? Lorelei told her stories?"

"Possibly," Josie agreed. "Other than her mother, there are no known relatives in this database. She's never been married. She lived in a series of apartments in Philadelphia in her twenties and early thirties. The next address listed is the house here in Denton. There are no other residents associated with it. No neighbors, even, as her house is so remote."

Mettner said, "Is it even possible for someone to be that isolated these days?"

Josie replied, "I checked all the social media platforms. She's not on them. I didn't expect her to be."

"What about work?" Gretchen said. "Did you find any records of employment?"

"That's where things get interesting," Josie said. "She was a licensed psychologist in the Commonwealth of Pennsylvania. She got her PhD from the University of Pennsylvania in Philadelphia. However, her license was revoked twenty years ago. She never practiced again."

"What was her license revoked for?" Mettner asked. "Can you find out?"

Josie shook her head. "The licensing board doesn't get into it, but I can check some other sources. It looks like she was practicing in Philadelphia at that time. If her license was revoked, it could have made the news."

Chitwood said, "You do that, Quinn. One of you should get a hold of her kids' birth certificates and see if she listed a father. I know women aren't required to do this in Pennsylvania, but it's worth a shot."

Noah said, "Once I get this warrant finished, we can access her medical records and see who she put as her emergency contact."

"There was a doctor prescribing her medication," Josie said. "We should contact him. Vincent Buckley. I'll look him up. I'm also going to check the deed on her house to see if it's in her name or not."

"Good idea," Gretchen said. "It seems like this woman has had no income for the last twenty years. How has she been surviving?"

Mettner said, "We can probably get a warrant for her financial records as well, but that will take some time, too."

Chitwood clapped his hands together. "Get going! I want this case solved as quickly as possible. Watts, do your thing with the press."

Amber said, "Tell them we can't comment on an ongoing investigation?"

"Right, right," said Chitwood.

Josie's desk phone rang. As the others got to work, she picked it up. "Detective Quinn?" said a familiar voice. "This is Dr. Nashat at Denton Memorial. We've got a problem."

CHAPTER TWELVE

Ten minutes later, Josie stood outside of Emily's hospital room once more. From inside, the sounds of the girl's shrieks cut through Josie's bones like a thousand tiny knives. Dr. Nashat and Marcie Riebe looked at Josie helplessly.

"She won't calm down," said Marcie.

"I can give her some Valium," Dr. Nashat explained. "Or some Versed. But I don't have a proper medical history for her. She could have allergies we don't know about. Plus, we'd have to hold her down. She lashes out anytime we try to come near her. I called again for the psych consult, but the doctor on call won't be here for another hour."

"I'm not sure what you expect me to do," said Josie.

"She asked for you," said Dr. Nashat. "Well, she asked for 'the angel lady cop with the scar on her face.'"

Self-consciously, Josie trailed her fingers down the right side of her face. "Was that before or after she started screaming?"

Marcie said, "We explained to her that you were working and couldn't come back. Evidently, she didn't want to hear that."

"We tried to talk her down," Dr. Nashat said. "She's not trying to hurt herself, but she won't stop… well, you can hear her."

Marcie said, "I've seen a lot of meltdowns in my work, but this is not that."

"What happened immediately before she started crying?" Josie asked.

"She was asleep," Marcie replied, mystified.

Josie turned to Dr. Nashat. "Could this be something like night terrors?"

"I don't think so. She's fully awake and cognizant. I mean, she's asked for you twice."

Josie left them in the hallway and pushed open the door. Emily wasn't in the bed. Instead, she was balled up in one corner of the room, curled around her stuffed dog, her knees drawn all the way up to her chin. Her mouth stretched wide as she screamed, took in a ragged breath, and screamed again. Josie panned the room as she walked slowly toward her. Rumpled sheet and blanket on the bed. Tray table with a cup of water and a small basin for vomit. Emily's sneakers were tucked neatly under the bed. Her duffel bag sat on one of the guest chairs. Josie stopped when she realized the zipper to the side compartment was open. She took a quick peek inside, noting that it was empty of all the strange treasures that Emily had insisted on bringing from home. "Shit," she muttered.

Kneeling in front of Emily, Josie waited for the next time Emily had to gulp in a breath, and said, "Emily, can we talk?"

Another shriek pierced the air. Emily's eyes locked onto Josie's in a look of terror and powerlessness. She couldn't stop it, Josie realized. The feelings were too big. There was no controlling them. There was only waiting until they petered out. Josie sat cross-legged in front of Emily and extended a hand, palm facing up. The shrill cries continued but in Emily's eyes, Josie saw the little girl trapped inside the hysterical body. Emily's fingers reached out and touched Josie's palm. Leaning closer, Josie dipped her head. Gently grasping Emily's fingers, she brought them up and guided them along the scar on her face. She started at the top, near her ear, and traced it down to under the center of her chin, then started again.

"Emily," Josie said softly. "You can survive the bad things. I promise you can."

After a long moment, Emily's fingers worked on their own, running over the scar. Josie's neck ached from staying in the same awkward position for so long, but Emily's cries had receded to moans and the occasional hiccup, so Josie held herself still. Finally, a raspy whisper came from Emily's throat. "One, two, three…" At six, she stopped and pulled her hand away from Josie's face.

Josie sat up straight and smiled. Emily clutched her stuffed dog to her chest. Her skin was pink and splotchy, eyes glassy. A look of complete exhaustion passed over her face. Josie said, "What happened, Emily? Why did you get so upset?"

"I couldn't help it," said Emily.

"I know."

"Sometimes I can't stop the… distress. That's what Mama calls it. Distress. Like bad, mad, and sad feelings all at once. They take over my body. I don't want to have them, but I can't stop them."

"What did your mom tell you to do when you feel distressed?" Josie asked.

Emily started to rock slowly back and forth. "She says I have to 'tolerate' it. Holly says that means I have to let the feelings feel until they're all done."

"That actually makes a lot of sense," Josie said.

"I don't feel upset now."

"That's good. Do you want to lay in the bed?"

Emily nodded. Josie offered her a hand and helped her to standing. Josie tucked her beneath the covers. "Your things aren't in your bag anymore," she said. "Was that why you got upset? Did someone take them?"

"I put them on the table next to my water cup. That lady was here but she fell asleep in her chair. I just wanted to see them. Then this other lady came with a cart filled with all kinds of cleaning stuff. She had a trash bag, and she wiped her hand across the table and right into the bag. I tried to tell her to stop, but the feelings came, and I—"

Her chest rose and fell more quickly so Josie cut her off. "I understand. I'm very sorry, Emily."

"I asked the computer lady and the doctor to get you. You're the police. Maybe you could get my things back."

Josie felt a little stab of pain in her chest. She couldn't imagine finding the five small items in the hospital's trash, and it would be hard to replace them. Why had they been so important to Emily in the first place? Lorelei hadn't allowed television or electronics, but both girls had plenty of toys, books, and arts and crafts supplies. They obviously had not wanted for much. Josie made a mental note to mention it to the psychologist when he or she came to do their consult. To Emily, she said, "I can try to find them, Emily, but there is a very good chance I won't be able to do so. This is a big hospital, and they have a lot of trash. Right now, we're trying to find the person who hurt your mom and sister."

Josie sensed that Emily wanted to argue, but fatigue was taking over. Her eyelids drooped and snapped back open as she tried to stay awake. "Okay," she said, resigned. "But can you stay in that chair and make sure nobody takes any of my other stuff?"

"Emily, I would love to, but I have a lot of work—"

"Can't you do it on your computer? Like that lady? Just until they take me to foster care?"

Josie looked at her watch. It was after one in the morning. The only work she'd be doing at this hour would be from her computer, chasing the leads she'd told the team about. She could have Noah bring her laptop to her. Josie smoothed the hair away from Emily's forehead. Her skin was feverish. "Okay, I'll stay for tonight."

CHAPTER THIRTEEN

Josie sat beside Emily's bed with her laptop open in front of her. One of the nurses had turned off the harsh overhead light, but it only succeeded in dimming the room slightly. Neither the light nor the noise of the Emergency Room on a Friday night just outside kept Emily awake. Curled on her side, her little stuffed dog clutched in her arms, she snored lightly. She hadn't moved since Josie tucked her in nearly two hours earlier. Josie was supposed to be scouring databases and other internet resources for information on Lorelei and her life, but she couldn't take her eyes off Emily.

"She's an old soul, isn't she?"

Dr. Nashat's voice startled Josie. He stood in the doorway, smiling.

"Yes," Josie agreed. "You're still here?"

"Until seven a.m.," he said. "The psychologist is here."

Josie looked back at Emily. "Surely, you don't want to wake her now?"

He shook his head. "No. Maybe you could talk to her while she's here, especially since Emily seems to have bonded to you. I'll ask her to come back later in the morning—at a more reasonable hour—for a formal consult. The social worker is coming back then, too."

Josie stood, left her laptop on the chair, and followed Dr. Nashat into the hall. She pulled up short when she saw Dr. Paige Rosetti standing outside. Her long wavy blonde hair was pulled back in a ponytail, and her thin frame was draped in a long tan linen dress accented by a white bolero sweater. Over one shoulder hung a messenger bag. Josie had gone to high school with Paige's daughter and had had to enlist her help during a case the year before. They'd had a connection. In a moment of weakness, Josie had shared some of her deepest fears with Paige. In spite of the embarrassment she felt over that moment, Josie genuinely liked the woman. Noah and Gretchen had been after her for months to go to therapy to work through some of her unresolved childhood issues. Paige's name had come up more than once.

"Detective Quinn," said Paige with a warm smile. "How nice to see you. I wish it was under different circumstances."

"So do I," said Josie.

"I'm sorry I'm so late. I was at Geisinger on another matter that needed my attention. It took far longer than I anticipated. Dr. Nashat said he didn't want to wake the patient, but if you have a minute, I could take some initial notes and come back in a few hours, after the sun is up."

"Sure."

Paige looked around, as if for a place for them to sit. "Would you like to go to the staff lounge?"

"I don't want to leave Emily that long. Here." Josie found the linen bin that Marcie had used earlier and pulled it over. "You can put your laptop here."

Paige laughed. While she removed her laptop from her bag and booted it up, they exchanged pleasantries. Josie asked about Paige's daughter and Paige asked about Josie's grandmother. Then it was time to get down to business. Josie described the case, the day, the circumstances of locating Emily and her unusual behavior throughout. Paige's expression didn't change as she listened, tapping away on her laptop the entire time. When Josie finished, she stopped typing and looked up, her brow furrowed. "Let's start with her mother. You said Lorelei Mitchell?"

"Yes," Josie said. "Did you know her?"

Paige folded her arms over her chest. "We went to the University of Pennsylvania together. Grad school. We were studying for our

PhDs. She's quite a bit younger than I am, but I took a break between getting my master's degree and my PhD. That's how we ended up in the program together."

Josie felt a spike of excitement. "Were you friends?"

"I wouldn't call us friends, but I knew who she was. She went on to specialize in adolescent and child psychology, but she was primarily focused on areas that included oppositional defiant disorder, OCD, ADHD, that sort of thing. She was very interested in cognitive behavioral therapy."

"For non-psychologists, if you would," Josie said.

Paige laughed. "CBT is a form of therapy that focuses on changing behaviors that are based on cognitive distortions."

"Dumb it down a little more," Josie said.

Now Paige gave a full-throated laugh, head tossed back, mouth wide open. "Most therapy is based on sort of unpacking your past, right? Exploring your childhood or things that have happened to you in the past that shape you emotionally and cognitively."

"I get it," Josie said.

"CBT is different. It assumes that your behaviors are based on distorted thinking or behaviors, and it tries to help you change them. It proposes strategies and coping mechanisms to meet those behaviors exactly as they are in your life."

"Was Lorelei good at it?"

"I don't know," Paige answered. "We lost touch after the PhD program. I had been splitting my time between Philadelphia and here while I completed the program. Lana and my husband were here in Denton—this is where we lived—so once I got my PhD, I came back permanently. Lorelei stayed in Philadelphia. I'm surprised to learn she's even here. I thought she'd be working for a large hospital by now, maybe teaching, speaking at conferences. She was very ambitious."

"Her license was revoked twenty years ago," Josie said.

"Oh my. Do you know what for?"

"I haven't found out yet. What can you tell me about Emily?"

Paige glanced down at her notes. "It sounds like she has obsessive-compulsive disorder. I'm no expert, but the counting, the hoarding, the meltdown—those are pretty classic signs."

"What do you mean?"

Paige closed her laptop. "People think of OCD as this disorder in which the person who has it is simply excessively clean, or that they insist on symmetry, right? Someone will say, 'oh, I have to straighten that painting out because it's bothering my OCD,' or 'I keep my house so clean because I have OCD.'"

"I've heard people say things like that, yes," Josie agreed.

"OCD has nothing whatsoever to do with cleanliness."

"Really?"

"Really. It's about certainty. A person with OCD usually has some form of intrusive thoughts or obsessions. Typically, they don't make sense. For example, if I don't step on my bathroom floor tiles in a certain order every time I'm in there, my friend might die. Or if I don't repeat the same phrase fifty-two times in my head, then my house might burn down. OCD is illogical that way, but the main thing to understand is that the obsessive thought will cause the person anxiety. In terms of the examples I just talked about, you would not want your friend to die or your house to burn down, right?"

"Right."

"So you have to do something to relieve that anxiety you're feeling. That's where the compulsion comes in."

Josie said, "The compulsion is stepping on the tiles in a certain order or repeating the phrase."

"Yes! Exactly. If you believe that stepping on your bathroom tiles in a certain order is going to prevent your friend's death, then doing that is going to relieve the anxiety you have which comes from worrying about your friend dying. The problem is that even if you step on those tiles in the perfect order, there's always this little voice in your head that is nagging and asking, 'Are you sure you stepped on those tiles in the right order?'"

"It makes you go back and do it again and again," Josie said. "Because the more your mind asks the question, the more uncertain you become."

"Precisely. So you keep carrying out the compulsion. It's all very ritualistic, and it takes so many different forms. It sounds like Emily has some intrusive thoughts and compulsions surrounding counting and hoarding. The problem is that no matter how many times a person with OCD carries out their compulsion, that anxiety is never going to go away because it's based on distorted thinking. That's why trying to reason with them or talk them out of their thoughts or compulsions won't work. Their brain is misfiring. Telling someone with OCD not to think obsessive thoughts or engage in the compulsive behaviors would be like telling a diabetic patient to produce more insulin."

"You said hoarding," Josie noted. "But she had five very random little objects. That hardly seems like hoarding."

"Hoarding doesn't always mean collecting hundreds or thousands of objects. What Emily was doing is a form of hoarding. Those objects are meaningless, aren't they?" Paige argued. "Most people would think they were trash. In fact, obviously housekeeping thought they belonged in the garbage. Yet she was hoarding them—keeping them—because to get rid of them would cause too much anxiety and stress. This is the distorted thinking. The brain is misfiring. Those items took on some significance to Emily, making it very difficult for her to part with them. The voice in her head was likely saying something like, 'if you throw that away, something bad will happen.' It's very nonsensical. That's why cognitive behavioral therapy works so well to change the behaviors and thinking."

"What about the meltdown?" Josie asked.

"OCD provokes a fight or flight response. While you or I might only have a fight or flight response to something like being assaulted, someone with OCD will have that response to something that seems very minor—like these objects being thrown away. Again, it's the brain misfiring, telling her that losing those objects is a life-or-death situation when it's not. Believe me, she can't control it. Stress and trauma, like the kind she experienced in the last twenty-four hours, will always make the obsessive thoughts and compulsions worse. OCD can be difficult to manage in the best of circumstances, let alone after a traumatic event. To be honest, she was lucky that Lorelei was her mom. She would probably be much worse without Lorelei to—"

Paige broke off and looked at the floor. Lines creased her face. Neither of them needed to say it. Emily was now a lot worse off without Lorelei. Clearing her throat, Paige changed direction. "The trick with cognitive behavioral therapy and OCD is exactly what Emily told you: if you can tolerate those feelings, eventually they decrease and even go away. For example, if she was afraid to touch a railing, you'd make her touch it over and over again and just sit with the feelings until her brain righted itself and realized that touching that railing isn't going to make something bad happen. The worst thing you can do is give in to the compulsions."

"So I shouldn't be digging through the dumpsters out back for a stone, sequin, feather, birthday candle and milk bottle cap?"

Paige smiled. "No, I would not recommend it."

"What else do you remember about Lorelei?"

"Not much other than that. As I said, we went our separate ways after the PhD program. I went into private practice here. I had no idea she was even in Denton. When did you say her license was revoked?"

"Twenty years ago."

"How strange," said Paige. "That must have been devastating for her. She was extremely passionate about her work."

"Do you remember if she had any family or friends she was close with?"

"No, I don't, I'm sorry."

"Have you ever heard of a Dr. Vincent Buckley?"

Paige shook her head. "That name doesn't sound familiar."

Josie thanked her for her time. Paige agreed to return in the morning to speak with Emily directly. Josie returned to the dimly lit room where Emily's snoring continued unabated. She was grateful that the girl was getting some rest. Soon enough, she would wake again to a world that was completely shattered.

CHAPTER FOURTEEN

It took a couple of hours of searching, and Josie had to subscribe to the *Philadelphia Inquirer*, but she found an article about Lorelei from twenty years earlier. The headline read: *Pennsylvania Psychologist Loses License After Preventable Murder–Suicide*. Josie gasped and sat up straighter in the guest chair. She glanced over at Emily to make sure she was still asleep, and read on.

The Pennsylvania Board of Psychology has revoked the license of Dr. Lorelei Mitchell after a long-time adolescent patient killed his mother in her home and then later attacked Dr. Mitchell at her office before killing himself. The patient had a history of oppositional defiant disorder and schizoaffective disorder with paranoid delusions. He was also being evaluated for bipolar disorder at the time of this tragedy. The patient's estranged father had filed a complaint with the disciplinary board following the incident. After a review of Dr. Mitchell's chart, the board deemed the tragedy "foreseeable and preventable", given Dr. Mitchell's credentials and experience with adolescent patients dealing with these and other similar disorders.

"It's unthinkable that something like this could happen," said the patient's father. "Dr. Mitchell holds herself out as an expert in ODD, schizophrenia and bipolar disorder, and yet she failed my son. She treated him for years. She knew him well enough that she should have seen this coming and had him locked up so he couldn't hurt anyone."

Dr. Mitchell, who is still recovering from her extensive injuries, had no comment.

"Good lord," Josie muttered under her breath.

That could explain the thirty-four stab wounds. Josie thought about the trajectory of Lorelei's life: losing her mother at nine; managing to become a successful psychologist only to be nearly killed by a patient; losing her license, and now, she and her daughter had been savagely murdered, leaving her other daughter alone, just like she had been. Sometime during her life, Lorelei had met someone and had his children. Had he abused Holly? Josie thought of the antipsychotics in the kitchen cabinet. Or had it been Lorelei?

"Angel lady," whispered Emily from the bed.

Josie set her laptop aside and leaned in toward Emily, offering her hand, which she took. "You can call me Josie."

"Josie. Are we still alive?"

Josie squeezed her hand. "Yes, we're still alive. I'll be right here until morning. You go back to sleep."

Emily nodded and closed her eyes. After a few minutes, she relinquished Josie's hand and turned onto her other side. Josie returned to her laptop, focusing her attention on Lorelei's property instead. It took an hour of digging through the Alcott County Recorder of Deeds and Tax Assessment records before she found what she was looking for—and that led her to an extensive search through the County Court records.

"Son of a bitch," she mumbled.

She looked at the clock in the bottom right-hand corner of her laptop. It was nearly five a.m. For a moment, she considered calling and waking Noah, but they couldn't do anything with this information for at least three hours. Shutting the laptop, she tried to go to sleep. She would need at least a few hours if she was going to function during the day. It seemed like an eternity since she'd stood before the mirror at her private suite at Harper's Peak, barely recognizable in her wedding dress and expertly done make-up. Soon she would return, this time in her capacity as a detective.

CHAPTER FIFTEEN

Josie sipped coffee from a paper cup and watched the vibrant scenery pass by the car window as Noah drove them out of central Denton toward Harper's Peak. He had arrived at the hospital with coffee and a cheese Danish—one of the many reasons she had planned to marry him—and served the warrant for Lorelei's and Holly's medical charts on the hospital. They made one stop at the stationhouse so that Josie could print out some documents. Then they headed toward Reed Bryan's Farm Fresh Produce Market and after that, Harper's Peak.

"Mett found birth certificates for both Holly and Emily Mitchell," Noah said. "It took a while, since all we had were their approximate ages and no birthdates. Anyway, no father listed on either one."

Josie sighed. "That's a dead end then. Still, it's strange. The birth certificates are a matter of public record. I'm sure there were copies at Lorelei's house, and yet, the killer destroyed every document in that house—and every photo."

"Makes you wonder what he was trying to hide," Noah said.

"Exactly. Oh, and I found some information for a Dr. Vincent Buckley in one of the counties outside of Philadelphia. He's a psychiatrist. I left him a voicemail."

As they pulled onto the road that led past Lorelei's home and on to Harper's Peak, the produce market came into view on the left. It was an old barn that had been converted to a market. The words "Farm Fresh Produce" were stenciled on the side of it in large green letters. Crude wooden tables and crates lined one side of the parking lot, filled with various fruits and vegetables. A tall, sturdily built teenage boy wearing a green apron over the top of a long-sleeved black cotton T-shirt and faded jeans moved watermelons from a wheelbarrow onto one of the tables. Shaggy brown hair hung over his eyes. Beside the produce displays were two vans parked side by side. Each one had a magnetic sign affixed to its body that read: "Bryan's Farm Fresh Produce."

They parked and headed inside. The building was cavernous and cool with rows of produce tables from one side of the building to the other. A counter with a cash register sat near the front doors. Arrayed across it were plastic containers filled with different kinds of nuts and candy. Next to the counter was a row of refrigerated display cases filled with milk, cheese, and eggs.

They looked around. Several people browsed the aisles, using plastic baskets to carry their selections. Behind them, the front door swished open, sending a bell overhead jangling. A large man in a tattered green T-shirt beneath overalls carried a bushel of corn. White hair hung from the back of his mostly bald head. Small brown eyes regarded them from over ruddy cheeks. "Help you?" he said gruffly, brushing past them to get behind the counter.

Josie showed him her credentials. "Is this your place?"

"Yeah. Reed Bryan. What can I do for you?"

"We came to talk to you about a woman named Lorelei Mitchell," she said.

"What about her?"

Noah said, "Do you know her?"

Josie knew he wanted to see if Reed was going to deny his association with Lorelei. Reed didn't know they'd found his prints inside the house. If he chose to lie about knowing her, they'd have to look much more closely at him for hers and Holly's murders.

He nodded. "Lives up the road. Something happen?"

Noah said, "I'm afraid she was murdered. So was one of her daughters."

The man went very still. His large, calloused hands were flat against the counter. Josie noted that there were no visible injuries on his arms or hands, although that didn't mean much. They knew the killer bled at the scene of Lorelei's murder, but they had no idea what body part had been injured. She counted off fourteen seconds before Reed spoke. This time his voice was softer. "What, uh, what happened?"

"We're still investigating," Noah said.

"Just the two of them were killed?"

"Lorelei and Holly," Josie answered.

"When? When did it happen?"

Josie answered, "We believe it happened yesterday morning."

Noah said, "Where were you yesterday morning?"

Reed's eyes sharpened. His voice took back some of its flintiness. "I was here, working."

"What time was that?" Josie asked.

"Got here at seven."

"Where were you before that?" Noah asked.

He hesitated a moment, looking back and forth between them, his eyes dark with suspicion, as though they were trying to trick him. "I was home," he answered.

Noah said, "Can anyone confirm that you were home until you arrived here at seven a.m.?"

"My son."

Josie asked, "Did you know Lorelei well?"

"No. She came in regular, but I didn't know her other than to say hi."

"Do you know where she lives?" Noah asked.

"Up the road aways."

"Have you ever been to her home?" Josie asked.

He shifted his weight uncomfortably. He looked past them, craning his neck to see through the front doors. Then he lowered his voice. "I mighta been there once or twice. What's any of this got to do with me?"

"When is the last time you were at her house?" Josie asked.

"Why do you need to know this?"

"We're investigating the murder of a mother and her child. You can tell us what you know here and now, or you can come down to the police station and make a more formal statement."

He glared at her. "I don't know, okay? It was a long time ago."

"What was your relationship with Lorelei?" Josie asked.

He squeezed the bridge of his nose between two fingers. "Wasn't no relationship between us, okay? I went to her house to get my son. Sometimes he goes off on his mountain bike and rides over there."

"Is your son's name Pax?" Josie asked.

"It's short for Paxton, but yeah, that's him. Now what else do you need to know?"

Noah asked, "Did you ever see her with anyone?"

"Just her kids. You about done?"

Ignoring him, Josie went on, "We believe that Lorelei and her children were targeted for personal reasons. You've been here a lot of years, right?"

"Twenty-two years. Used to run this place with my wife till she passed. Now it's just me and my boy. I got a farm outside of the city. Got a few people I pay to work it. Get the rest of our stuff from local farmers, other places."

"That's a long time to be in business," Noah said. "You don't ever remember seeing Lorelei or her children with anyone else?"

"She talked to some other customers now and then, but no, she never came here with anyone besides her kids, and usually they weren't with her. Most of the time it was just her."

"How often was she here?" Josie asked.

"Couple times a week."

"Is your son here?" Noah asked. "We'd like to confirm with him that he was with you yesterday morning."

Reed responded with a grunt. He moved back around the counter and out the door. Josie and Noah followed. He walked over to where the teenage boy was now arranging apples, oranges, and bananas on the outdoor tables. Every so often he seemed to get stuck on a particular row of fruit. He would take the entire row off the table, put it back into the bushel, and start again. Reed leaned down and said something in his ear. Then he snatched the basket away and tossed it to the ground. The boy winced.

Josie and Noah walked over with their credentials out for the boy to peruse as they introduced themselves. Wide-eyed, he studied their IDs. Up close, Josie saw that his face was covered in acne. His eyes were brown and wide with what looked like a combination of fear and uncertainty. Reed nudged the back of his neck. "Tell 'em."

Josie said, "Hello, Paxton."

Mumbling a hello, he looked down and jammed both hands into his apron pocket.

"How old are you, Mr. Bryan?" asked Noah. If he was a minor, they wouldn't be able to speak to him without his father present.

"Eighteen," said Pax. "You can call me Pax."

Josie and Noah looked at one another. He gave her the nod to continue. "Pax," Josie said. "We had some questions about friends of yours: Lorelei Mitchell and her daughters, Holly and Emily. Can you tell me—"

"Hey," Reed said, cutting her off. "You're not asking questions here. You said you wanted him to confirm I was here and at home yesterday morning. That's what you'll do."

Quietly, Pax said, "My dad was home with me yesterday. We woke up at five. Then at six thirty we drove here to the market. I was with him the whole time."

"Thank you, Pax. When was the last time you saw Lorelei, Holly, or Emily Mitchell?"

Reed stepped in front of his son, fists clenched. "What the hell do you think you're pulling here? I didn't say you could ask my son questions."

Josie stood her ground, hands on her hips, chin thrust outward. "Emily Mitchell said that he was a friend. You said you had been to the Mitchell house on more than one occasion to retrieve your son. I'm trying to figure out who killed Lorelei and Holly. Your son might have information we need."

Pax's voice was still quiet as he spoke from behind his father. "No," he said. "I have no information. We weren't friends. I wasn't friends with them."

Noah said, "Then why were you at their house—more than once?"

Reed took a deep breath. On the exhale, he said, "This is on me, okay? Pax is right. They are not friends. I didn't want him being friends with the Mitchell family."

Josie said, "Why not?"

"Pax," Reed said. "Go on inside and put out the rest of the lettuce."

Reed stepped aside so that Paxton could get past him. Paxton scurried toward the doors to the market, stopping briefly to look back at them. Once he had disappeared, Reed turned back to Josie and Noah. "My son ain't right, okay? You couldn't tell from talking to him?"

"He seems perfectly normal," Josie said. *Terrified of you, though*, she added in her head.

"Well, he ain't, okay?" Reed said. "He's always been a little off. His mama used to see to him right up till she passed on. She had him to a bunch of different doctors over the years, couldn't nobody fix what's wrong with him."

"Did you get a formal diagnosis?" Josie asked.

He waved a hand in the air. "I don't know. It don't matter, though, does it?"

Noah said, "Maybe it does. There might be treatment for whatever he's dealing with."

Reed lifted an index finger and pointed it at Noah's chest. "Ain't no one gettin' in my boy's head. You got that? No talking doctors, no social workers, no teachers. Nobody. I take care of him now. That's all he needs. I don't need nobody messin' with him, especially nosy bitches like Lorelei Mitchell."

Both Josie and Noah remained calm. Josie said, "Lorelei thought she could help him?"

"Yeah, she did, but she couldn't. No one can help him."

"Is he violent?" asked Noah.

Reed's eyes narrowed. The finger came back up, this time inches from Noah's nose. "Don't you try putting whatever happened to that bitch on my kid. He would never kill anyone. Sometimes he gets upset. Has little meltdowns, but he's only ever tried to hurt himself. Banging his head against the wall sometimes. That's all. If I keep things just the way he likes them, he's fine. That's what Lorelei didn't understand."

Noah didn't step back. Slowly, Reed lowered his arm.

Thinking of Emily and her OCD, Josie asked, "How does he like things?"

"That's none of your damn business, now is it?"

"Maybe Lorelei just wanted to offer him friendship," Josie suggested. "Emily said Pax used to come to the house, bring fruit, and play games with her."

"I put a stop to that soon as I found out. It ain't right for a young man of his age to be playing around with young girls."

"I thought you said he wasn't dangerous," Noah said.

"He's not. It ain't him I'm worried about. It's other people. Like you. You don't understand him. You don't know him. I can tell what you're thinking—that because he's got problems in here—" Reed tapped his finger against his temple. "That he would hurt people. You just assume that's what would happen. I knew if he hung out at Lorelei's house, not only would she be gettin' into his brain, someone would get the wrong idea about him being around a little girl."

Josie had an uncomfortable feeling in the pit of her stomach. She didn't know Pax at all, but what would lead Reed to believe that his son might be accused of inappropriate behavior with Lorelei's girls? Had Pax done something to put that into Reed's head, or was Reed projecting his own sick thoughts onto his son?

"Is he still in school?" Noah asked.

"He dropped out after his mama died. Couldn't do it without her."

Josie's heart broke a little for Paxton—losing his mother and now being raised by a man who felt he wasn't "right" in the head. Lorelei and her girls must have seemed like a breath of fresh air to the boy. Josie wondered if there was any truth to Reed's assertion that Pax struggled with some sort of mental illness. Or did he just have a disorder of some kind? Perhaps Pax had no illness, disorder or condition that needed managing. Maybe he was merely different; and required more care, work, and effort than Reed was willing or able to give the boy. What had Lorelei seen in him? If there was something affecting Pax, then surely she'd come to a conclusion or made a diagnosis even if it was only in her own mind. Josie bet his school had done some kind of evaluation, perhaps even made a diagnosis back when his mother was still alive. But it wasn't Josie's job to interfere with Paxton Bryan and his father. Her job was to find the person who killed Lorelei and Holly.

"Did Pax sneak off to their house?" Josie asked. "You said you didn't want him to go."

"Yeah, he'd disappear on me when I was busy or when he was on his own. Ride his bike up there."

Noah said, "Do you leave him on his own often?"

"It's a lot of work dealing with him and trying to keep my farm and business going. Yeah, sometimes he has to be on his own. Can't be helped."

"Was he on his own at any time yesterday morning?" Noah asked.

Josie counted off the seconds of hesitation before Reed answered. One, two, three. A vein in his neck throbbed. "No, like I told you and like he told you, he was here with me."

"When is the last time you saw Lorelei Mitchell here at the market?" Josie asked.

"Few days ago," he answered instantly.

"Mr. Bryan, could you tell us yours and Paxton's blood types?" Noah asked.

His face reddened. One hand fisted at his side. "What in the hell do you need to know that for?"

Josie said, "It's for our investigation."

"Bullshit. I ain't gotta tell you that kind of stuff. That's medical. It's private."

"How about your shoe sizes?" Josie pressed.

Color rose in his cheeks. "I ain't tellin' you nothing private. Now get the hell out of here and leave me and my boy alone."

Without missing a beat, Noah said, "Thank you for your time." Calmly, he handed Reed a business card and told him to call if he thought of anything that might help the investigation. Josie suspected the card was going directly into the trash as soon as Reed got back inside.

They returned to the car. Reed stood outside the doors of the produce market, burly arms crossed over his chest, glaring as they pulled away.

Josie said, "Why wouldn't he tell us their blood types or shoe sizes? If he hasn't got something to hide?"

"Maybe he does. Unfortunately, I don't think we can get a warrant for their blood types or shoe sizes since he and Pax alibi each other."

Josie sighed. "You're right. No judge will sign off on a warrant if they've both got alibis. We can have Hummel or Chan come over here and lift prints from something Pax has touched—maybe from the trash or something inside the market—to match up his prints to the scene."

"He's already admitted to being in the house, though," Noah said. "You think he killed Lorelei and Holly?"

Josie took out her phone and fired off a text to Hummel. They didn't need a warrant to pull prints from something that Pax had touched and then discarded. Someone from the ERT could hang around the market until he threw something away and then they could take it and get the prints. They didn't even need to tell him. "I'm not ready to rule anything out yet," she said. "I just know that if we can figure out which prints are Pax's, and we already know which prints are Reed's, then we're down to two sets of unidentified prints at Lorelei's house instead of four."

"True," Noah said. "I'm not sure about the kid, but the dad seems to have a lot of pent-up anger. You think he was mad enough with Lorelei interfering with his son to kill her?"

"I don't know, but his son sure is terrified of him."

CHAPTER SIXTEEN

With the paperwork Josie had printed out under her arm, she strode into Griffin Hall in search of Celeste Harper. Noah jogged to keep up with her. Celeste was dressed in a skirt suit, her hair pulled up in a French twist. Heavy make-up covered her pallor but not the bags beneath her eyes. She smiled wanly as Josie approached, but the corners of her mouth turned down when Josie slid one of the documents across the counter toward her. Tom, who had been standing behind her, tapping away on his iPad, leaned forward to pick up the document. Celeste grasped his forearm, stopping him from touching the pages. "Not here, Tom," she said.

His brows shot up in surprise, but he withdrew his hand, keeping his eyes glued to her face. Several emotions flashed across his own face: confusion, irritation, anxiety. Clearly, he was used to taking charge and giving orders, even though Celeste was his boss.

He continued to stare at her, not moving a muscle. Celeste kept her eyes on Josie, drew herself up straight, cleared her throat, and said, "If you wouldn't mind, I'd prefer to discuss this matter at our private residence."

"Lead the way," said Josie.

They walked single file with Celeste in the lead, then Tom, and Josie and Noah bringing up the rear. Celeste was surprisingly agile on her six-inch heels, even in the grassy areas. The private residence she shared with her husband, which was the original stone Harper house, was a fifteen-minute walk from Griffin Hall. There was a wide path for resort cars to travel back and forth. Josie knew that Celeste could have had Tom or any member of the staff retrieve one for them to drive to the residence, but she chose to make them walk. The house was surrounded by forest on three sides, but from the front door, they were able to see all of the other buildings that comprised Harper's Peak. Josie imagined Celeste's father, Griffin Harper, standing here and surveying his little empire. Celeste likely did the same each morning as she emerged to go to work. Inside, it looked like little had changed since the house was originally built. Everything was rustic wood and antique furniture. Fresh flowers sat on a round white oak table in the center of the foyer.

Celeste held an arm out to the right, indicating a parlor. Inside, two large gray upholstered Chesterfield sofas faced one another, a large oval cherry coffee table between them. Adam sat on one of the couches, a mug of coffee in one hand and a newspaper in the other. As Josie, Noah, and Tom walked in, he stood, setting his things onto the table. His smile seemed forced. He looked beyond them to Celeste. "What's going on? Have you found something out about the girl at the church?"

Celeste strode over to him. "They found something out, all right, but not about that girl." Glaring at them, she said, "Go ahead, say whatever it is you've got to say."

"I don't understand what's going on," said Adam. He glanced at Tom, who stood just behind Celeste, always at her heels. "Does he need to be here?"

Celeste didn't answer.

Tension filled the room like a thick, noxious gas. Adam looked from Celeste to Tom and back. Tom stood perfectly still, hands holding his iPad at his waist.

Adam said, "Celeste, what happens in this house doesn't concern him."

Celeste narrowed her eyes at her husband. "But what happens on the resort does. He's the manager. He needs to know everything that might be of concern to the business."

"It's our business, not his," Adam said.

Celeste sighed. "Tom has been with me almost as long as you have, don't forget."

Adam pressed an index finger to his own chest. "But I'm your husband. He's an employee."

Celeste gave him a cool glare. "This is my business. Mine. I decide what's ultimately best for it. Tom needs to hear this."

Adam opened his mouth, as if he were going to argue more, then clamped it shut, shook his head and gestured toward Josie and Noah. "What is it?"

Noah said, "Yesterday, Lorelei Mitchell was shot and killed in her home."

Josie saw the tremor in Celeste's lower lip even as she fought to control her emotions. "What did you say?"

Adam looked at Celeste. "Did you know about this?"

"Know about it? How the hell would I know about it?"

Josie said, "We looked into the property records. Her home is so remote, and we haven't been able to find a single close relative. That's when we found out that the house she lived in, the land she lived on, was given to her nineteen years ago by Harper's Peak Industries."

Celeste narrowed her eyes. "So?"

"So," said Noah. "She paid one dollar for twenty acres of land. That's pretty unusual."

"Very unusual," Josie said. "Which made us wonder why Harper's Peak Industries would give a woman twenty acres of land for one dollar."

"Get to the point," Celeste snapped.

"We checked court records. They're a matter of public record, but they're also extremely old and some of the pleadings were sealed for privacy, but there was enough information for us to figure out the relationship between the two of you," Josie said.

Celeste rolled her eyes. "There is no relationship."

"Really?" Noah said as Josie handed him a legal pleading from the stack of documents she had brought with her. He made a show of studying it before holding it out to Celeste. She refused to take it. "It says here that she was your sister."

"She was *not* my sister."

Tom surged forward and tried to get a look at the document, but Adam snatched it from Noah's hand and made a sound of exasperation. "Celeste, that's enough."

She shot him a glare but kept silent.

He said, "Lorelei Mitchell is—was—Celeste's half-sister, but she's right. They didn't have a relationship."

Tom said, "Adam, let me see that."

Adam ignored him.

"Did you?" Josie asked Adam. "Have a relationship with Lorelei?"

Adam shook his head. "I never met her." He pointed to the date on the document, which was a property deed. "This was all arranged the year before we married. My wife is correct in one sense: she and Lorelei did not have a relationship of any kind, even though they were technically half-sisters."

"All these years she lived just down the road," Josie said, "you never had any contact with her at all?"

Tom said, "No one on this resort had contact with her."

Finally, Adam looked at him. "What did you say?"

When Tom didn't answer, Adam looked at Celeste. "You told him?"

Tom took a step toward Adam, his face impassive. "Of course she did. I am the managing director of this resort. I need to know about anything that could negatively impact the business."

"This has nothing to do with the business," Adam growled, poking Tom's chest hard, sending him stumbling back a step. "My wife's personal life is none of your concern."

Tom held his ground. "This has everything to do with the business," he said, brushing his jacket where Adam had pushed him. "What will happen when the press finds out that Celeste Harper had a secret half-sister who was murdered? If the police found this out just by searching public records, the press will be right behind. The resort doesn't need this type of scandal, Adam."

"There is no scandal," Adam spat.

"I'll be the judge of that," Tom said. "You stick to cooking."

Adam lunged for Tom, a fist flying. The property deed sailed through the air, fluttering to the floor. Noah launched himself between the two men. Adam's blow glanced off Noah's shoulder. Tom staggered backward, nearly falling. His hand shot out and grasped the arm of one of the couches, regaining his balance. His face went white with shock. "How dare you?" he spluttered.

"Me?" Adam said, still straining to reach Tom, chest to chest with Noah. Over Noah's shoulder, he pointed an accusing finger at Tom's face. "You have some nerve. Did you hear what they said? A woman is dead. All you care about is public relations. How dare *you*?"

Every head turned when Celeste spoke, her voice high and reedy. "Lorelei Mitchell is—was—a horrible person."

"Celeste," admonished Adam, brushing himself off as Noah released him.

He stepped toward her and reached out to touch her shoulder, but she slapped his hand away. "No, I won't lie and pretend that she was some wonderful person just because she's dead. I've had to lie my entire life because of her. I'm finished."

"No one is asking you to lie, Celeste," Tom said.

Josie expected Adam to lash out at the younger man once more, but he kept his attention on Celeste. "I love you dearly, Celeste, you know that, but how can you say such a thing about a complete stranger? I know you two had issues when you were young women, but this deed is nineteen years old. You haven't talked to her since this was signed. How do you know what kind of person she was?"

Celeste plopped onto the couch and rested her head in her hands. Tom started to move toward her but then thought better of it, staying where he was beside the couch. Adam stooped to pick up the deed, leaving it on the coffee table, and then lowered himself next to her. He started to rub her back, but she shrugged him off and scooted away from him. Josie and Noah gave her a moment. Adam looked on helplessly. Finally, she lifted her head. Her eyes were dry. She looked at Josie and Noah and then to her husband. "I knew her well enough. She tried to take everything from me. My parents. This place. Everything."

Josie said, "She sued you for a share of Harper's Peak Industries."

Celeste nodded. "She thought she deserved it."

Adam said, "Celeste, I think you're forgetting your father's role in all of this."

"All of what?" Noah prodded.

Celeste took in several deep breaths, as if she was trying to maintain her composure. Josie could see her mentally erecting walls around her most vulnerable places so that she would be able to talk about what came next in a matter-of-fact way. Emotionless. Detached. Josie recognized the trick because she had spent a lifetime doing it herself. Like Celeste was doing this very moment, Josie knew what it felt like to systematically push the trauma down so deep inside yourself that you couldn't even reach it yourself anymore. You had to do it in order to survive, to keep functioning, but Josie also knew that, as much mental strength as it took to compartmentalize that trauma and lock it away, something as simple as a word or image, an errant memory or phrase, could spring open that lock and unleash the trauma in a split second, causing a roaring tidal wave of hurt.

Josie said, "Take your time, Celeste."

Celeste's eyes traveled to the ceiling. Adam shifted closer to her and she edged away until she was pinned up against one of the arms of the couch. The side where Tom stood, a silent sentry. One of his hands touched her shoulder lightly. She didn't shrug it off. In a clipped tone, she said, "We were happy. My mother, my father, me. We lived here. My father had opened the larger resort just before I was born. As soon as I was old enough to walk, I went with him everywhere. All over this property. He showed me everything, all the inner workings of this place. When I got old enough to go to school, my mother would pick me up at the bus stop and bring me home, and I'd be off, searching for him. Every day was an adventure. My mother often worked alongside him. She was happy. So happy."

Celeste's voice lowered to a whisper. She blinked rapidly, and Josie knew she was trying hard not to let her feelings bubble to the surface.

Noah said, "We were able to find your mother's obituary. She passed when you were ten years old. I'm sorry. That must have been horrible."

Celeste nodded. Swallowing, she tried again to speak. "My mother killed herself."

This time, when Adam placed one of his hands over hers, Celeste made no move to push him away.

Josie said, "I'm very sorry, Celeste."

Celeste's face hardened. "It was because of Lorelei. You see, my father had a second family in town. He'd been seeing Lorelei's mother at least as long as he was married to my mother. He impregnated the woman. Funneled money from the resort to her. Then she died of cancer. He could have, and should have, let her offspring go into foster care, but he didn't. He brought her home."

As she talked, Celeste's eyes glowed with barely concealed rage. "That's how my mother found out about his infidelity, his betrayal, when little Lorelei Mitchell showed up on her doorstep. My father expected her to take care of Lorelei like she was her own. My mother should have left, but she didn't. Instead, she hung herself."

Celeste motioned toward the large front windows. "From a tree out there. Right in the front yard. I had it taken down after my father died. Even after my mother's suicide, my father insisted on keeping Lorelei. He wanted her to be an equal part of this family. As she got older, she expected it, too."

It seemed to Josie that none of what had happened in the Harper family was Lorelei's fault, but she sensed that Celeste wouldn't accept that. Perhaps it was easier to blame Lorelei as an outsider than to lay the fault where it really belonged—at her beloved father's feet.

Noah said, "Your sister left Denton and became a psychologist. Obviously, she didn't expect to have a future here at the resort."

"She couldn't even do that right, could she?" Celeste spat. "She came back here disgraced, her license revoked, her career over."

Josie said, "She came back here with thirty-four stab wounds in her neck and back. She was attacked by a patient."

Tom didn't look surprised, but Adam gasped. "You never told me that, Celeste."

Celeste turned toward her husband. "Who cares, Adam? I told you when we met that she was not a part of my life and never would be. I took care of all of this"—she flicked the pages that Adam had placed on the coffee table after he tried to attack Tom—"before we were married. I only told you what you needed to know. She was an illegitimate product of an affair my father had. She didn't belong here. She failed in her career as a psychologist and then she came back here, begging for money."

Noah said, "You didn't give her any. That's why she sued you for her share of the estate."

Bristling, Celeste said, "Because she knew she had no right to a single dime my father made. We settled out of court."

"Because you didn't want bad press," Noah asked, "or because you didn't want your father's reputation sullied?"

"Both," Celeste admitted.

"What were the terms of the settlement?" Josie asked. "Was she still receiving payments from you at the time of her death?"

Celeste waved a hand in the air. "Goodness, no. She was given a cash settlement plus the land. Enough to build a house and live comfortably for many years. I never saw her again. We never spoke. I never went to her house. She never came here."

Noah said, "You're telling me in all the years that your sister—"

"Half-sister," Celeste corrected.

"In all the years that your half-sister was only a few miles down the road, on property that used to be part of Harper's Peak, you never once saw her?"

"That is correct," Celeste said. "Neither of us had any desire to see or speak to one another."

Josie eyed Tom. "What about you, Mr. Booth? Did you ever meet Lorelei Mitchell?"

"No," he said. "I never had any cause to meet her." He looked down his nose at Adam. "I only knew about her because when I first came on as managing director, Celeste and I talked about expanding the resort again, and the issue of property boundaries came up."

Adam withdrew his hand from Celeste's. "You were going to expand the resort? Again? Without discussing it with me?"

Celeste waved a dismissive hand and made a noise of exasperation in her throat. "We never got anywhere with it. There was no point in discussing it since we weren't going through with it." She looked at Josie and then Noah. "Now that you know my life story, can you tell me if there's a point to all this besides the fact that Lorelei has been murdered? Surely, you don't think I had anything to do with it."

"We haven't ruled anything out," said Noah. "But the real reason we're here is because one of Lorelei's children is still alive, and unless her next of kin takes her in, she'll go into the foster care system."

At this point, the very last thing Josie wanted to do was hand Emily Mitchell over to this woman, but she didn't get to decide. The laws of the Commonwealth dictated what would happen to Emily now that Lorelei was dead. Marcie Riebe would be in charge of placing her, whether it was with Celeste and Adam or someone in the foster care system.

Adam said, "Lorelei had children? Celeste, did you know that?"

Celeste shook her head. "Of course I didn't know."

He shot a glare at Tom but Tom only shrugged. "I never even met the woman. I didn't know either."

Celeste asked, "What does this have to do with us?"

"As Detective Fraley said, we're here because you're her next of kin," Josie said.

"How many children did she have?" Adam asked.

Celeste shot him a dirty look. "Who cares, Adam?"

Noah said, "Two. Holly was the girl found on your property."

"Wait, what?" Celeste said, springing up from her seat. "That girl was her—her daughter?"

"Your niece," said Josie.

Celeste's mouth clamped shut. Her lips pressed into a thin line. Josie could see her losing control of her emotions. "She was just a… just a kid."

"Oh my God," said Adam. His tears flowed freely down his face. "And she was—someone murdered her?"

"Yes," said Josie. "I'm very sorry."

Tom said nothing. His face showed no emotion. On the couch, Adam's shoulders shook. Celeste was still on her feet, staring at them, her eyes filling up even as Josie could clearly see her trying to hold back the emotion. "How old was she?"

"Twelve," said Noah.

"Oh God," Celeste said, covering her mouth with one hand.

Adam looked up. "You said there was another one? A girl?"

"Yes," said Josie. "Emily. She's eight."

"Wait. She was the Amber Alert we got last night," he said. "You found her?"

"Yes," Noah answered. "She was hiding. She was safe."

"But we didn't know that," Josie said. "So the Amber Alert had to go out."

"Of course," said Adam.

"What about their father?" Celeste asked.

"Evidently, he wasn't in the picture," said Noah. "There was no father listed on their birth certificates. Emily said she didn't have a father. We found no evidence in the house to indicate that a male was living there."

"The poor girl," Adam said. "She must be traumatized."

"Yes," said Noah. "She lost her mother and sister all in one day and now she has to leave her home. She hid in a closet during the murder. She was in there for several hours and ate some spoiled food. She's been at the hospital with food poisoning, but she'll need a place to go soon. Child Services is already involved. They prefer that a family member take her until more permanent arrangements can be made."

"We can't take her," Celeste said. "She doesn't even know us!"

"Celeste," said Adam.

She looked down at him. "No. I don't mean that we can't take her because she's Lorelei's child. I only mean that she'll need some support, someone with her, and we're working almost around the clock. We can't leave her here in this house alone, Adam."

He stood up and looked into his wife's eyes. "You heard them, it's only temporary. We can figure something out for a few days. There are plenty of staff to fill in for us. We can even take shifts if you'd like."

Tom stepped forward, moving closer to Celeste. "I don't think this is a good idea."

Adam whirled on him. "You stay out of this."

Celeste touched Adam's arm. "Stop."

"No," said Adam. "I've had enough of him. What we're talking about right now is between the two of us. It has nothing to do with him. This is our decision to make."

Tom said, "You have to think of the public relations implications."

Adam stabbed a finger in the air in front of Tom's face. "Shut up. Not another word. I'm talking to my wife."

As he turned back to her, Celeste shook her head. "We can't—"

"She has nowhere else to go, Celeste," Adam implored. "Don't you want to at least meet her?"

They gazed at one another for a long moment. Josie could tell there was a silent flood of communication happening between them. It was couples' shorthand. She and Noah had it as well. Finally, Celeste took his hand, lacing her fingers between his. Turning back to Josie and Noah, she said, "Fine. A few days. That's it. We're not prepared to have a child full-time. But only if all of this stays out of the press." She spared Tom a glance. He didn't look happy, but kept silent. Celeste continued, "Not to sound callous, but I don't want any bad press to fall on Harper's Peak. It's one thing for us personally, but we employ hundreds of people here, and it's my job to protect them and make sure they continue to have income."

"We'll do our best," Noah assured her. "Right now, we'll need to speak with the social worker. It will ultimately be up to her to approve Emily coming here temporarily. She may want to meet with you."

"You can give her our cell phone numbers," Adam said. "We're always here."

Noah's cell phone chirped. Josie recognized it as his text notification. He took it out and glanced at the screen. "Hospital," he said. "They've got those records we requested."

"Let's go," Josie said. To Adam and Celeste, she added, "Marcie Riebe from Child Services will be in touch."

CHAPTER SEVENTEEN

They left Celeste and Adam's residence and walked back to the parking lot adjacent to the main resort building. As they were about to get into the car, a white van flashed past, headed around the rear of the building. "Noah, look," said Josie.

"That's one of the vans from the market," he said, and read the words off the side of it. "Bryan's Farm Fresh Produce. Did you see who was driving?"

"No," Josie said. "It went by too fast. You?"

Noah shook his head but started walking toward the rear of the building, following the asphalt drive. "There's one way to find out."

Josie followed. They rounded the back of the resort building to see a loading dock. The van was backed up to it, doors open. Reed stood on the dock with a resort staffer. As the two of them studied a clipboard, the staffer checking off items with a pen, Paxton unloaded boxes of produce from the van, setting them at his father's feet. He lined them up in rows of four, taking time to make sure each box was lined up precisely beside the next with exactly one index finger's width between them. Josie watched him put his finger in the gaps between the boxes once, twice, then a third time. One of the boxes was too close to the other. He adjusted it and started all over again, counting and measuring with his finger again.

"Dammit, Pax," Reed yelled. "I told you to knock that shit off. Come on now, we don't have all day."

Pax jumped and quickly turned back to the van, grabbing more boxes. A resort staff member then helped Reed carry each one inside. Josie could see him surreptitiously adjusting the boxes when his father was inside the building. As she and Noah drew closer, Paxton looked up and spotted them. His brown eyes went wide with panic. He looked over at the dock, but his father was still inside. He put a finger to his lips. *Shhh.* Then he shook his head.

Josie kept walking. She would not be intimidated by Reed Bryan. She was only a few feet from the front of the van when she felt Noah's hand on her forearm. "Look," he said.

Pax had stopped unloading the van. His hands were jammed into his apron pockets, rooting for something. One hand emerged with a crumpled piece of paper. With a jerky motion, he tossed it to the side. It fell next to the van between the back and the driver's side door but out of the line of view of where Reed had been standing on the loading dock. Pax met Josie's eyes, making the hush motion again with his index finger. She nodded. As Reed came back out of the building, she and Noah crowded against the front of the van. From where Reed stood, he wouldn't be able to see them.

"What the hell, Pax? Come on. We don't got all day. We got more deliveries after this," they heard Reed complain.

"Sorry, Dad."

Noah peeked around the side of the van. "It's right there," he said. "I can get it."

"This is ridiculous," Josie said.

"Maybe, but when are we going to get to talk to this kid without his dad around? He's obviously trying to tell us something. Hang on."

Lightning fast, he crouched low and sprinted around the side of the van, scooping the crumpled paper and bringing it back. From behind them, they could hear Pax dropping boxes onto the surface of the loading dock, followed by grunts as Reed and the resort staff member hefted them into the building. Noah used the snub-nosed hood of the van to smooth out the paper. Most of the document was gone, burned away or blackened from fire. In many places, where Pax had crumpled it, pieces of it had flaked away. Only a few bits of text survived.

"This came from Lorelei's house. The greenhouse, maybe," Josie said softly.

Noah nodded. "This is handwritten. Hard to make out. Maybe a letter of some kind? '… *don't want to involve you. I never did. I thought I could do this on my own, but I was wrong. I won't be able to…*' I can't make out the rest of that sentence. Then: '…*we made a deal but if you'd just give it a chance, you might feel…*' More of this is unreadable. Looks like, '… *know the truth about you, and I don't care…*' Can't read the rest of this paragraph, but then down here it says, '…*can't just do the right thing? Why are you forcing me to make this choice? This is an impossible choice. I don't want to tell, but …*' The rest is just gone, burned away. The page is dark. I can't make it out."

"Do you see any names?"

"Nothing, you?"

Josie leaned closer. "I don't see anything."

Reed's booming voice startled them. "Boy, get this van started while I square up the paperwork."

"Yes, Dad," replied Pax.

Quickly, Noah placed the page into his pocket. Paxton came around toward the front of the vehicle. His eyes widened when he saw them. "You have to go. My dad is going to flip his lid if he sees you here."

Josie said, "Pax, you know you can legally talk to us without your dad's permission."

"I have to live with him. He'll kick my ass if he sees me talking to you," Pax pointed out. "Look, please just go. Don't make this worse for me."

Josie held up her hands. "We're going, Pax. Thank you for this. Where did you find it?"

"The woods. It was near Miss Lorelei's house. I found it. I knew something bad happened because she didn't come for her fruit like she always does on Fridays."

"You were at her house yesterday?" Josie asked.

Pax looked back toward the dock. His fingers rested nervously on the van's door handle. "My dad was busy with a big order. He was on the phone. I took my bike through the woods like I always do. I smelled fire. Miss Lorelei doesn't like fire near her house. Someone had been burning something in the greenhouse."

"Did you go inside?"

He shook his head violently. A tear streaked down his face and he wiped it away quickly. "There was blood on the back porch. I got scared. I got away from there, rode my bike back into the woods."

"Did you see anyone, Pax?" Josie asked.

"Please," he said. "You have to go."

"Just tell us one last thing," Noah said. "Did you see anyone?"

"Nobody. Just this paper in the woods. I was upset and I got lost. I had to turn around to go back to the market. But I found this. I thought it was important, and I'd give it to Miss Lorelei when I saw her next, but then today when you came to the market, you said she was dead. Holly, too."

Another tear rolled down his face.

"I'm sorry, Pax," Josie said.

"Is Emily okay?"

"Yes," Josie said. "She's fine. Thank you for this. You did the right thing. Pax, was there ever anyone else at the house with Lorelei, Emily, and Holly when you were there?"

His chin dipped to his chest. "I'm not supposed to say. My dad doesn't even know."

They heard Reed hollering goodbye to someone on the loading dock. "Just take the paper and go, okay?"

Noah said, "This paper, do you know who wrote it?"

Reed's voice boomed from the loading dock. "Boy! Why isn't this van started! Pax?"

"Miss Lorelei, probably. Looks like her handwriting. She had secrets. All adults have secrets. They're liars, every one of them, even my dad. You can ask Emily. Ask her what grown-ups do."

"Pax! Where the hell are you?"

"Now, please, go!"

Josie pressed a business card into his hand. "You call us if you need us or if you think you can talk, okay?"

While Pax walked to the rear of the van to distract Reed, Josie and Noah sprinted around to the front of the building. Once in their car, Noah threw it into gear and took off down the long drive.

CHAPTER EIGHTEEN

Emily had been moved to another area of the Emergency Department. Now she lay on a gurney behind a curtain. Her duffel bag sat at the foot of her bed, and her stuffed dog was clutched tightly to her chest. Someone had turned on the television on the wall and she was transfixed. In the chair beside the bed sat Marcie, tapping away on her phone. When she spotted Josie and Noah, she jumped from her chair. "Oh good," she said. "I was just texting you. We're getting close to overstaying our welcome here. I've got to get Emily settled in somewhere. I've found a spot for her at a nearby group home. Did you get anywhere with next of kin?"

"Yes," said Josie. "Could we talk privately?"

Noah said, "I'm going to run up to Health and Information Services and get those records. I'll be right back."

Josie and Marcie stepped out of earshot of Emily so that Josie could give her a recap of the meeting with Celeste and Adam. "It's not ideal," Marcie agreed. "But it sounds like they might be more sensitive to her recent trauma than a stranger. Well, I suppose they are strangers as well, but if they've shown interest in taking her for now, I should at least meet with them. The group home I have in mind is run by a lovely woman, but she's got a lot of kids on her hands."

"Did Dr. Rosetti come by this morning?" Josie asked.

"For the psych consult? Yes. Other than OCD and some obvious emotional trauma from losing her mother and sister, Emily has no issues."

"Did Dr. Rosetti happen to ask her about what she saw yesterday?"

"Yes. I was in the room with them. Emily wouldn't say. Dr. Rosetti said she is obviously still processing everything that happened, and it's best not to push."

"Right," said Josie. "But someone has been making Emily keep secrets. Those secrets may have gotten her family killed."

"Look, I realize you're trying to solve a case, but my job is to find a place for this little girl to stay until we can make permanent arrangements. You're welcome to speak with her again if you think it will help, but I am asking that you do not put any additional stress on her."

"I won't," Josie promised. "Will you meet with Celeste Harper and Adam Long today? They said they'd be available."

"Do you have their numbers?" Marcie asked.

Josie gave her both Adam and Celeste's cell phone numbers. Marcie disappeared down the hall. Josie slipped inside the curtained-off area and perched on Emily's bedside. "I met your friend Pax today," she said.

Emily's eyes looked from the television to Josie. "Is he sad?"

Josie nodded. "I'm afraid so, yes."

"Me too," said Emily, clutching her dog tighter.

"Emily," Josie asked, thinking of what Pax had said. "Pax told me to ask you a question. He said to ask you what all grown-ups do?"

"They lie."

"What makes you say that?"

She looked back at the TV. Someone had put Nickelodeon on. With a shrug, she said, "Because it's true."

"Did your mom lie?"

"Only because she had to."

"Why did she have to lie?"

"It's a secret."

"Who told you it was a secret?"

"Mama."

Josie tried to catch the girl's gaze once more. "Emily, it's really important now that you don't keep secrets from the police. We're trying to catch the person who did bad things to your mom, and that's why we need to know any secrets your mom told you."

"I can't tell secrets."

Josie tried a different tactic. "Emily, did anyone else ever live with you, Holly, and your mom?"

Emily's eyes snapped toward Josie. "I can't tell secrets. If I tell secrets, more bad things will happen."

"I promise you that nothing bad will happen if you tell me these secrets," Josie said.

"I can't tell secrets," Emily repeated, curling in on herself.

"Okay," Josie said. Shifting away from the subject, she asked, "Did you ever meet Pax's dad?"

"He came to get Pax and make him go away. He didn't want us to be friends."

"Did he ever hurt any of you?"

"Maybe he hurt Pax. He was mean."

Marcie appeared in the opening of the curtain. "I'm going to go to Harper's Peak now for that meeting. The nurse is aware that Emily will be here for a while longer."

Emily's voice was small. "Can Josie stay until you come back?"

"I don't think she can, Emily. I'm sorry, but she's got police work to do."

"I can stay," Josie said. "My colleague is upstairs getting some information. I've got to wait for him anyway."

Marcie smiled. "I'll be back as soon as I can."

Josie sat in the chair next to the bed. Emily went back to watching TV. Within minutes, she was asleep. Noah appeared at the entrance to the curtained area, a flash drive in one hand and a small stack of pages in the other.

"What took so long?" Josie asked.

He lifted his chin to motion toward Emily. "I had a feeling we weren't getting out of here anytime soon. I asked the clerk in Health

Information Services to print out the registration form from the last time Lorelei was seen in the ER."

He pulled the curtain closed behind him and walked over, handing Josie the stack of pages. "It was a year ago. She was here for a spider bite. Evidently, she had a severe reaction. Anyway, her emergency contact is there."

Josie turned the pages until she found it. "Vincent Buckley."

"The psychiatrist who lives two hours away from here and is prescribing her anti-psychotics and anti-anxiety drugs is her emergency contact. That strike you as odd?"

Josie handed the pages back to him and took out her phone. "You know it does. I'm calling this guy back. Stay here."

Phone pressed to her ear, Josie paced the hallway, avoiding nurses and doctors as they walked to and fro. This time, Vincent Buckley answered. "Dr. Buckley here. Can I help you?"

Josie identified herself. "I need to talk to you about Lorelei Mitchell."

There was a hesitation, but Josie could hear him breathing on the other end. Then he said, "What is this about, then?"

"Lorelei was murdered yesterday. So was one of her daughters. We found medication in her home that was prescribed by you. She also put you down as her emergency contact. I need to meet with you as soon as possible to discuss anything you can tell us about Lorelei and her family situation."

More silence. His breathing quickened. "M-m-m-my," he stammered. "I don't know what to say. I—what happened? Can you tell me what happened?"

"We don't know what happened," Josie said. "That's why I called. What can you tell me about Lorelei's living situation?"

Instead of answering, he said, "Can you describe the scene for me?"

"I'm sorry, what?"

"The, uh, crime scene."

"I can't give out that information, Dr. Buckley. This is an open investigation."

"I understand. Her living situation? She lived with her children."

Josie held back a sigh of exasperation. "Dr. Buckley, we've got a murderer on the loose. Time is of the essence. If you could tell me everything you know about Lorelei then I can decide what information is useful and what's not."

"What, specifically, would you like to know?"

He wasn't going to make it easy. "Are you the father of her children?"

A chuckle. "Goodness, no. Lorelei and I were colleagues back when she was practicing. That's how I know her."

"All right," Josie said. "Do you have any idea who might have wanted to kill her?"

"I live two hours from her. I didn't see her often. I was not privy to the minutiae of her daily life."

"She was your patient and you were her emergency contact. She must have confided in you about many things."

Another long hesitation. Just as Josie was about to ask if he was still there, a long sigh came over the line. "Detective, Lorelei Mitchell was not my patient."

"What? We've got medications with your name on them."

"Right. This is a lengthy conversation that is best had in person. Unfortunately, I'm not in a position to drive just now. My car is in the shop. But I'll have it back by the end of next week. Perhaps then we could—"

"I'll see you in a few hours," Josie said, and hung up.

CHAPTER NINETEEN

Vincent Buckley lived on a sprawling farm in Bucks County surrounded by a low, crumbling stone wall. The driveway to his large farmhouse was at least a half mile. On either side of it were rolling fields of verdant green dotted by the occasional tree. While it didn't offer the kinds of views Harper's Peak did, it was very beautiful. She and Noah parked in front of the house and climbed the steps to the large wraparound porch. A man in his seventies with thick, wavy white hair and a neatly trimmed white beard sat in a rocking chair. Beside him was a small circular table with an ashtray on it. In one hand he held a half-finished cigar and in the other, a book. Tendrils of smoke rose from his cigar, sending its strong scent in their direction.

"You must be the detectives from Denton," he said, not getting up.

Josie and Noah both showed him their credentials. He studied each one for a long moment. Then, apparently satisfied, he put his cigar into the ashtray and his book into his lap. He motioned toward a wicker bench across from where he sat. "Please," he said.

"Dr. Buckley," Josie said. "On the phone you said Lorelei wasn't your patient, yet you've clearly prescribed medication to her. That's a pretty serious admission. Your license could be revoked or suspended."

"Will you report me, then?" he asked in a tone that sounded like he almost wished they would.

Noah said, "We have to discuss it with our Chief. For now, we just need to know why you would be prescribing medications for someone who was not a patient."

"Her son was my patient."

Josie felt a tickle at the back of her neck. "I'm sorry, Dr. Buckley. You said her son?"

"Rory Mitchell." He put his book onto the table and leaned forward, resting his elbows on his knees. "I can tell by the looks on your faces that news of Lorelei's son is a complete shock to you. This is exactly how she wanted it, although ultimately, I'm not sure that it served her all that well. She is dead, after all."

Noah asked, "How old is her son?"

"Oh, he would be fifteen by now, I imagine. Detectives, if you want to know who killed Lorelei and anyone else living in her house, you need look no further than Rory."

"He wasn't there," Josie said. "There was no evidence that he even lived there. No one has even mentioned him."

Buckley gave a pained smile. "Because he was her secret."

Noah said, "How and why would you keep a child a secret?"

"Have you found out about Lorelei's past? I assume you have if you're here talking to me."

"She was a psychologist," Josie said. "She specialized in adolescent abnormal psychology, and she was attacked by a patient who killed his mother and then, later, himself."

Buckley nodded. Gone was his smile. "I've already admitted to prescribing medications to someone who isn't my patient, and now I'm going to tell you something else that would end my career, except that I will retire now that Lorelei no longer needs me. I haven't treated patients in over five years. Rory was my last patient. Only Lorelei didn't want him in any system—not the medical system, not the mental health system, and certainly not the criminal justice system—so I prescribed his drugs to her, and she dispensed them to Rory as needed."

"What's the other thing you were going to tell us?" Josie asked, sensing he was losing track of his thoughts.

He raised a finger in the air. "Oh right. Yes. Here it is." He put his hand back into his lap. "Lorelei and I were colleagues. She was a great deal younger than I was, but so brilliant. Very successful treating even the most difficult patients. Her specialty was cognitive behavioral therapy. She didn't like to medicate patients. That was my job. We often disagreed on when or whether to medicate patients. We had many arguments. Then there was a particularly troublesome patient. She had worked with him for just over three years. She'd made great progress."

"What was his diagnosis?" Josie asked.

Buckley waved a hand. "Oh dear. Is there ever one single diagnosis for the children most afflicted in mind and heart? Many children have several comorbidities. Therefore, it becomes difficult to treat one without somehow worsening the other—or others. The trickiest cases are the ones that you cannot pin down to one single cause. Imagine, if you will, a child who comes to a clinic with a general feeling of malaise. He doesn't feel well. Perhaps he is achy or his stomach bothers him. Perhaps he has headaches or fatigue. Overall, he simply doesn't feel right. He's not able to function well. What do you do?"

He went silent, as if waiting for an answer. Finally, Noah ventured a guess. "Try to rule out different causes until you've narrowed it down to one or two?"

Buckley smiled. "Yes. Indeed. That is part of what I tried to do. If you have a child who is experiencing episodes of extreme rage, who is acting out violently, you might say perhaps this child has intermittent explosive disorder, conduct disorder, or oppositional defiant disorder, or a number of other things. It will help to pinpoint which one, if possible. But what if you've got symptoms and behaviors that are more consistent with ADHD, OCD, or even bipolar disorder? What if you believe there is some combination of these at work? What if that child also displays indicators of schizophrenia?

What if he has fixed paranoid delusions? We do try to narrow it down, but sometimes we cannot. Sometimes the inner workings of these various syndromes and disorders on a child's mind are so complex, we can only treat them through trial and error."

Josie said, "You're saying the patient that you and Lorelei treated twenty years ago suffered from multiple diagnoses, some of which caused him to have violent episodes?"

"Precisely, yes."

Noah said, "Lorelei didn't want to medicate him?"

"Quite the opposite. She did want to medicate him. She'd gotten as far as she could with him using her therapies, and she believed he was declining. Headed toward some kind of psychotic break. She wanted me to medicate him."

"But you didn't," said Josie.

"I did not."

Noah said, "If she believed this patient was that much of a danger to others or himself, couldn't she have him committed?"

"She did. But you must understand, there are few structures, if any, in place to deal with children who have these sorts of problems. He was out within a week. He'd done fine in the hospital. Lorelei believed it was because it was a controlled environment where he didn't have access to the things he needed in order to carry out a violent act. She still wanted to start him on a medication regimen beyond what he was given in the hospital to treat him acutely."

"You said no," Josie said. "Why?"

He gave a heavy sigh and his gaze drifted over the tops of their heads. "Why? The question that has plagued me for nearly twenty years. Why? Because I was a drunk. I was lazy. I was stubborn, and I was a lecherous old fool. I didn't want to help Lorelei with her patient because I had made a pass at her, and she'd turned me down. The truth is I was too wasted during that time in my life to remember much of it. It was a blur. She tried to find another psychiatrist to treat the patient, but before she could find anyone, he had carried out his attack."

"How was that her fault?" Josie asked. "Her license was revoked. Her career was destroyed."

Buckley sighed again. "It wasn't her fault. It was just so egregious that the powers that be felt something had to be done. Even then, she was only to get a slap on the wrist. Then the boy's father got involved. A man who had not even seen his son for ten years because he couldn't handle his behaviors. This man gave up on his son, but when there was money to be had in suing our clinic, he was front and center. Made a cool million from our insurance policy. Lorelei's license was just a casualty."

"But not yours," Noah said.

"No. Not mine. Lorelei could have taken me down with her, but she didn't. Of course, I've spent a lifetime repaying that debt. Until today. Now I am free. So is Lorelei. Finally."

Josie didn't think that Emily would see it that way, but she didn't say that. Instead, she turned the conversation toward the case, and finding out everything they could about Lorelei's life and who had been in it. "Were you in touch with Lorelei through the entire process? The lawsuit and licensing hearings?"

"No. I didn't hear from her until Rory was about six years old. He had been throwing tantrums. Severe tantrums. Destroying toys and anything he could get his hands on. He was spiteful. If she told him to brush his teeth, he might try to throw her hot coffee in her face. She could not manage him—not with a toddler in the house."

Josie said, "The children's father wasn't involved?"

"No. She said he was a non-factor. He had shown some interest in Rory when he was an infant but once the difficulties started, he did not want to be involved. Very much like the father of her last patient, sadly. I don't think that Lorelei wanted him involved anyway. She had serious trust issues when it came to men. Well, not only men, I suppose, but let's say she trusted men least of all. She was the expert, she said, and she didn't want another person there making decisions for her children."

Noah asked, "She never told you anything about the father? His name? Anything at all?"

Buckley shook his head. "All she would say is that he was a mistake. That was it. I used to joke that he was clearly a mistake she liked to make over and over again. She didn't appreciate that."

"What happened when she called you about Rory?" Josie asked. "What did she want?"

He spread his hands. "Help. She had already evaluated him and thought he probably had oppositional defiant disorder. I went there and evaluated him. I agreed with her assessment, although I also suspected that he might have comorbidities like conduct disorder, autism, and ADHD, which made things much more complicated for him. One thing was for certain: he had uncontrollable aggression. Most of the time, these children with disorders that cause violent ideations don't actually act on them. Sometimes they'll destroy property but violence against other people is extremely rare, believe it or not. But Rory was not responding to Lorelei's efforts. She wanted to medicate him. I do not typically medicate children that young."

"So you didn't?" Josie asked.

"I didn't. I told her to keep working with him. She had been out of practice for some time. I made some recommendations based on studies I had read."

"But that didn't work," said Noah.

Again, Buckley's gaze went over their heads, as if he were looking into his past. He didn't like what he saw. "No. It didn't. I was back there within a year."

"You prescribed medication," Josie said. "Why?"

"Rory had injured his sister, Holly. Badly. He routinely beat her, shook her, pushed and pulled at her. He was out of control. Lorelei could not manage him."

"What did you do?" Josie asked.

Buckley waved a hand toward the grounds all around them. "I brought him here. Got him stabilized. Worked with him until I felt it was safe for him to return to Lorelei's care."

"Lorelei just gave you her child?" Josie said.

"You must understand how desperate she was, how exhausted, and how frightened."

Noah said, "Why didn't she just have him admitted somewhere?"

"Because she knew what would happen to him. It would be a lifetime of him being in and out of institutions with no continuity of care. He would frequently be placed far away from her, because facilities equipped to deal with his range of issues are few and far between. Then, once he became a teenager, he would do or say something that would land him in the criminal justice system. That is where this story ends for children like Rory. Jail. They don't get help. They don't get care. At least, not into adulthood. There are not structures in place in this country to support these kids. Lorelei knew that first-hand. She didn't want to lose her son."

"Is that why you prescribed the medication to her and not him?" Josie asked.

"She didn't want him to have the stain of taking those kinds of drugs so early in life. It was easier, fewer questions asked, if I prescribed them to her rather than to a young boy. There are also drugs and certain combinations of drugs I could not prescribe to a child, but could to an adult. We had to take some extraordinary measures to bring Rory to a place where he was functioning without violent outbursts. She was always afraid that if even one person saw him when he was at his worst, they would call the authorities, and he would be placed into the state system, and out of her reach, especially given her history of having her license revoked."

"That's why she was so secretive about him?" Noah asked.

"If you were in public somewhere, and your son began punch-ing and slapping your younger daughter, shaking her, pushing her down, pulling at her limbs and saying things like, 'I'll find the knives and stab both of you to death. I'll cut you into pieces. I'll kill you,' do you think people around you would walk on without doing anything?"

"Probably not," Josie said.

"As I said, Rory could not control these rages or impulses. Just because they were out in public didn't mean he would behave. If violent ideations overcame him, he would try to act on them. He once beat Holly bloody in the car on the way home from the playground. I believe that was the last time Lorelei ever took him out in public."

Noah said, "It didn't bother her that he was hurting her other child?"

"Of course it did," Buckley said. "But what was she to do? They're both her children. Both her responsibility. She wanted to protect both of them."

"She thought she could save Rory," Noah said, a slight edge to his voice.

"Noah," said Josie.

"I'm sorry," he said to Buckley. "I'm trying to understand. How do you protect both children when one of them is trying to kill the other?"

"Well, that's just it, isn't it? It's an impossible situation. Both are your children. Must you choose? If you choose the one who doesn't have psychological issues, then what do you do with the afflicted one?"

"Lorelei didn't feel she had a choice," Josie said softly.

"She loved her children," Buckley said. "Intensely and passionately. More than anything or anyone else in the world. Holly could be insulated from harm to a large degree with an effective safety plan. But Rory was more difficult to protect. Lorelei felt she had to keep him away from a world that would not understand or accept him. She did not want a repeat of what had happened with her last patient."

Josie and Noah were silent for a long moment, taking in this information. Then Josie said, "Holly's autopsy showed chronic signs of physical abuse. It was from Rory. Not from Lorelei or the children's father."

"Correct."

"You and Lorelei weren't able to manage his violent behavior," Noah said. "Not if there were still safety plans in place in the home. What was Lorelei's long-term plan for Rory? He couldn't stay there in the woods with her forever."

"I often asked her that myself, but she was so exhausted and frazzled from being in a constant state of crisis with him, I don't think she had thought that far ahead. I think she truly believed she could get him to a place where he would become high-functioning and non-violent. It's certainly possible. One should never count these children out. But treatment is difficult. It's very complicated. With these kids, it's often like throwing spaghetti at the wall and seeing what sticks."

"That's reassuring coming from a psychiatrist," Josie said.

Buckley laughed. "I only mean to say that every person is different. What might work for one, might not work for another, even if they've got the same diagnoses. As I said, I suspect Rory had several comorbidities, and some we hadn't yet fully addressed. With someone who is in almost a constant state of crisis, you're always trying to put the fire out, and it becomes more and more difficult to find the time to look beneath and address all the things that continue to cause those fires in the first place. We did not learn to manage his violent behavior in the sense that we made it go away forever. It may never go away. But we managed to get him to a point where his outbursts were less frequent and less intense, where he had more control over them. Lorelei and her girls had a safety plan for when Rory would act out. Also, to my knowledge, he rarely hurt the younger one. What was her name?"

"Emily," Josie supplied. "Have you met her?"

"Only twice, very briefly. Years ago. She was probably too young to remember me."

"The safety plan," Josie said. "Would that involve hiding? Keeping all dangerous or sharp objects away from Rory?"

"Yes, indeed. I had brought Rory here again when he was a bit older after some particularly violent episodes with Holly. His meds needed to be adjusted. Lorelei said she was going to convert her bedroom closet into some sort of hiding place for the girls to go while I had him here with me. After I sent him home that time, I didn't hear from her again, other than to check in and refill Rory's meds."

"Does Rory have OCD?" Josie asked.

"Rory has many diagnoses, but no, that's not one of them."

Noah said, "You said you haven't had contact with Rory for several years now, but you think that he killed Lorelei?"

"It would be the most obvious explanation. The last time I saw him, I believe he was starting to experience hallucinations as well as paranoid delusions. I spoke with Lorelei about it, but she believed she could still manage him with medication and her own efforts. However, I do not believe that Rory one day just stopped having violent outbursts or uncontrolled aggression."

Josie said, "Lorelei had a gun. Did you know that?"

Buckley raised a brow. "No, I did not. That's surprising. I assume she kept it out of Rory's reach, however."

Not far enough, Josie thought. "Where were you yesterday morning, doctor?"

"I was here. I'm always here. As I said, my car has been in the shop."

"Does anyone live with you?" she asked. "Anyone who can corroborate that you were here?"

"No, it's just me."

Noah said, "Do you have any photos of Rory?"

Buckley shook his head. "I do not. Lorelei had many, though. Albums and albums of them."

Josie met Noah's eyes and she knew he was thinking the same thing: those albums were gone or destroyed. She asked, "Would Rory have destroyed them if he were having some kind of outburst?"

"Certainly. He destroyed many things over the years."

"Can you tell us what he looked like?" Noah asked.

"Last I saw him he was tall and gangly. He strongly resembled Lorelei. Brown eyes. Brown hair. Oh, he's got a lock of white hair right here." Buckley pointed to the center of his forehead where his hairline started.

"Poliosis," Josie said.

He smiled. "Yes! He had the white forelock and Holly the white eyelashes."

Noah asked, "Did Lorelei have poliosis, do you know?"

"I don't believe so," said Buckley.

"The children got that from their father, then," said Josie.

"I can't say for certain," said Buckley. "I'm no geneticist or expert on poliosis, but perhaps, yes."

Emily had no white forelock or white eyelashes. "Do you know if all three of Lorelei's children were fathered by the same man?" she asked.

"I have no idea. I assumed they all had the same father. It's not like Lorelei got out much. Her entire life was those children. Could she have met someone else after Holly was born? I suppose. We never discussed it."

Josie thought about what Paxton and Emily had said about adults lying. Buckley had been quite forthcoming with them even at the risk of tarnishing his career. With Lorelei dead and him retiring, the damage to his career would be moot, even if Josie and Noah reported him to the state. Without Lorelei alive, there would be no one to bring criminal charges or to file any civil suits. In a sense, now that she was gone, the only thing he had to lose was his reputation. Still, Paxton and Emily were both right—it seemed every adult in Emily's life at least had lied about many things.

"Do you know a man named Reed Bryan?" Josie asked.

There was no flicker of recognition in his face. "No. I do not."

Noah asked, "Did Lorelei ever talk about her family?"

"Her evil half-sister?" he laughed. "Yes, in broad strokes. When I first visited her, I wondered how she'd gotten her house and all that land given she had no job and no prospects. If you're wondering what other secrets Lorelei shared with me, there are none. Only Rory."

Josie said, "Dr. Buckley, what's your shoe size?"

He raised a brow but answered, "Nine."

"Can you tell us your blood type?"

"B positive," he answered easily. "Would you like my fingerprints as well?"

It was a joke. Josie could tell by his smile. She said, "Actually, yes."

CHAPTER TWENTY

"You think that guy's the father of Lorelei's children?" Noah asked as he pulled out of Vincent Buckley's long driveway and back toward Denton.

"I don't know," Josie said. She tucked a brown evidence bag holding one of her business cards with Buckley's prints on it into the glove compartment. She'd have Hummel process the card when they got back, see if any of his prints matched up to those found in Lorelei's house. "It seems like he would have confessed that. He told us every other damn thing, including that he made a pass at Lorelei."

"All the stuff he told us means nothing now," Noah said. "Not if he's stopped practicing medicine. But if Rory and Emily are his children, that makes things a lot more complicated for him."

"True," Josie said. "But he screwed Lorelei over. He actively blocked her attempts to help a patient, and people died because of it. Then he let her lose her license and her career. I don't know if that's something any woman would be able to forgive—not enough to have three kids with him. Anyway, right now we need to focus on finding Rory. Can you drop me off at the hospital? My car is there. I'm going to drive over to Lorelei's house and see if I can find anything that belonged to Rory."

"While you do that," Noah said, "I'm going to see if I can find a birth certificate for Rory Mitchell and draw up a warrant for any medical records. I know Lorelei kept him a secret, but she had to give birth to him somewhere. I know a lot of women give birth at home, but she had both of his sisters at Denton Memorial so maybe he was born there, too. If he was, his blood type will be on file. Also, I'll see if I can get the Sheriff to send Deputy Sandoval and her dog Rini over to you. Using the dog would probably be the fastest way to find this kid if he is out in the woods."

"Update the team," Josie said. "We'll need bodies out there with the K-9 unit. It's a lot of area to search, and if this kid is as violent as Buckley claims, it might be better to have some back-up."

"Remember when we were talking with Pax and he said something like, 'my dad doesn't even know.' He meant his dad didn't know about Rory, didn't he?"

"I think so," Josie said. "If Reed is telling the truth and he was only at Lorelei's house a couple of times just to get Pax, it's possible he never met Rory. But Pax also said his dad was lying, too. I'm just wondering what he was lying about, and it if has any bearing on this case."

"You mean you think Reed was involved?"

"I don't know," Josie said. "Buckley made it sound so simple. Lorelei has a teenage son she's kept from people for years because he has violent outbursts. This time things went too far."

"If that's what happened, why wouldn't Emily just tell us that she has a brother, and he killed their mother and sister?"

"I don't think that Emily actually saw the murders. I think that Holly told her to hide before anything happened."

"Still, she knew about Rory and didn't tell us. Why couldn't she just tell us she had a brother?" Noah asked.

Josie thought about Emily's reasoning for not telling secrets. It would make the bad things happen. That was her OCD. The irrational worry and the voice whispering in her ear, "Are you sure the bad things won't happen if you tell these secrets?" Josie had explained to her repeatedly the need to tell the police whatever she knew, and yet, she could not bring herself to do it. Doing so would provoke her fight or flight response. Panic. Josie had seen and heard her in the throes of it the night before. Feeling all her feelings until they went away. No wonder she didn't want to go through that again. There was also the issue of bad things happening in her household on a regular basis if Rory was as aggressive and uncontrollable as Buckley made him out to be. Rory's outbursts would certainly reinforce the distorted thinking and the need for secrecy. "I think that's her OCD," Josie told Noah. "Remember what I told you about my conversation with Paige?"

"Yeah. That makes sense. But what about Pax? Why wouldn't he just tell us about Rory? He has no stake in any of this, especially with Lorelei gone. It's one less thing for his dad to be angry about."

"I don't know," Josie answered. "But if Pax is riding his dirt bike through the woods on that mountain, there's a chance he could run into Rory—who now has a gun."

"All the more reason for Pax to tell us about Rory. Unless Pax is hiding something."

"It seems like everyone we talk to is hiding something," Josie groused. An image of Pax fitting his index finger between the boxes of produce on the loading dock flitted through her mind. "It might be worth trying to talk to Reed again, but right now, Rory is our main suspect and the only member of Lorelei's household not accounted for."

Noah pulled up beside Josie's vehicle in the hospital parking lot. Before she got out, he leaned across the center console and kissed her deeply. Then he pressed his forehead against hers. "I'll get the team on this right away, and when this is over, I'll make you my wife."

CHAPTER TWENTY-ONE

Crime scene tape fluttered around the perimeter of Lorelei Mitchell's house. Josie parked in front of the porch steps and got out. Gone was the creepy pinecone doll. Chan had taken it in for processing. A light breeze sailed through the trees surrounding the house. Birds sang. The sun shone down overhead. Josie paused to take it all in. It was so peaceful here, and so secluded. There were no neighbors. The property went for acres in every direction and where it ended, the land owned by Harper's Peak Industries picked up. Even so, the house was still miles from the main buildings on the resort. There was no chance of anyone accidentally pulling into her driveway, as even that was well hidden. This was a well-loved sanctuary that had been turned into a small pocket of hell.

Josie walked up the steps and let herself inside. The house was silent. She moved through the living room to the dining room, noticing that the basement door was open. Had they left it open? In the kitchen, Lorelei's blood had dried on the floor and the side of the island countertop. Someone had closed the back door. The shattered glass on the other side of the island had been pushed aside, almost as if to make room to get to the sink. Josie's heartbeat ticked up as she approached the sink. Inside was an empty mason jar turned on its side, the lid a few inches away. Had this been in the sink yesterday, or had someone been here?

She turned back and went to the stairs, now wanting to get out of the house as quickly as she could. All she needed was some item that she could reasonably conclude belonged to Rory. Something for the dog to scent. It also wouldn't hurt if she found some other evidence of his existence—like a photograph of some kind. She started in the last bedroom—the one with the bare twin mattress, poster, and the drawing of the angry face. Josie wondered if Rory had drawn it. Was it a representation of the rage he sometimes felt? She stood in the middle of the room and turned in a circle. How could a fifteen-year-old boy live here without any personal possessions? Josie could understand wanting to keep any objects from him that could be used to injure others, but surely he had had clothes. She made a mental note to check the closets downstairs to see if there were winter coats stored away somewhere. She was beginning to get the creeping sense that he didn't really exist. If Vincent Buckley hadn't seen the boy, Josie might be inclined to believe that Lorelei had made him up completely and that the drugs in her medicine cabinet really belonged to her.

On the other hand, all of Lorelei's documents and photographs had been destroyed. Had Rory done it? Did Lorelei's attempts to keep his existence from being known to anyone but her daughters and Buckley extend even to Rory's own mind? Had he felt the need to destroy all traces of himself once he'd killed his mother and sister? Surely, he would have known that eventually Emily, Dr. Buckley or even Pax would tell the police of his existence. Did that mean that someone else had destroyed all of Lorelei's things?

A loud creak jarred Josie from her thoughts. Her hand went to her holster, unsnapping it as she crept into the hallway. Had it come from up here or downstairs? She didn't know the house well enough to say. Keeping one hand on the handle of her pistol, she took slow and silent steps back down the hall, toward the top of the staircase, head swiveling to look into the bedrooms as she went. As she came to the end of the hall, something in the bathroom caught her eye. On top of the sink was a toothbrush holder. It held four toothbrushes. Lorelei, Holly, Emily, and Rory. If someone had been trying to remove all evidence of Rory's existence, they'd overlooked this one detail. Josie would have to take them all into evidence and see if they could get DNA and prints from whichever brush belonged to Rory.

Another creak drew her attention back to the hallway. Heart thundering, she took her pistol out and held it pointed downward. She was turning to press her back to one of the hallway walls when something heavy landed on her shoulder from behind. The gun dropped from her grip. She tried to turn to see what or who was behind her, but punches rained down on the back of her head and neck. It was only then she realized she was dealing with a person. A very angry person. Josie's arms immediately went up, trying to block her head from being clobbered. She dropped down, hoping to catch sight of her gun, to retrieve it, but the person kicked her, sending her sprawling on her stomach, and straddled her. Fists pelted her. Her head snapped from side to side. All she was aware of in that moment was trying to stay alive and the sound of grunting above her.

There weren't many fighting options for her, pinned on her stomach with fists smashing into the meat and bones of her arms where they shielded her head. Still, her lower body struggled to somehow wriggle out from beneath the man, to get her knees under her so she could buck him off, anything to slow him down or stop his assault. Nothing worked. Although her arms absorbed most of the attack, she wasn't sure how much more she could withstand. But if she used her arms, her head would be exposed. Would he wear himself out? Could she wait that long? Trying to overcome her internal panic, she concentrated on the hands pummeling her. She couldn't stay here all day, she told herself. He'd beat her to a pulp. She would have to be fast.

Keeping her face toward the floor, she quickly pulled her arms in and down so they were between her and the floor, elbows bent. Pushing up on her forearms, she used the leverage to send him off-balance. There was a two-second-long delay in the punches, which she used to her advantage, bucking with her hips and sending him over and into the wall. On her back, she kicked at him to keep him away, one of her hands searching for the gun. Her fingers closed over it and as she brought it up at the man, he launched himself onto her again, knocking the pistol out of her grip once more. She was in a stronger position on her back, however. Using her arms to shield her face this time, she bent her knees and pushed with her feet. She tried to buck him off again, but the hallway was too narrow. Instead, they just moved in one mess of fused bodies toward the top of the steps. The next time she tried to buck him off, he fell away from her. He was falling down the steps, she realized, but a split second later, she felt her own body begin to tumble. His hands gripped her shirt, pulling her with him.

Together, they tumbled to the bottom. Josie's adrenaline kept her from feeling anything on the way down. Once at the bottom, Josie realized she was suddenly free. She looked up from where she'd landed on her back in time to see the shadowy figure bolt out the front door. Scrambling to her feet, she limped after him, only then realizing her left ankle was throbbing. Ignoring the pain, she picked up her pace, banging out the front door onto the porch. Her eyes searched the front yard where her vehicle sat a few yards from Lorelei's truck. A mountain bike lay between the two. That definitely hadn't been there before.

She hurried down the steps, rubbing an ache in her shoulder. "Pax?" she called.

There was the snap of a branch to her left, so she went that way, following the sound into the trees. Her feet staggered over pine needles and an area of thick brush. Every few seconds she stopped, ears straining to hear any movement. The ground rose and then fell again. She had no idea which direction she was going. Her labored breath roared in her ears. The ache in her shoulder spread across the back of her neck. The throbbing in her ankle grew worse. She heard another branch snap to her right and turned that way. She thought she saw a flash of brown fabric in her periphery and adjusted course. As she went, her mind tried to work through any details her subconscious might have picked up about her attacker while her conscious mind and body fought him off. He'd been wearing earth tones, she remembered that much. Brown sweatpants, she thought. Possibly a drab-green hooded sweatshirt.

The sound of ragged breath that was not her own invaded her ears. She froze and tried to slow her racing heart. Turning toward her left, she saw him, back leaned against an oak tree. His chest heaved. His head dipped downward. A fine sheen of sweat covered his thin, pimpled face.

"Rory," Josie said.

His head snapped up, and Josie saw the white forelock. A perfectly white lock of hair in the center of his forehead. *Striking*, she thought. Lorelei had probably loved it. Josie took a step toward him, keeping her movements small. He watched her warily but made no move to get away. She stopped about five feet away from him, staying in place, letting them both catch their breath.

"Rory," she said again, "my name is Detective Josie Quinn. I'm here to help you, I—"

Again, she heard the telltale sound of a branch snapping and her words stopped in her throat. This sounded like a bigger branch. Closer. She took a quick look around but saw nothing. Her gaze went back to Rory. He stood up straight, moving a step away from the tree, to his full height, which was easily a foot taller than Josie. The fine hairs on the back of Josie's neck stood up. She had the sense of someone or something watching them. Closing in on them. Rory's eyes were brown, the same as Lorelei's. Buckley was right. Aside from the white forelock, he was the spitting image of his mother.

Slowly, his index finger lifted and pressed against his lips.

Hush.

Josie felt a thin ribbon of fear wrap itself around her spine. Footfalls, soft and careful, came from behind her. She whipped around and they stopped. No one was there. When she looked back toward the oak tree, Rory was gone.

"Pax?" Josie called. "Rory?"

Reflexively, her hand went to her holster, but it was empty. Patting her back jeans pocket, she felt the reassuring square of her phone. Except she might not get service out here. She'd have to go back to Lorelei's house if she hoped to get any bars. But perhaps Pax didn't know that. She slid the phone out of her pocket and held it in the air. "I'm calling my team," she yelled. "They'll be here in a few minutes. It's best if you come out now and talk with me before they get here. We can work this out, you and me."

A gunshot shattered the air. Bark from the oak tree Rory had just been leaning against exploded. Josie dropped down to a crouch and started running. No conscious thought drove her body forward, only a primal instinct to get away from the direction of the gunshot. She ran until her lungs burned, her knees ached, and her ankle throbbed mercilessly. When she could barely catch her breath, she stopped, folding herself down beneath a tree trunk that had fallen over a small gully. She tried to listen for footsteps over the sound of her own breathing. She took out her phone and checked for service. One bar.

She didn't want to make a phone call. Not if Paxton or Rory were still out there—one of them armed. Instead, she sent a text to the team. She watched the little circle next to the text spin as her phone tried to send the message. Seconds later, a red exclamation point appeared beside her message. Failed.

"Shit," she muttered.

Two more attempts to send the message failed. Josie staggered to her feet. She couldn't stay out here forever. Her phone wouldn't send or receive data at the moment, but her GPS still worked. She pulled up the app and studied it, trying to orient herself. Once she had a pretty good idea of where Lorelei's house was, she began walking in that direction, trying to stay quiet and alert for any noises around her.

She had almost reached the clearing she believed to be Lorelei's house when she saw a flash of red ahead of her. She raced ahead, weaving among the trees until she saw a figure walking ahead of her in a red shirt and jeans. His head hung low. Paxton Bryan. He had changed clothes since she last saw him. Josie snuck up on him, drawing parallel to him. His hands were empty. He didn't seem to notice her presence at all, unless he was just pretending. Josie fell back and shifted directly behind him. She waited until there was a small clearing ahead and then tackled him to the ground.

He went down hard, crying out. Josie straddled him and twisted his arms behind his back. "Stop!" he cried. "Stop!"

"Where's the gun, Pax?" she demanded.

He twisted his neck, trying to look at her. "What gun? I don't have a gun."

"What did you do with it?"

"I don't have a gun."

"You shot at me."

"No, no, I swear. I didn't. It wasn't me. Please, let me up."

"Were you following me?"

"What? No." His voice was pleading.

"Then what were you doing out in the woods, Pax?"

"I was—I was—I can't tell, okay?"

"I know about Rory," Josie said. "You can stop lying."

He said nothing.

"Were you looking for him?"

Again, no response.

Josie sighed. "I'm going to let go of you now. Do you promise not to hurt me?"

"I wouldn't hurt you. I promise you. I wasn't doing anything."

Josie stood. She took a few steps back and watched as he got to his knees and then his feet. He brushed dirt and leaves and pine needles from his pants and shirt. Josie was startled to see tears glistening in his eyes. She watched his Adam's apple bob a few times as he swallowed, pacing in a tight circle, until he calmed down.

"Pax," she said. "What are you doing out here? Where's your dad?"

He kept pacing, eyes down. "He's back at the market. It was busy so I snuck out."

"You went to Lorelei's house," Josie said. "I saw your bike there. Were you looking for Rory?"

He nodded.

"What were you going to do when you found him?"

"I don't know," he said. "I just needed to talk to him."

"You knew about him, but your dad didn't."

He stopped pacing and met her eyes. "Yeah."

"How is that possible?" Josie asked. She wondered how she hadn't known he was there when she visited.

"Rory spends most of his time in the greenhouse. That's his thing. He kind of lives out there. He doesn't like being around the girls, so he just stays out there. I mean, sometimes Miss Lorelei makes him come inside but mostly, that's where he stays. He grows a lot of stuff out there, does experiments. He's really good at it. You should have seen the peppers he grew last summer. They were huge!"

Before he could get off on a tangent, Josie said, "He was in the greenhouse when your dad came looking for you?"

"Yeah. He knew that Lorelei didn't like people to meet him, so he stayed out there. He's got anger issues. Did you know about that?"

"Yes," Josie said.

"He's my friend. I know that he can't control it when the creature comes."

"The creature?" Josie said.

"That's the name we made up for his rage—the creature—because it's, like, not him, you know? It's something inside him that he can't get a hold on. He doesn't want to say terrible things.

He doesn't want to hurt anyone but sometimes, it's like there's this thing inside him that overtakes him."

He must have seen her brow furrow because he said, "I don't mean in a split personality way, if that's what you're thinking right now. Rory doesn't have that. It was just this thing we did to make it easier for us to talk about the feelings he gets. Miss Lorelei taught us. He's got the creature and I've got the palterer."

"The what?"

He gave a small smile. "The palterer. It's a great word, right? I read it in this super-old book I got from the library. It's considered archaic now."

"What does it mean?"

"A palterer is someone who talks or acts insincerely."

"A liar."

His smile widened. "Right."

"Who is your palterer?" Josie asked. "Are we talking about a person?"

"No," Pax said. "You know how I said Rory gets this rage inside him that he can't control and he doesn't want? I get this, like, thing inside me that's always giving me trouble. Always telling me crazy things that don't make any sense, but they scare me even though I know they're wrong, so I have to do what the thing—the palterer—says. Miss Lorelei made us name them so we would understand that they were not the entirety of our identities. Like, that's not who we are. Rory isn't just his rage, and I'm not just the palterer. These things are apart from us. Rory even drew his."

Josie thought of the disturbing drawing in the barren bedroom at Lorelei's house.

"Yeah, I think I saw that," she said. "The palterer told you to make sure the boxes on the loading dock this morning were exactly one finger's width apart, didn't he?" she asked. "Or something bad would happen."

His eyes widened. "How did you know?"

Ignoring his question, she said, "But the palterer isn't an actual voice or identity or person, is it?"

He shook his head.

"You have OCD."

His entire face changed. He took two steps toward her, his arms opening, as if he were going to embrace her. Instead, he placed them on her shoulders. Josie held still, divining no threat from the boy. "That's what Miss Lorelei said!" he told her.

If Pax was not a threat to her, maybe he was telling the truth about not having a gun and not having shot at her.

"Emily has OCD as well," Josie said.

He dropped his hands and stepped back, his look of relief tempered with something else. Something dark and uncertain.

If Pax wasn't the one who had shot at her, then who?

"Pax," Josie said. "Remember when you told me that even your father lied?"

His head bobbed in acknowledgment. Even as she watched him and worked out the scenario in her mind, her ears were tuned to the forest around them, listening for even the slightest noise. A soft footfall. The snap of a branch. An exhale.

"Emily is your sister, isn't she?" Josie asked. "That's what he's lying about. He did have a relationship with Lorelei, and Emily was the result of it. That's why you kept going there to see her."

His face went ashen. "You can't tell," he whispered.

Josie thought she heard something swish through the brush to their right. She surged forward and grabbed Pax's upper arm, pulling him along. "Come on, we have to get out of here."

CHAPTER TWENTY-TWO

Josie found her pistol inside Lorelei's house, put the toothbrushes in a paper bag she found in the kitchen, threw Pax's bike into the back of her vehicle, and drove directly toward the stationhouse. It could take hours for the K-9 unit to arrive. They served the entire county and were often out on other calls when Denton PD asked for assistance. Josie would instruct one of her team members to search the house for some personal item belonging to Rory. Right now, she just wanted to get away from the house. In the passenger's seat, Pax was silent. As they passed the produce market, he looked at it. Josie glanced over as well, noting that one of the vans was missing. Was Reed out looking for him?

As if reading her mind, Pax said, "My dad's gonna be really mad."

Josie said, "Pax, does your dad hit you?"

"Only a couple of times," he said, his eyes still glued to the outside as the market faded into the distance.

"You know you're eighteen now," Josie said. "You don't have to stay with him."

"Where else would I go? I didn't even finish high school. This problem I have, it can make things really difficult for me. Miss Lorelei was helping me, and for the first time since my mom died, I started to feel normal. But then my dad found out she was 'messing around in my head.' That's what he calls it. He said I couldn't see her—or Emily—again."

Josie glanced over at him to see him shrug his left shoulder twice.

"Do you feel nervous?" she asked him.

"Anxious," he said.

Josie said, "I can talk to your dad for you, if you want, when we're done at the station."

His shoulder shrugged again, but he said nothing.

"Pax, can I ask you a couple of questions that are important to our investigation?"

"Sure, I guess."

"Do you know what your blood type is?"

"No," he said. "I have no idea."

"How about your shoe size?"

"Well, yeah, I wear a size ten, just like my dad."

Josie felt a small jolt but then reminded herself that it could mean nothing. Lots of men wore size ten shoes. Noah wore a size ten. "Do you know Rory's shoe size?"

"No. We're friends, but I don't know that kind of stuff about him."

"Fair enough," said Josie.

Ahead, Denton's quaint, historic Main Street came into view. Josie saw Komorrah's Koffee on their right, and had a terrible craving for coffee. It would have to wait. She pulled into the municipal parking lot behind the station and parked. "Pax, how do you know about Emily? That your dad is her dad, too."

He looked at his lap. "I see things. I hear things. I'm not an idiot. I know he thinks I am. Always telling people I'm 'not right in the head.'" He lowered his voice in a comical impression of Reed that Josie also found sad. Then he continued, "Yeah, I didn't finish school, but I go to the library all the time. I read a lot. Miss Lorelei said I was brilliant."

"She was right," Josie told him. "I mean, come on, 'palterer' is a great word!"

He laughed. Josie noticed his shoulder-shrugging had gone away for the moment. She wanted him relaxed, especially now that she was going to ask him to come into the police station and make an official statement about all the things he'd told her.

He said, "I saw him and Miss Lorelei back in the office once, at the market. It was right after my mom died. They were having sex. They did it a few times at the market after that, and then it just stopped."

"Did he go visit her?" Josie asked.

"No. I don't think it ever went anywhere. I don't think it was more than those few times. She kept coming to the market for food, but she avoided him and he avoided her. Then, as the months went on, her stomach got bigger and bigger. It was pretty obvious what was going on. The other thing about my dad? He thinks I don't understand anything so he has conversations with people while I'm around and thinks I don't get what's happening."

"He confronted her about the pregnancy," Josie supplied.

"Yeah. She said the baby was his—that she hadn't been with anyone else. I'm not sure he believed her—or maybe he just didn't want to—but then he got mad at her. He said she should have 'gotten rid of it.' She asked him how he could say that about his own baby. Then he said—"

Paxton broke off. His shoulder jerked up and down again. Josie reached over and touched it lightly, glad that he didn't flinch. His Adam's apple bobbed in his throat again. Then he said, in a croak, "He said, 'I already got one broken kid, why would I want another?'"

"Oh, Pax," Josie said. "I'm so sorry."

He waved a hand in the air, as if to dismiss her words. Josie kept her hand lightly on his shoulder, feeling it twitch under her palm. "You know you're not broken, right?"

He nodded, not convincingly. "Miss Lorelei took an interest in me after that. Every time she came in, she'd talk to me. When I got older and got my bike, I'd ride over to see her, and I'd visit with Emily. Hold her and stuff. Play with her. Then I got old enough to work at the market, and it wasn't easy to get away anymore. You have to understand though, I don't have anyone in my life but my dad. My dad's sister, my aunt, she wanted to see me all the time after my mom passed, but he won't let her visit. She lives far away in Georgia. I wish she was closer. I'd try to see her, too. She always treated me well."

"I'm sorry to hear you haven't been able to see her," Josie said. "Pax, is it possible that your dad was... seeing Lorelei for many years before Emily was born? Is it possible that Rory and Holly were also his children?"

"I don't think so. He was married to my mom."

While Josie knew that to be true, she also knew it didn't mean a damn thing. As Pax had told her himself, if there's one thing that all adults do, it's lie.

CHAPTER TWENTY-THREE

Josie sat in her chair, her left foot bare and resting on top of her desk. Beside it, Noah perched, holding an ice pack over her ankle and intermittently shaking his head. Josie had an urge to stand up and smooth the worry lines from his forehead. Mettner had taken Pax down to their conference room to try to get a full statement from him about the Mitchell family and his father's relationship to them. Gretchen had gone back to Lorelei's with several patrol units. Sheriff's deputy Sandoval and her K-9 companion, Rini, were going to meet them there so that they could try to find Rory before nightfall. Amber had gone to Komorrah's for coffee.

Noah said, "I should have gone with you."

"Don't be ridiculous," Josie said. "I went there looking for a personal item. I didn't expect to get my ass kicked by a fifteen-year-old boy, chase him through the woods and get shot at."

"It just seems to me that if anyone should expect something like that to happen, it should be you."

Josie tried to slap him from her seat, but he laughed and moved out of reach.

"By the way," he told her. "Hummel got Buckley's prints from your business card. They're not in AFIS and they don't match any of the unidentified prints in Lorelei's house."

"But Buckley said he was there," Josie said.

"He said he hadn't been there in years. Hummel says it's entirely possible for none of his prints to remain if he hadn't been there in years. He also lifted Pax's prints from a water bottle he threw away at the produce market. He went there right after you texted him this morning. As expected, Pax's prints match up to one of the unidentified sets of prints in the house."

"Which means we're down to two sets of unidentified prints in the house," Josie said. "One of those has to be Rory's, which leaves who?"

Noah shook his head. "I don't know, but of the other two sets of prints, one set is found all over the house. The other set is only found on the front door and in the kitchen."

"I'm guessing the set found all over the house is Rory's," Josie said.

"Right. But the other set—it could mean nothing. Maybe it was a delivery person or someone who only came over once. It could be unconnected."

"I doubt that," Josie said. "I don't think Lorelei would have things delivered to her home."

"We thought Lorelei was exceptionally private—that she had no visitors at her place—and then we found out that Pax was there regularly, and that Reed would go to get him," Noah pointed out. "Hell, we didn't even know about Rory until a few hours ago. We really don't know what else Lorelei was doing out there or who else she entertained. Also, I did manage to find out Rory's blood type from his birth records. Guess what?"

"It's O positive. Same as the blood found on Lorelei's truck," Josie guessed.

"Yes."

That put Rory right back at the top of their suspect list. Not that the list was very long to begin with.

Noah said, "When you saw him, did he look banged up at all? Have any scratches or lacerations?"

Josie shook her head. "No, but he was wearing long sleeves and pants. There was no way for me to tell. Hey, did anyone ever hear from Dr. Feist about the bloody footprints leading from the kitchen out the backdoor of the house? The barefoot prints?"

Noah nodded. "She confirmed they're Holly's footprints in Lorelei's blood."

"What about Emily?" Josie asked. "Any word on her?"

"Adam and Celeste took her. Ms. Riebe met with them and said she felt comfortable leaving Emily with them temporarily."

"Great."

A door slammed and the Chief appeared before them, arms crossed over his thin chest. "What the hell is this, Quinn?"

She brought him up to speed, watching as his face reddened with each word. "Gretchen's going to need more people out in those woods," he said. "If this kid is running around with a damn gun shooting at my detectives."

"I wanted to talk to you about that, Chief," Josie said. "I don't think it was Rory who shot at me."

Noah said, "You said you looked away from him, looked back, he was gone, and then came the shot."

"Right," said Josie. "But I'm not sure he could have circled me that quickly and gotten off a shot. Besides, he didn't have a gun the whole time I saw him. Not in the house and not while I was chasing him."

The Chief said, "What if he hid it out in the woods? Maybe that's why he stopped at that spot. You thought he was catching his breath, but maybe he was getting you close enough so he could grab the gun and take a shot."

Josie pictured the scene again in her mind. She tried to calculate how long it was between the time she looked back at the tree to discover that Rory was gone and when the shot rang out. Would it have been enough time? She was already full of adrenaline at that point. Time was meaningless. Things that took only seconds would have felt like an eternity, and things that took a long time would have felt instantaneous. The only real way to tell if the Chief's scenario was possible would be to go back out to that spot, try to figure out exactly where she was standing, as well as the bullet's trajectory and origin using the marks left on the trunk by the bullet.

"You're not going back out there," Chitwood said, as if he could see her mental calculations floating above her head. "Not tonight, anyway. Look, I'm going to call the state police and see if we can get some more bodies out in those woods. Maybe if there are twenty cops out there instead of just one, he'll be less inclined to take a shot. Once we nab him, we'll see if we can get him to talk."

Something in the back of her mind was irking her. "Can you get someone to find Reed Bryan? If he's looking for Pax and finds out he's here, he's going to be a real shitstorm. Maybe we can head him off at the pass?"

"Fine," said the Chief.

Josie's desk phone jangled. Noah lifted the ice pack. She put her foot down and leaned over, snatching up the receiver. "Quinn."

Adam Long's voice came over the line. "Detective Quinn?"

"Mr. Long."

"Do you think you could come up to Harper's Peak? We have a bit of a situation."

Josie wondered if Emily was having another meltdown. She had no idea whether or not Marcie had prepared Adam and Celeste for her OCD.

"What's the problem, Adam?"

"It's just that, well, Emily is missing."

CHAPTER TWENTY-FOUR

Josie stood in Celeste and Adam's parlor again, hands on her hips as she and Noah watched Celeste pace frenetically before the large picture window. Black six-inch heels sank into the thick oriental carpet as she moved back and forth. A sleeveless purple wrap dress clung to her angular frame. Strands of her hair had come loose from her chignon, floating around her head no matter how many times she slicked them back. Josie watched her reflection in the glass. Outside, there was only darkness punctuated by the lights of the resorts downhill. In the distance, Josie saw the strobe of blue and red police lights. Celeste followed her gaze and froze in place. She waved a pale arm toward the window. "Would you tell them to turn off the lights? Jesus. I don't want police vehicles on this property. I'd have Tom do it, but he's out in the woods looking for Emily, too."

Noah said, "With all due respect, Ms. Harper, we've got a missing eight-year-old girl last seen here on these premises. She's vanished only a day after her older sister was found murdered on Harper's Peak's grounds."

Celeste's voice shook. "I'm well aware of what's been happening in the last twenty-four hours, but I have a resort to manage. I have guests. They paid for a certain standard of luxury, and police vehicles do not meet that standard."

Josie said, "Our priority is to find Emily Mitchell. You'll have to handle any issues relating to your guests."

Celeste glared at Josie. "This was not my idea. It was my husband's. Now he's out there with Tom and half of my staff and the police looking for that girl while I've got a business to run. How am I supposed to do this?"

"Emily Mitchell could be in danger," Noah pointed out.

"That is not my problem or my fault," Celeste spat. "That girl walked out of here. We spent the entire afternoon trying to make her comfortable and getting her settled in. Do you know what she did?"

Neither Josie nor Noah responded.

Celeste walked past them, toward the coffee table bracketed by couches. Josie noted that several pieces of copy paper were spread across its glossy wooden surface. Some were cut into shapes and others had been used to draw butterflies and what looked like renderings of Emily's stuffed dog. A pair of scissors rested on one end of the table. There were easily four dozen crayons. These had been lined up precisely according to color. A row of greens, a row of blues, reds, yellows, et cetera. Josie hid her smile.

Noah said, "She colored?"

Celeste rolled her eyes. "No. That was Adam's idea. We don't know the first damn thing about children, you know. He got the crayons from a staff member. We made do with printer paper. He thought he'd have craft hour, or something. Well, he left her alone. We have work to do. He was needed in the main building, so he went there. Emily cut almost every tufted button from our couches!"

Now Josie's eyes traveled the length of each of the Chesterfield sofas, noticing that they looked much puffier than they had this morning. Without the tufted buttons, the couches looked somehow naked and incomplete.

Celeste said, "Who *does* this?"

When Noah spoke, Josie could tell that he was just barely holding in his laughter. "To be fair, there are a few buttons left on the arms of the couches."

"Do you know what she told me when I asked her why she would do such a thing?" Celeste went on, ignoring Noah. "She told me that she had to cut them off because she was afraid she would choke on them."

Josie and Noah stared at her. Noah's eyebrow kinked. "Are you sure that's what she said?"

Celeste huffed. "You think I got that wrong? Yes, that's what she said."

Josie knew it was an exceptionally odd thing for anyone to say and do but she suspected it had something to do with Emily's OCD. She'd have to ask Paige or an OCD specialist about it later. Or she could ask Emily, hopefully, when she found her.

"Did you ask her what she meant by that?" Josie asked.

"Why would I? It doesn't matter. She destroyed our property!"

Before Celeste could continue, Josie changed the subject. "How do you know she walked out of here?"

"When Adam left, I was here with her. I had to take a call. It was… a rather long one, but I was only in the kitchen. She's not an infant. I thought she'd be fine in here for a little while, so I didn't worry about it. Except that when I came back, she was gone. The front door was open. She'd taken that ratty old stuffed dog with her, and my tufted buttons!"

"You don't actually know that she left of her own volition," Josie pointed out. "You don't have cameras out front?"

Celeste huffed. "Not out here. This is our private residence. *Private* being the operative word. In all the years I've lived here—my entire life—we've never had an issue. Until now. It had to be Lorelei's little girl, didn't it?"

Keeping to the task at hand, Josie asked, "Did you look for her when you realized she was no longer in the room and the door had been left open?"

"Of course I did. I'm not a monster. I walked around the perimeter. I called for her. When I couldn't find her here, I went down to the resort area and searched. I spoke with Tom and the two of us asked several of the staff to help. Once I located Adam,

I asked him as well. When we could not find her on the premises, Adam called you."

"You didn't actually see her leave though," Josie clarified.

Celeste returned to the front window, taking a moment to gaze outside. "No. I'm sorry. I didn't. My God. Who knew having children was so fraught? She's eight years old. It seems like they should be easier to manage. Lorelei came to us when she was nine, and while I always despised her and all that she represented, as a child of that age she was fairly well behaved."

"How long ago did she go missing?" Noah asked.

Celeste looked up toward the ceiling. "Oh, I don't know. Maybe a half hour ago. Forty-five minutes? I spent some time looking for her before Adam called you."

Josie said, "Do you still have Emily's duffel bag?"

Without looking at them, Celeste motioned over her shoulder. "Upstairs, third bedroom on the left. She didn't take that with her."

Josie nodded to Noah and he disappeared upstairs, returning moments later with one of Emily's shirts. "I'll get this to Sandoval," he said.

"Tell her to prioritize finding Emily," Josie said. "I'm not even sure if Gretchen found anything of Rory's for Rini to scent, but even if she did, put her off him for now. I want Emily found safely. We'll deal with Rory later. Call and ask the Sheriff's office if they can spare another K-9 unit. Once they get here, they can search for Rory."

"You got it," said Noah and walked out the front door. From behind Celeste, Josie watched him recede through the front window.

Bitter laughter drifted over Josie's shoulder. "That's your future husband?"

"Yes," Josie said. "You know that."

"You've got him well-trained. He follows instructions precisely, doesn't he?"

Josie's head reared back slightly. "He's not well-trained, nor is he following my instructions. We're colleagues. We're just on the same page."

"On the same page," Celeste muttered. "If only my parents had been on the same page. We wouldn't be standing here, would we?"

Josie didn't answer. She was too busy watching two figures shuffle up the walk from the resort area to Celeste and Adam's house. One of them had a familiar gait and pushed a walker in front of her. What was her grandmother doing here?

Josie left Celeste at the window and went outside. Sure enough, Lisette was steadily making her way toward the house. Behind her was Sawyer. Josie walked to meet them, but Lisette didn't stop. Instead, she kept motoring toward Celeste's door, even as Josie asked questions. "Gram, what are you doing here?"

Lisette smiled as Josie fell into pace beside her. "Some of us were booked to stay at this beautiful place for your entire wedding weekend, dear. Myself included."

Behind them, Sawyer muttered, "She wouldn't go back to Rockview."

"Why should I?" Lisette said. "I was meant to stay the weekend here. Even if my granddaughter didn't get married, I still fully intend to make the most of this rare treat."

In the dim light coming from Celeste's house, Josie saw her grandmother wink. Celeste met them at the door. A cell phone dangled from one of her hands. "Just come in then. Do what you must. I've got guest issues to attend to. It's a disaster with Tom off looking for that child and not carrying out his usual duties. Let me know when you're done here, would you?"

"I'll need to sit a spell," Lisette said as she pushed into the living room. She took a moment to stare at the couches before sitting down. "Interesting what she's done here, isn't it?"

Josie waited until Lisette was firmly seated on one of the couches with Sawyer beside her before repeating, "Gram, what are you doing here?"

"Word spreads like wildfire on this resort," Lisette said. "We all know you're looking for a little girl. I saw her."

Josie perched on the coffee table and leaned in toward her grandmother. "When? Where?"

"A couple of hours ago," Lisette explained. "I was down at Griffin Hall with everyone else. I'd managed to get away from the crowd for a little while." She gave Sawyer the side-eye. He just shook his head. "I was walking around outside in the garden in front of Griffin Hall, and I saw this little girl. She was up this way, actually. She had on a blue shirt and gray sweatpants. Her pockets were bulging. In her arms was a little stuffed dog. I might not have paid it any mind at all except she reminded me of you, dear."

Josie splayed a hand across her chest. "Me?"

Lisette smiled. "Yes, you and your little stuffed dog, Wolfie. You probably don't remember. He disappeared when you were six." At this, Lisette leaned forward and traced her warm fingertips over the scar on Josie's face.

Josie swallowed. "He didn't disappear. Where was the girl going? Was she with anyone?"

Lisette said, "As far as I could see, she was alone. She walked right off into the woods."

Josie stood up. "Do you think you could show me where?"

"Let me rest a minute, dear, and we'll walk back toward Griffin Hall. If I recall correctly it was about halfway between here and there."

"You said this was a couple of hours ago?" Josie asked.

"Yes. I mentioned it to the staff at Griffin Hall, and they said they would call the private residence. If your team is here then she obviously hasn't been found yet."

Josie said, "You're absolutely sure it was a couple of hours ago. Not just one hour?"

"Yes. I'm old but I can still tell the time, dear."

Why would Celeste lie? Josie wondered. Or had she been on her call far longer than she originally told them, and simply lost track of time? It would be easy enough to determine if she lied by speaking with the staff member that Lisette had talked to and finding out what time they'd called the residence.

Josie fired off a text to the rest of the team, letting them know there was a discrepancy in the timing of Emily's disappearance. Noah texted back that he would track down both the staff member and Celeste and ask them about it.

Sawyer disappeared into the kitchen and came back with a bottle of water, which he handed to Lisette. "I figure when Celeste said 'do what you must,' she meant it was okay to raid her fridge."

Lisette shrugged and took a sip. A few minutes later, she was on her feet, shuffling toward the door.

The path from the residence to the resort buildings was only partially lit by solar-powered lights sunk into the ground on either side of the strip of asphalt. Every few feet, Lisette stopped and peered into the night. Then she said, "A little further."

Sawyer said, "Lisette, I know you're trying to be helpful but from what I'm hearing, there are already searchers in the woods. Maybe it would be best if you just came back to the hall for now and tomorrow morning, in the daylight, we can try to pinpoint where you saw this girl go into the woods."

"I've got to get back to Griffin Hall no matter what, haven't I?" she replied. "Why not show Josie where I saw this child?"

Josie said, "The dogs do like to work from the last place the person was located."

"The dogs can work from the house then," he said. "That's the last place she was located before she walked into the woods."

Lisette raised a hand in the air. "Now you two, stop it. There's no harm in me showing Josie where I last saw this girl. It will only take a moment. We're passing by it on the way back to Griffin Hall anyway."

Sawyer made a noise in his throat. Josie looked over and saw his eyes gleaming in the dim light. She realized then that he was just concerned about Lisette making it all the way back under her own steam. Josie was surprised she'd made the walk to the private residence without assistance. She'd be paying for it the next day. Josie said, "It's a long walk, though. Why don't you and I stay here and try to find that spot while Sawyer sees if he can get the staff to bring around a resort car to take you back?"

"Sure," Lisette said. "That sounds good."

Josie knew she must be getting tired when she didn't argue. Lisette waited until Sawyer was out of earshot to say, "He's a good boy, but he hovers a lot."

"That's not the worst thing," Josie said.

"Didn't say it was," Lisette said. She maneuvered her walker through two of the small lanterns staked alongside the path and pushed it into the grass.

"Just a minute, Gram," Josie said. She took out her cell phone and found the flashlight app. Turning it on, she caught up with Lisette and shone the light ahead of them. The tree line was about thirty feet off. "How do you know where you saw her?"

"There's a tree trunk that looks like someone set it on fire, like it's covered in soot."

Josie panned the trees with her flashlight. "Not soot," she said. "Black sooty mold. It's from spotted lanternflies. When they eat, they produce this stuff. It's sugary. I think it's actually called honeydew. Anyway, it gets all over everything. That's why the trees they feed on look like they survived a fire."

Lisette kept pushing her walker along, now and again, when the grass was thick, picking it up and thrusting it forward. "To your left."

Josie panned left with her flashlight.

Lisette stopped walking as they came within ten feet of the tree line. "There!"

The flashlight landed on a young birch tree, its trunk blackened. "You sure this is it?" Josie asked.

"I think so."

They moved closer to the trees. "You're sure she was alone?"

"Yes. I think so."

Josie used her flashlight to pan the ground. Why had Emily left? Why would she walk into the woods within hours of nightfall? Was she running away? Was she looking for Rory? "Once Sawyer comes back, I'll take a closer look, although by now she could be anywhere."

A rustling sound came from within the trees. Josie swung her phone upward, but not before she saw a small pile of gray tufted buttons in her periphery. It lay at the base of the birch tree. Had Emily left them on purpose, or had she just dropped them?

"Emily?" Josie called, swinging the light back and forth.

"Josie," said Lisette. She stepped away from her walker and placed a hand on Josie's free arm. "Josie, we need to—"

More rustling sounded from beyond the ruined birch tree. Josie kept shining the flashlight but could see nothing besides low-hanging branches and tree trunks.

Lisette's grip tightened, and Josie could only remember one other time in her life when she had felt her grandmother's fingers dig into her skin so sharply. Josie had been a child and they were about to be separated. Josie had been going back to a house of horrors, and Lisette knew there was nothing she could do to stop it.

Josie turned her head and met her grandmother's eyes, registering the fear in them. "Gram?" she said.

Lisette tipped her head ever so slightly toward the trees and mouthed the word *gun*. Josie's heartbeat stuttered. She wanted to ask Lisette what she'd seen. A person? Rory? Josie wanted to sweep the light over the trees again but if Rory was there with a gun, only a few feet from them, they were sitting ducks. He'd already attacked Josie once that day without provocation. Josie wasn't sure she could reason with him under the best of circumstances. What was he doing here anyway? Did he have Emily? Had he lured her into the woods? Josie used one hand to unsnap her holster and pull out her pistol, holding it in one hand while she shone the flashlight with the other. She kept the barrel pointed downward. She didn't want to risk hitting someone who wasn't a true threat, but if someone was in the woods pointing a gun at them, she wanted him to know she was prepared.

There was only one problem. Whoever was in the woods, she couldn't capture him with the beam of her flashlight. It wavered under the weight of Lisette's hand on Josie's forearm.

"Police," she called out. "Whoever is there, come out where we can see you."

Lisette pulled at Josie's arm and the flashlight beam jerked downward. "We should go back."

In front of them, something moved, a dark blur. Lisette yanked at Josie's arm with surprising strength, throwing her off-balance and sending her flat on her ass. Josie's phone fell into the dirt, the flashlight facing down, plunging them into blackness. A gunshot cracked through the air. Josie sensed, rather than saw, Lisette's body crumple. She placed both hands on the handle of her Glock and pointed it upward toward the trees. But she couldn't shoot blindly. There were other police officers and searchers in the woods. She couldn't risk it. Through the rushing in her head, she heard an unmistakable sound that turned her blood to ice. A shotgun being racked. Another shot was coming.

"No!" Josie screamed.

She scrambled onto her knees, taking one hand off the pistol grip to feel her way toward Lisette. Josie was aware that everything was happening in a matter of seconds and yet, time seemed to stretch out in an agonizing drip, like sap from a tree. Josie's hand brushed against Lisette just as her body rose up. The second shot pierced the air. Lisette fell back, knocking Josie down and falling on top of her.

"Gram! Gram!"

Ears perked for the sound of the shotgun racking again, Josie squirmed from beneath Lisette. Her mind was overwhelmed. On some gut level she knew she had to choose between pursuing the threat in the woods—which could still kill her—or tending to Lisette. Her hands had already made the choice as they tossed her pistol aside and began to feel Lisette's body for wounds.

"Gram!"

Lisette was on her back. Profound, visceral relief flooded Josie's veins when her trembling hands reached up to touch Josie's face. "Jos—"

Her breathing was ragged. Josie's fingers traveled down her grandmother's wrists to her shoulders, caressing her face, her hair. Nothing wet or sticky. No head or face wounds. Her chest and torso were another story. Hot blood clung to Josie's fingers. Had the shooter used a slug or buckshot? The more her fingers explored, the more Josie was convinced it had been buckshot, which meant multiple wounds.

"Jesus," she cried. "Gram! Hold on."

She couldn't see. Her hands scrabbled through the grass. She needed her phone. The flashlight. Or she could call her team.

"Gram!"

Every nerve ending in her body buzzed. She couldn't find the phone. Lisette coughed. Josie turned back toward her and had the sensation of leaving her body. Suddenly, she was floating just over herself and Lisette. It was like looking through night vision goggles, both of them dark forms against a glowing green backdrop. Josie saw herself on her knees, hands gliding across the grass, finding nothing. Lisette lay on her back, eyes staring upward. One of her arms reached out, searching for Josie.

There was no time.

Josie snapped back into her body. Felt the terror choking the air from her lungs, the hot blood on her hands, the adrenaline making her entire body feel like a live wire. She heard noise in the distance. Someone moving away, through the woods. A motor whirring in the opposite direction. Then, as sure as if he were standing over her, whispering into her ear, Josie heard the voice of her late husband, Ray.

"*Focus*," he said.

"I'm trying," Josie cried, aware for the first time of the tears streaming down her face. Had she said it out loud? She didn't know, didn't care.

"*Jo*," the voice said again. "*You have to scoop her.*"

Scooping was a term used in law enforcement. When a victim of violence—usually a shooting—was losing blood too fast to wait for aid, the police literally picked them up and carried them to their vehicle and then rushed to get them help.

Josie crawled toward Lisette, found her shoulders and hips and slid her arms beneath her, scooping her up. She stumbled to her feet, swaying, trying to find her balance on the grass with a swollen, aching ankle. Then she ran.

CHAPTER TWENTY-FIVE

Sawyer pulled up along the path in a resort car as Josie reached the asphalt. Josie watched the emotions pass over his face in seconds: confusion, alarm, fear, and then his training took over. He threw the car into park before it even stopped moving and jumped out, running toward Josie. He met her in the grass and took Lisette from her. "What the hell happened? Were those gunshots I heard?"

Josie followed him as he ran toward the resort car. "Someone was in the woods. They shot at us. I couldn't see, I—"

"You have to drive," Sawyer said, cutting her off. He tried to sit Lisette up in the back seat of the car and then he slid in beside her. "Can you do it? They didn't have the staff to spare, so they gave me the keys."

"Yes," Josie said.

In the low light of the path lanterns, Josie could see the blood. It soaked Lisette's torso. It streaked over the gear shift and the steering wheel as Josie put the cart in motion and turned it around. She had never driven a resort car before but this one was just like an extremely large golf cart. It was similar enough to a car that her body went onto automatic pilot.

"Lisette," Sawyer said. "Jesus. She's bleeding everywhere. Everywhere, Josie. How many times was she shot?"

"It was buckshot," Josie said.

"Oh my God. Lisette!"

Josie punched the gas pedal as hard as she could and zoomed back down the path to Griffin Hall, headed for the flashing red and blue lights of one of Denton's police cruisers. She glanced briefly over her shoulder to see that Sawyer had pushed Lisette's shirt upward in his attempt to find the wounds. One hand held pressure on the left side of her chest while the other tried to find a pulse in her throat. Josie hadn't heard a sound from Lisette in what seemed like an eternity but was probably less than a minute. She tried not to think about what that meant.

Sawyer said, "She's not going to make it if we wait for an ambulance."

"I know," said Josie. "We're taking a police vehicle."

In front of Griffin Hall, a crowd of people stood, many of them Josie and Noah's own family members who had stayed for the weekend. They all looked nervous, eyes searching the horizon. They'd heard the shots, Josie realized. She heard several cries as they pulled up in front of the building, but the faces were a blur. People crowded her but she pushed through them. Behind her, Sawyer had gotten out of the car and now carried Lisette. The uniformed officer asked no questions. He took one look at Josie's face as she approached and held out his keys. Josie opened the back door and helped Sawyer get Lisette inside, sprawled across the seat. While they were doing that, the uniformed officer popped the trunk and riffled around until he found a first aid kit. He gave it to Josie, who handed it over to Sawyer. Then she got into the driver's side.

As she turned on the siren and backed out, she heard Lisette cough. The sound sent a jolt through her. "We'll be there in a few minutes, Gram," Josie said. "Just hold on."

From the back, Josie heard the squeal of a zipper and the ripping of Velcro as Sawyer tore into the first aid pack. "Jesus," he said. "I don't have anything. I can't take her vitals. I can't—"

"Do whatever you can," Josie told him. "I'll get us there as fast as I can."

"Hang on, Lisette," he muttered. "Her airway is clear. Pulse is thready. Multiple wounds to her chest and abdomen. I've got gauze. Not a lot, but I can use what's here to pack some of these. No sucking wounds, thank God."

"QuikClot," Josie said. "We all carry it in our cars. There should be some in the kit."

QuikClot was a hemostatic dressing. It looked like gauze, but it had an agent in it that stopped bleeding more quickly in wounds. Soldiers in combat often carried it with them. When it became available for civilians to purchase, the Chief had added it to the first aid kids carried by all officers on Denton's force.

"Got it," Sawyer said. "This will help. Lisette! Lisette! Stay with me."

Josie pushed the patrol car as hard as she could, doing nearly eighty miles an hour down the long mountain road into town. Once she hit the residential area, she slowed only enough so that she didn't hit anyone or anything. It felt as though the hospital was hours away, when they'd only been driving for minutes. Josie took the long hill up to the hospital at sixty miles per hour and screeched into the Emergency Room ambulance bay. The patrol officer whose vehicle she'd taken must have called ahead, because Dr. Nashat and several of his staff members were already outside with a gurney, waiting for them. By the time Josie got out of the driver's seat and limped around the car, they already had Lisette strapped in. Dr. Nashat, one of his residents, and four nurses jogged alongside as they rushed Lisette inside. Josie looked to her right to see Sawyer standing there, arms slack at his sides, covered in Lisette's blood.

He turned toward her. His expression was a combination of fear and anger. "What the hell happened out there, Josie?"

Josie swallowed the hysteria that rose in her throat. "Someone was in the woods and they—"

He advanced on her, cutting her off. "Someone was lurking in the woods and they decided to shoot an eighty-four-year-old woman?"

"No, I don't know. We were just standing there, and she saw something, a gun."

"I thought you guys were looking for an eight-year-old girl, Josie."

"We were. But there's more to it—"

He pointed a finger toward the Emergency Department doors. Josie noticed his entire arm shook. "What kind of person would shoot an eighty-four-year-old woman, Josie? She walks with a goddamn walker. She's not a threat. You're a police officer. Didn't you have your gun? What in the hell happened out there? You're not hurt. You're not shot."

Josie couldn't seem to push the words out. How it had been so dark and happened so quickly, and how she couldn't see anything. How she'd already been shot at once that day. How the killer was aiming for her, not Lisette. The feeling of Lisette's steel grip on her arm, the way that Lisette had whipped Josie off-balance like she weighed nothing, how her body rose up in front of Josie before the second shot—all of those things kept repeating in Josie's mind. Sensory memories, shadows across her shock-addled brain.

"She put herself in front of me," Josie choked.

"What?"

"She was protecting me."

"Bullshit," Sawyer spat.

But he hadn't been there. He was Lisette's grandson by blood, but he didn't really know her. He hadn't spent a lifetime knowing her. He had no idea the lengths that Lisette would go to protect the ones she loved. He had no idea the things she had done to protect Josie from the very moment that Josie came into her life. If he did, he might not look at Lisette the same. Of course Lisette would protect Josie—instinctively and reflexively. Completely without thought or regard to her own safety. In that horrible moment, Josie was a scrawny kid again and Lisette was imbued with the strength of a mighty lioness whose ferocity overcame any physical limitations she might have.

"She shouldn't have been out there," Sawyer said. "In the dark, out in the woods. What is wrong with you?"

"Me?" Josie shouted. "My grandmother is a grown woman. No one has ever told her what to do, and no one is starting now."

"*Our* grandmother," Sawyer said. He turned away from her and brushed his cheek with his sleeve. When he turned back, Josie saw that he had left a streak of Lisette's blood below his eye.

"I'm sorry," Josie said. "Our grandmother."

She walked over to him and tried to touch his hand, but he jerked away from her. He turned away again, his shoulders trembling. Josie waited a moment. She tried to touch him again, but he moved out of reach. "Just go," he said. "Go check on her. I'll call Noah."

Josie realized then that she didn't have her phone. It was somewhere along the tree line with her gun. "Tell him he has to secure the area where she was shot. It's a crime scene."

Without looking at her, he nodded. Josie ran through the trauma bay doors. She followed the sounds of tense shouting and Dr. Nashat's voice barking instructions. They had taken Lisette to one of the glass enclosures, but the door stood open. Lisette's clothes had been cut off and discarded on the floor. Her arms, chest, and abdomen were peppered with small round wounds where the buckshot pellets had penetrated her clothes and skin. Blood leaked from each one and smeared across her flesh. Some bled faster than others, and two of the nurses worked quickly to staunch the flow. Another nurse tried to get her vital signs. Dr. Nashat tweezed pellets out of her arms and dropped them into a basin. An oxygen mask covered her face. Her skin was as pale as her gray curls.

"Gram," Josie croaked.

One of the nurses shouted out her vitals. Dr. Nashat dropped the basin and tweezers onto a nearby tray table. "We have to get her up to CT. We need to know what's going on inside."

Lisette's head turned slowly. Her eyes searched the room until they locked onto Josie. Everything around them faded for a few precious seconds. Lisette's mouth moved but beneath the mask, Josie couldn't make out what she was trying to say.

"Detective."

Josie tore her eyes from Lisette long enough to see Dr. Nashat standing before her.

"We need to get this woman upstairs. She needs a CT scan, and, given the placement of some of these wounds, I'd say she'll most definitely need surgery."

Josie stepped aside. "Would you please keep me updated? She's my grandmother."

Dr. Nashat froze momentarily, his professional demeanor slipping for just a moment. Then he patted her shoulder. "You'll know everything I know."

The nurses wheeled Lisette out the door. Josie managed to touch her bare shoulder as she went past. Her skin was cold.

CHAPTER TWENTY-SIX

Josie felt a paralysis unlike any she'd ever known. Thoughts escaped her mind. She stood in the hallway until a security guard appeared and ushered her into another area of the Emergency Department. It was a small, private waiting area. She was aware that he said something about her not going into the main area because she would frighten everyone else, looking as she did. He planted her in a chair and handed her a towel. She held it limply in her lap, eyes staring straight ahead but seeing nothing. Nurses, doctors, and other patients passed by. Some asked if she was okay, to which she simply nodded. Her mind replayed the scene at Harper's Peak over and over, trying to figure out what she could have done differently.

They shouldn't have been out there.

She should have sent Lisette back to Griffin Hall with Sawyer. Emily would have been long gone from the place Lisette had last seen her. What did it matter where she went into the woods?

But what was Rory doing there? Why was he at Harper's Peak? He couldn't have known that Emily was there. Could he? Why had he shot at them? Maybe it hadn't been Rory. But who else would be wandering around in the woods with a shotgun? Mettner had driven Pax back to the produce market after he gave his statement. Had Josie misread Pax? He had been in the woods earlier that day the first time Josie was shot at.

"Josie!"

She looked up, fighting her mental fog, and saw Noah rushing toward her. Behind him was Trinity, Drake, Shannon, Christian, Josie and Trinity's brother, Patrick, and Misty.

Misty's hand flew to her mouth.

Trinity said, "Is any of that your blood?"

Shannon leaned down and put her arm across Josie's shoulder. Into Josie's ear, she said, "Where's Lisette?"

"Mom," Trinity said. "Don't."

Christian said, "I'll go find a doctor or something and see what we can find out."

Josie wanted to tell him to ask for Dr. Nashat, but her mouth wouldn't work. Noah knelt in front of her. In his hands were her phone and gun. She made no move to take them. He pocketed them and touched her face. "Josie," he whispered. "Can you talk to me?"

She said nothing. He palmed her cheek. "Sawyer told us what happened. He's outside."

Finally, words came. "Someone should be with him," Josie said. "Gram would want someone to be with him."

Christian appeared again with Dr. Nashat by his side. "I didn't have to look far," he said.

Dr. Nashat looked down at Josie, concern creasing his features. "Detective, are you okay?"

Josie looked at Noah. "Sawyer," she said. "He shouldn't be alone."

Shannon said, "Let's hear what the doctor has to say, and then Drake and your father can go sit with Sawyer."

Dr. Nashat said, "Mrs. Matson is in surgery. While most of the buckshot injuries were superficial, and I was able to remove the pellets myself, she did sustain severe damage to her right radius and ulna. We'll have an orthopedic doctor look at it, but right now the priority is trying to repair the internal damage. Scans show multiple perforations of her liver and intestines. There are two bullets lodged within her anterior inferior right ventricular wall."

Trinity said, "For non-medical professionals, please."

Shannon said, "Her heart wall."

"Oh my God," Misty squeaked.

Dr. Nashat said, "The good news is that there's no active arterial hemorrhaging in her chest cavity. But she'll be in surgery for some time. She's quite advanced in age, and while she was very lucky—these were not close-range shots—the odds of her making it through the stress of multiple surgeries to remove the pellets and repair the internal damage are, I'm afraid, quite low. If she does survive, post-surgical complications could—"

Trinity said, "That's enough. We get it. Is there somewhere we can wait or get updates from the surgeons?"

Dr. Nashat nodded. "Fourth floor. There's a surgical waiting area. She's the only one on the floor right now. Dr. Justofin is the trauma surgeon. He'll either send someone out to update you or see to it himself. It will be several hours, though."

Josie heard footsteps behind Dr. Nashat. Dr. Feist pushed her way past him and rushed toward Josie. "My God. I just heard what happened. Josie—"

She stopped and looked around at all of them. Meeting Dr. Nashat's eyes, she said, "I just spoke with the surgical resident. She let me know what was going on. I'll show them to the waiting room upstairs."

Dr. Nashat nodded and left. Drake nudged Christian's ribs and said, "Why don't we see if we can find Sawyer."

As they walked off with Patrick in tow, Dr. Feist put a hand on Noah's shoulder. He stood and moved away. Dr. Feist said, "I don't suppose anyone assessed you, did they?"

She placed two fingers on the side of Josie's throat.

"I'm fine," Josie rasped.

Trinity said, "You're a mess. We have to get you out of these clothes."

Dr. Feist slid a warm hand under one of Josie's armpits and drew her to her feet. "Come downstairs to my office. I've got an extra pair of scrubs that will fit and a private bathroom."

"Josie," Noah said.

Her mind fought to focus. "I think it was Rory," she told him. "Maybe. I don't know. I didn't see anyone, but it was a shotgun. Lorelei was killed with her own shotgun. Rory's out there."

"We're working on it," Noah said. "That mountain is crawling with police. Anyone who's out there will be found. I'll call Mett and Gretchen. They wanted an update right away."

"Emily?" Josie asked hopefully.

He shook his head.

"Let's go," said Dr. Feist. "Lieutenant, you know where to find us when you're done."

Noah leaned in and kissed Josie's forehead. "I'll find you," he said.

Surrounded by Shannon, Trinity, Misty, and Dr. Feist, Josie found herself herded into an elevator. A few minutes later they were in Dr. Feist's office. Josie's gaze fell on her wedding dress hanging in the corner. She should have gotten married, she thought dimly. She should have let Mettner and Gretchen handle the case; walked down the aisle, and watched Lisette beam as they exchanged vows. Instead, she'd been plunged into her own personal hell.

Misty placed a hand between Josie's shoulder blades and gently nudged her in the opposite direction, toward Dr. Feist's private bathroom. "Don't look at it," Misty said. "One thing at a time, okay? First, we get you cleaned up."

The women crowded into the bathroom. Although it was the same as all the other sterile bathrooms in the hospital, Dr. Feist had added a few personal touches including a small bench and cabinet. While she took towels and a set of scrubs from the cabinets, Misty sat Josie on the bench. Shannon and Trinity began peeling her shirt off. Then Misty was back with a warm, wet towel, carefully wiping away Lisette's blood.

Shannon held up Josie's shirt. "What should we do with this?"

"Throw it away," said Trinity, now kneeling in front of Josie to take her sneakers off.

"No," Josie cried. "Don't!"

She couldn't bear the thought of losing the shirt she'd been wearing the last time she was close to Lisette. What if that was the last time she would ever hold her grandmother? Misty, Trinity, and Shannon all stared at her. A long moment stretched out, filling the room awkwardly. Finally, Dr. Feist said, "There are patient belonging bags in the exam room. I'll go get one."

Silently, the women scrubbed away the blood until there was a pile of white towels stained red in the corner of the bathroom. Dr. Feist took each piece of Josie's clothing and placed it into a bag, as promised. Josie did everything they told her to do until she was clean, her skin was damp, and she was dressed in Dr. Feist's scrubs. Misty brushed her hair while Shannon and Dr. Feist used washcloths to clean her sneakers. They only talked to ask where something was or to give each other instructions. No one demanded anything of Josie, and for that she was glad.

Then they were back in the elevator, Josie buffeted by the four women as though they were her bodyguards. In the fourth-floor surgical waiting room, Noah waited. "No news yet," he said.

She sat down on one of the couches and Noah sat beside her. Curling up, she rested her head in his lap. She didn't want anyone to talk to her. She didn't want to answer questions. She didn't want to think. Still, a voice in her head spoke on a loop: *they shouldn't have been out there.*

CHAPTER TWENTY-SEVEN

Josie woke with a start. In her dreams the gunshot had gone off again and again. Lisette fell. Lisette rose. She fell again. No matter how many times it happened, Josie couldn't change the outcome. Noah's hand stroked her hair. "Hey," he said.

Josie blinked and sat up. All around the room, her family dozed. Dr. Feist was no longer there. Misty had gone, probably to be with Harris and Trout, but Christian, Patrick, and Drake had brought Sawyer to sit with them. Only he was awake, slouched in his chair and staring straight ahead with glassy eyes. She looked at the clock. It was after five a.m. Eight hours had passed. "No updates?" she asked.

Noah shook his head.

She didn't know whether to take this as a good sign or a bad sign. They were still working on Lisette, which meant she was still alive, but no updates one way or the other in over eight hours couldn't be good, could it?

As if reading her mind, Noah said, "I'll go see what I can find out."

He returned twenty minutes later with a nurse. Behind them trailed Misty, who had come with a box of coffee and several breakfast items from Komorrah's which she placed on one of the tables. As everyone began to wake up, stretch, and fix their coffees, the nurse gave them the update that Lisette was still hanging on. They'd gotten most of the pellets out and repaired as much of the damage as they could, but part of her bowel had to be resected. It would be a few more hours before she went into recovery.

Josie sat back down on the couch, waving off coffee and food until Misty insisted she eat, sitting beside her and watching her chew each bite like a mother hen. People drifted in and out, but Josie stayed on the couch, sleeping when she could because her reality was so horrific, she didn't want to stay in it.

Finally, four hours later, a tall, burly doctor in blue scrubs and a surgical cap with dolphins on it came into the room. "Josie Quinn?" he asked.

Josie raised her hand. "I'm here."

He walked over and shook her hand. "I understand you're Mrs. Matson's granddaughter."

Josie nodded. Her gaze found Sawyer across the room and she pointed to him. "This is her grandson, Sawyer Hayes."

"Very good. I'm Dr. Justofin. Your grandmother is in recovery in the ICU right now. We had to remove a portion of her liver, and she ended up needing two bowel resections. Then ortho came in and did their best to reassemble her arm. She's got rods and pins in it. Your grandmother was extremely lucky to survive this, but she is in critical condition."

Noah said, "Will she live?"

Dr. Justofin frowned. "She's alive now. If you're asking for a long-term prognosis, I can't tell you with any degree of accuracy. A lot will depend on the next couple of days. She's in her eighties and this has been a lot of stress to put on her body. Risk of infection is extremely high, and we're still worried about internal bleeding. I've seen a few hunting accidents by way of shotgun in my time. Younger, healthier people have died with far less serious injuries. I hate to be the bearer of bad news, but I think you should be prepared that the next few days with your grandmother may be her last."

Josie swallowed. She was so dehydrated, her tongue stuck to the roof of her mouth. "When can we—when can we see her?"

"A few hours," said Dr. Justofin. "You can go downstairs to the third floor where the ICU waiting room is and someone will come get you when it's time."

Someone thanked him, and Josie watched him walk out of the room.

Sawyer stood up. Glaring at Josie, he said, "She's going to die. We have a few days with her, if we're lucky. I hope this case—whatever the hell you people are working on—was worth her life."

"Hey," Noah said. He put himself between Sawyer and Josie. "I know you're suffering, but you're way out of line."

Sawyer's voice was so calm, it felt like a knife straight to Josie's heart. "She didn't have to be out there. No one did. You two could have had your wedding like normal people, but no, the great Josie Quinn couldn't stay out of the spotlight."

A chorus of protests went up around the room. Drake tried to insert himself between Noah and Sawyer, but it was too late. Josie never even saw Noah's hand leave his side, but then his fist smashed into Sawyer's face. Misty cried out, then clamped her hands over her mouth. Shannon said, "That's enough."

Drake dragged Sawyer toward the door while Christian and Patrick restrained Noah.

A hand slid into Josie's. She looked over to see Trinity beside her.

One of Sawyer's hands shot over Drake's shoulder, pointing an accusing finger at Noah. "You know I'm right. She's nothing but trouble, man. You're lucky you didn't get married. She'll probably get you killed, too."

Drake pushed Sawyer through the doorway and out into the hall, leaving the rest of them in silence. Noah stood behind Christian and Patrick, chest heaving, fists clenched at his sides. "You better hope he doesn't press charges," Christian muttered. "Your career will be over."

"I don't care," Noah snapped.

Shannon said, "Everyone just needs to calm down. Take some deep breaths. Has everyone eaten?"

Taking her cue, Misty opened another of the boxes of food and offered some to Christian, Patrick, and Noah. Noah refused and went to sit in the corner of the room. Josie stood up, sliding her hand out of Trinity's grasp. "I need to get some air."

Everyone stared at her, but no one argued or tried to go with her, for which she was glad.

She went through the Emergency Department, striding through the lobby doors unnoticed. Outside, she walked several feet from the doors, sucked in the cool, fresh air and turned her face to the sun. It was amazing the way things worked, she thought. Her entire life was being shattered into pieces and the sun still came up, still shone indifferently onto the world.

"Quinn."

Josie looked over to see Chief Chitwood walking toward her. Dread settled in her stomach. For the first time in hours, sensations returned to her body again and she felt like she might pass out. She should have eaten more. She didn't want to, but whether she liked it or not, her body demanded it.

"Sir," she said.

He kinked a bushy brow as he looked down at her. "I'm not going to ask you a bunch of dumb questions," he said. "I was just up in the ICU waiting room looking for you. Got a full report."

"Then you know that Noah hit Sawyer?" Josie asked.

He waved a hand in the air. "I don't care about that right now." He held out a set of car keys. Her car keys. "Brought your car back from Harper's Peak. It sat there all night. I thought you might want it. You know, in case things get too intense in there and you need a break. Parked it in the visitor's lot."

Josie took them. "Thank you, sir."

"Something else." He dug into his jacket pocket and came up with what looked like a set of thick beads which he deposited into her hand.

"What's this?"

"Rosary bracelet," he said.

"I'm not Catholic, sir," Josie said.

"Neither am I."

She stared at the bracelet. There was a medal with a woman in flowing garb on it. Around her were the words: "Our Lady Untier of Knots."

Josie was too tired to figure out what Chitwood was doing. "I don't understand, sir."

He reached forward and curled her fingers over the bracelet. "Someday, I'll tell you the story of how I got that thing. All you need to know right now is that even if you never prayed a day in your life, when someone you love is dying, you learn to pray pretty damn fast. Someone who believed very deeply in the power of prayer gave that to me, and at the time, it was a great comfort. Maybe it won't mean shit to you. I don't know. Regardless, if this is Lisette's time, nothing's gonna keep her here, but you? You're gonna need all the help you can get. You hang onto that until you're ready to give it back to me, and Quinn, I do want that back."

"How will I know when I'm ready to give it back?" Josie asked.

Chitwood started walking away. Over his shoulder, he said, "Oh, you'll know. See you in the ICU?"

"Yeah."

When he was gone, Josie opened her hand and stared at the bracelet. The beads were green and polished and warm against her palm. It was quite beautiful. She squeezed it again and put it into the pocket of Dr. Feist's scrubs. She had prayed to God so many times during her childhood to save her from so many horrific situations. It had almost never worked. Even Lisette, in spite of all her machinations, had not been able to save Josie from the worst of what happened to her. Josie had learned to rely on herself. Still, she appreciated whatever it was Chitwood was trying to do. Offer her comfort in his own bizarre way, from what she gathered.

Fingering her car keys, she took a walk through the parking lot until she found her vehicle. She always kept a change of clothes in a bag in the back. As she got closer to the SUV, she hit the unlock button on her key fob. She heard the metallic clink of the locks disengaging. She looked up, something on the driver's side window catching her attention. For a second, she wasn't sure exactly what she was seeing. Then a gasp escaped her lips. Her keys fell to the ground.

There, on the windshield, was a pinecone doll.

CHAPTER TWENTY-EIGHT

A half hour later, Josie, Noah, Chitwood and Gretchen crowded inside the hospital's security CCTV room and watched as the security manager on duty brought up black and white footage from the parking lot. The angle was from a light post that extended high above the ground and sat several yards away from where Chitwood had parked her vehicle. They had waited until Hummel arrived to take the doll into evidence before requesting the CCTV footage. Josie doubted they would get anything useful from either the doll or the footage, but Chitwood wanted everything documented nevertheless. Gretchen had arrived in the ICU when Josie went back there to get Noah and Chitwood. Her khakis and Denton PD polo shirt were wrinkled and covered in dirt. Her brown and gray spiked hair was unusually unkempt, and the dark circles under her eyes told Josie that she hadn't slept in at least twenty-four hours. She was probably going off shift but had detoured to the hospital to check on Lisette. Josie felt relief at her presence, although now she was maybe looking at another seemingly endless shift on the Mitchell case.

"Here we go," said the manager, pointing to the screen. "This is the Chief pulling in and parking."

They watched the screen as Josie's car pulled into the spot. Chitwood got out, clicked the key fob and walked off. The manager fast-forwarded the footage. About ten minutes later, a hooded figure appeared on the edge of the screen, walking down the row of cars. The hood was pulled too low to make out any of his features. His hands were jammed into his hoodie pockets. Josie noted that he wore jeans and a pair of boots. Not what she'd seen Rory wearing the day before when she'd encountered him. Unless he had gone back to his house and changed. But Josie didn't remember seeing any clothing that looked like it belonged to him in the house.

"Here he goes," said the security manager.

The figure stopped at Josie's car and stared for a few seconds, as if trying to decide something. Maybe whether or not he had the right vehicle? Then he panned the area and quickly pulled the pinecone doll from his hoodie pocket and put it on the windshield. Checking all around once more, he ran out of the frame.

Chitwood said, "What in the hell is going on here?"

Noah said, "Why is this kid going to all this trouble to come here and leave the doll? Why Josie?"

"The doll means he's sorry," Gretchen said. "That's what Emily told us. Rory leaves them for her when he's sorry."

Chitwood said, "Is he trying to say he's sorry for shooting Mrs. Matson?"

Noah said, "A crazy-looking doll is not going to fix this. That kid needs to be in custody. Now."

"That's not Rory," Josie said.

They all turned toward her.

"Rory's only fifteen. He can't drive yet. Even if he could, where would he get a vehicle? He didn't even have a bicycle. Lorelei kept him on her property. He was her big secret, remember?"

"If that's not Rory," Gretchen said, "who is it?"

"Paxton Bryan," Noah said. "It has to be. He's got a driver's license and access to his dad's vans."

Chitwood said, "What was Paxton Bryan doing out in the woods by Harper's Peak last night? How did he know where to find Quinn today?"

"And if he's protecting her, why is Emily leaving the buttons behind?" Gretchen added.

Josie said, "Emily went into the woods. We know that. We also know that Pax is frequently out there on his bike, and he also drives up and down the road from the produce market to Harper's Peak often. He would have seen all the police vehicles. All he would have had to do is ask any of the searchers what was going on. Maybe he went out to look for her."

"I'll buy that," Chitwood said. "But why is Pax leaving the pinecone doll? I thought that was Rory's thing."

Josie scrubbed her hands over her face, trying to rub away her exhaustion. Her mind felt foggy. "Emily never said Rory's name. Jesus. We've been looking at the wrong person this entire time."

"Shit," Gretchen said. "The boss is right. Emily said 'he.' She never said a name. We just assumed it was Rory based on the fact that he had a history of violence."

"And his blood type," Josie pointed out.

"We don't know Pax's blood type," Gretchen said. "It could also be O positive. Pax wears size ten shoes."

Noah said, "Emily said Pax was her friend. Would she say that if he had killed her mother and sister?"

Josie said, "That's a good point. She knew to hide when Rory got violent. That was part of the safety plan."

"But she didn't actually see the murders," Gretchen said. "That's the theory we're operating on. Things got violent and she hid."

"Still, the safety plan applied to Rory," Josie insisted.

Chitwood said, "Maybe the Pax kid was there that morning. Maybe things got heated and Emily just went to her hiding place because that's what she'd been conditioned to do."

"Then why wouldn't she just tell us Paxton was there?" said Gretchen.

"She didn't even tell us she had a brother," Chitwood pointed out. "But she did mention Paxton. She told the social worker about him, didn't she?"

Josie nodded.

Noah said, "Paxton Bryan has an alibi for the time Lorelei and Holly were killed."

"His dad," Josie said. "Reed Bryan isn't going to win any awards for father of the year, but I believe he'd lie to protect his son. Still, something about all of this doesn't fit."

"Then we don't have all the pieces yet," Chitwood said. "We'll bring Reed in for questioning. We also need to find all three of these kids: Pax, Rory, and Emily. We need to do it now before anyone else gets hurt. I'll send patrol over to the Bryan farm and the market right away."

Noah said, "If Pax isn't there and he's driving around in one of his dad's vans, we need to put a BOLO out on whatever vehicle he's using. We've still got the issue of Rory Mitchell, who may or may not be homicidal, wandering around in the woods." He turned to Gretchen. "What happened with the searches?"

"Nothing. Nothing happened. All we found were the spent shotgun shells near where Lisette went down. As you know, we can't get prints from them once they've been shot from the gun, so they're useless."

Noah said, "What about the dogs? They didn't find anything?"

Gretchen shook her head. "We've had three dozen people and two K-9 units out working all night long. They've got nothing. We had clothes for Emily's scent, and we found a coat at Lorelei's house that we believe belongs to Rory that we used for his scent. Those dogs ran for miles through the woods, until they were almost falling over from exhaustion. They lost both scents."

"Dogs don't lose scents very often," Josie said. "Unless there are certain weather conditions—of which there were none—or the person is carried off in a vehicle."

Noah said, "Whose vehicle would they get into?"

"As far as we know right now, Paxton is the only person in this entire scenario with access to a vehicle," Josie said.

Chitwood said, "Which is another reason why we're going to find that kid as soon as possible."

Josie asked, "Did anyone find out whether Celeste was lying or not about what time Emily disappeared?"

Noah said, "I found the employee Lisette spoke with. He called Celeste a full two hours before Adam called us. I asked her about it, but she would only say that she lost track of time."

"Bullshit," Josie muttered.

Gretchen said, "Both Rory's and Emily's scents were found at Harper's Peak."

Chitwood said, "We know why Emily's was there. But why would Rory be up the mountain that far? He wouldn't have known that's where she was."

Josie said, "Neither would Pax. No one told him where Emily was going. Even if he'd driven up there to deliver something for his father, Emily was at the private residence. He couldn't have seen her."

Gretchen said, "Unless he overheard someone on the staff talking about it."

Chitwood said, "All right. What we've got here is the following scenario: the girl was at the private residence at Harper's Peak yesterday. Rory Mitchell was out in the woods. We know that because he beat the hell out of Quinn, and she chased him. Pax was at the stationhouse giving a statement for some of yesterday and then Mettner dropped him back off at the produce market. Shortly after that, Emily walked out of the residence and into the woods. Lisette saw her. It appeared as though she was alone. When Lisette took Quinn to check out the spot where the girl went into the woods, someone shot at them. Searchers trawled the mountain from the Mitchell house to Harper's Peak looking for Rory and Emily and found nothing. Next thing we know, Pax shows up here and leaves the creepy doll on Quinn's car."

"Yep," Gretchen said. "That's where we are."

Josie's phone buzzed in her scrubs pocket. She took it out to see a text message from Trinity. "We can see my grandmother now."

CHAPTER TWENTY-NINE

Lisette was still sleeping. She looked tiny and frail in the hospital bed, dwarfed by all the equipment attached to her. For the first time, she looked old, Josie realized. In her seventies and eighties, even with a walker and terrible arthritis, Lisette had always seemed so vital to Josie. In Josie's mind, she had never aged. She was always the woman who took Josie roller skating and to the beach for the first time. Full of energy. A mischievous sparkle in her eye. Josie wished she would open her eyes, but the medical staff had told them it could be hours before she woke.

Her right arm was in a thick cast and propped on a pillow. At least someone had taken the time to clean her up. Gone was all the blood, although Josie could still see some wounds starting to scab over where Dr. Nashat had removed the buckshot on her good arm and on her chest where the hospital gown had drooped. The ICU nurse only let two of them in at a time and only for ten minutes each. Noah stood behind Josie as she stared down at Lisette. Her tears came hot and fast. They were unstoppable. Compartmentalizing was one of Josie's special skills, but looking down at her grandmother—easily the most formidable woman Josie had ever known—she felt like her heart was splintering into a million pieces. She would never be able to put them back together.

Josie reached through a mass of wires and IV tubes to find Lisette's left hand. Squeezing it, she leaned in and whispered into Lisette's ear. "Gram, I'm here. Everything's going to be okay. I just need you to stay with me."

Lisette slept on, the steady rise and fall of her chest of little comfort to Josie. As the surgeon had made clear, it was her insides that had been ravaged by the shooting. It remained to be seen whether her body would heal completely or fall victim to complications or infection. Noah put his arm around Josie, holding her from behind, resting his head on top of hers. Josie kept hold of Lisette's hand until the nurse came in to shoo them out. Outside the room, Sawyer waited to see Lisette. He glared at them. She noticed some slight bruising under his left eye where Noah had punched him. Josie felt a sudden uptick in her heartbeat. Even though Lisette wasn't awake, she didn't want a scene right outside her room. Thankfully, neither Sawyer nor Noah spoke, and Sawyer disappeared into Lisette's room.

The day was filled with waiting. Every hour, the nursing staff let her go into Lisette's room to spend ten minutes with her. Josie spent the rest of her time in the ICU waiting room. Noah had found her spare set of clothes in the back of her car so she could change. The rest of her family, friends, and colleagues flitted in and out all day, trying to feed her, keep her hydrated, and get her to talk. Josie had nothing to say other than they shouldn't have been there. She shouldn't have had Lisette out near the woods. She didn't say this to anyone because she knew they would have a thousand justifications as to why Lisette's shooting was not her fault.

Josie believed none of them.

Finally, around three in the afternoon, Lisette woke. It was Sawyer's turn to go into the room, so he went first. Josie hoped he wouldn't say anything to upset their grandmother. She had no idea how lucid Lisette was or how much she remembered. When he came out, his face streaked with tears, she and Noah went in. Lisette lifted her good hand and Josie rushed to the bedside to take it. Josie met her eyes.

She said, "It's not your fault, Josie."

"I'm sorry, Gram," Josie squeaked.

"No, it's not your fault. You must remember that."

For a moment, Lisette's face went pale and a grimace of pain passed over it, deepening every line in her face.

"It's okay, Gram," Josie said. "We don't have to talk. You need to rest."

Lisette's grip on Josie's hand tightened. "I didn't see his face," she told them. "Only the barrel of the gun."

"I know," said Josie. "It's fine. We're going to find him. There are dozens of people out there right now looking for him. Mettner and Gretchen are handling it. Don't worry about that."

Lisette gave a small nod. Josie could see the toll it took on her body to speak. Josie didn't press her. She was just happy to see her eyes open, to feel her warm hand. Lisette's gaze drifted away from Josie and Noah and down to the foot of the bed. Then she looked back at Josie. "I'm not going to make it, dear."

More tears streamed down Josie's face. She couldn't control the sob that erupted from deep within her. "What? No, Gram. Don't say that. You can survive this. The worst is over, the surgery—"

Lisette squeezed her hand hard, and Josie stopped talking. "Two things: I don't want you and Sawyer to fight. He'll blame you but that's his burden to bear, not yours. This was not your fault."

She paused and her chest rose and fell more quickly as she tried to catch her breath. Josie waited.

"Second, I want you two to get married."

"We will," Josie promised.

"Absolutely," Noah agreed.

Lisette shook her head, the movement small. "No. Now. I want you to get married. I want to see it. I don't want to go without seeing you two get married. Josie, he's the best one."

Josie couldn't help but laugh. "I know, Gram."

"If you don't do it now, before I'm dead, you won't do it."

"That's not true," Josie said.

Lisette's hand squeezed hers again. "Yes, it is."

Noah reached over and touched Lisette's shoulder. "We'll get married, Lisette. I promise."

"I just want to see…" she said, eyelids fluttering. They waited to see if she would continue, but her eyes drifted closed. Josie felt her grip loosen. For a second, Josie's heart skipped, thinking Lisette had passed. Then she looked up at the screen showing Lisette's vital signs, comforted by the steady numbers.

They were ushered back out of the room shortly after that. As they approached the waiting room, Josie could see through the glass that everyone was waiting for news: Trinity, Drake, Shannon, Christian, Misty, Chitwood, and even Dr. Feist. She pulled up short, not ready to face anyone. Wiping away her tears, she looked up at Noah. "I have to use the bathroom. I'll be right back."

She let him go ahead and found the nearest bathroom. She splashed cold water on her face and sucked in several deep breaths. When she had composed herself, she went back into the hall and ran smack into Mettner. She bounced off his chest and he grabbed her by her upper arms before she could fall backward.

Righting her, he looked down, his brown eyes deep pools of concern. "Boss," he said. "I'm sorry. Didn't mean to bump into you. I was looking for you, though. I'm really sorry about your grandmother. Chief says she's still hanging on."

"Yes," Josie said. "So far. Thank you."

"I came to tell you that, but also, I thought you and Noah would want to know—we found Reed Bryan at his farm. He was in the barn. Someone bludgeoned him to death."

CHAPTER THIRTY

Josie, Noah, Mettner, and Chitwood huddled in a corner of the hallway, out of earshot of the waiting room. Only Dr. Feist was privy to what they'd just learned, as they'd called her out of the room so she could respond to Reed Bryan's death. Mettner held his phone in one hand and scrolled through his notes with the other as he spoke. "Searchers are still combing the mountain between the Mitchell place and Harper's Peak. We couldn't justify keeping the dogs any longer, but we do have officers out in the woods searching. I don't think we're going to find anything at this point. Not if we haven't already."

Chitwood said, "Tell us about Reed Bryan."

Mettner scrolled some more. "I just came from the scene. Hummel and his team are processing it. Patrol went to his house earlier. Knocked on the door. No answer, but there was a truck parked on the premises. They ran the plates. It's his personal vehicle. The officers had a look around, didn't see anyone. The barn door was partially open so one of them went inside and found Reed deceased on the ground with severe trauma to his head. Looks like someone went completely off on him, and most of the blows were to the back of his head. At least from what I could tell. He's a big guy, so to take him down whoever did it blitzed him from behind and didn't stop until he was gone. Dr. Feist will examine him but from what I saw, it didn't look like he stood a chance."

"Any idea what the killer used?" Noah asked.

"There was a shovel nearby with his blood and some of his hair on it, so it looks like the killer left the weapon there."

"Pax?" Josie asked.

"Not there. The house was searched, as were the rest of the grounds. No sign of him."

"What about the vans?" Noah asked. "He's got two vans for his produce business."

Mettner nodded. "We found one of them. Actually, several people reported seeing it driving erratically through town. About a mile from the produce market, it crashed into someone's front porch. Plowed right up over the grass and into the house."

"Oh my God," said Josie. "Was anyone hurt?"

"Thankfully, no," Mettner said. "Homeowners reported seeing a teenage boy stumble out of the driver's seat and take off running. They called it in, but we're short with everyone searching the mountain right now, so by the time patrol got there, he was long gone."

"Did they get his description?" Chitwood asked.

Mettner went back to his notes. "Caucasian male, about five foot nine, five foot ten, wearing baggy jeans and a blue hooded sweatshirt. That's all I got."

"So we don't know if that was Rory or Pax," said Josie.

"My money's on Rory," Noah said. "The erratic driving. He's only fifteen. Maybe Lorelei taught him to drive a little, but he really wouldn't have a good grasp on it, theoretically."

"Or it could be Pax," Chitwood said. "Maybe he's injured. Quinn, you said the relationship between him and his dad was strained. Is it possible Reed got mad at him, hauled off and hit him and Pax fought back?"

"I suppose," said Josie, but she was thinking of the method of killing. Head and neck. Blitz attack. From behind. When the person wasn't looking and didn't expect it. A lot like the patient who had nearly killed Lorelei almost twenty years ago. Also a lot like the way Rory had attacked Josie in the hallway of his home. Josie thought about Lorelei and Holly's autopsies. Lorelei had had a head injury before she was shot. Emily had shown years of trauma to her head which they now knew was from Rory, based on what Dr. Buckley had said.

"Do you have any photos?" Josie asked. "From the scene?"

Mettner said, "Hummel took photos."

"But you always do a sketch," Josie pointed out. "On your computer. I know you take your own photos with your phone for reference in case the ERT takes too long to upload to the file."

Mettner swiped a few times and turned his phone toward Josie. It was exactly as he had described. In the center of the barn, on the dirt floor, Reed Bryan lay face down in a pool of blood. The back of his head was a pulpy mess, what white hair he'd had left dark with congealed blood. His arms were extended, almost as though he had tried to crawl away from his attacker. The shovel lay discarded next to him.

"I'm not sure what you're looking for," Mettner said.

Josie studied the rest of the photo, using her thumb and index finger to zoom in and out on the other areas of the barn depicted. "I think Rory Mitchell did this."

"Based on what?" Chitwood asked.

Josie explained the connection she had drawn from the method of attack.

"That's thin," Mettner said.

"Maybe," Josie said.

Chitwood said, "What would Rory Mitchell be doing at Reed Bryan's farm? You're saying now that Pax picked up both Rory and Emily and took them home? Then Rory killed his dad?"

A small blur in the corner of the photo caught Josie's eye. She zoomed in on it as close as she could. "Is this the only photo of the scene, Mett?" she asked.

"Swipe to the left," he said, sounding impatient.

She found a better photo and zoomed in on the same area, finding exactly what she'd expected to find. She turned the phone around so the rest of them could see it. "Yes. Pax had both Rory and Emily with him. See that?"

Chitwood took some reading glasses from his shirt pocket and positioned them on his nose. Squinting, he put his face only inches from the screen. "What the hell are those? Buttons?"

"Gray tufted buttons from the couches in Celeste Harper and Adam Long's parlor, yes. Emily was there. Whether she left that pile there on purpose or they fell from her pockets, she was there. You need to call the dogs again. We need them back up near Harper's Peak in case that's where Rory went, and also down by Reed Bryan's farm in case Emily is still in that area. People saw a teenager who could potentially be Rory get out of the crashed van and head back in the direction of Harper's Peak, but there was no sign of Emily, so she could still be in the area of the farm in South Denton."

Mettner took his phone back and peered at the photo. "I don't think we can get the dogs back. They had a couple of other calls elsewhere in the county."

"Try," said Chitwood. "Quinn's right. We need to cover the area around Harper's Peak and Reed Bryan's farm. Move some of the searchers from the Harper's Peak mountain to the farm."

"There's still the matter of Paxton," Noah pointed out. "If it was Rory who crashed the van into a house and then ran back up the mountain, that means Pax could still be out there driving the other van. Do we have any leads on that vehicle?"

"We're still looking," Mettner told him. "We've got a BOLO out. City and state police are looking for it."

Josie said, "Has anyone checked the produce market?"

Mettner raised a brow. "You're kidding, right?"

"Paxton Bryan's world is narrow, Mett. Home, the market, Lorelei Mitchell's house. That's it. That's what he knows."

Chitwood said, "He drives all over town with his dad delivering produce. It's not that narrow."

"But he's on the run," Josie said. "Think about it. Everyone he cares for has either been killed or gone missing in the last forty-eight hours. He won't be thinking straight. Even if he had something to do with these murders, it's a stressful time for him. He's going to go somewhere he finds comforting. Mett, you said you've got searchers out in the woods between the Mitchell house and Harper's Peak. That's a huge area to cover. When's the last time anyone looked inside any of the structures on Lorelei's property?"

He looked at her as if he wanted to argue. He often argued with her. It drove Noah crazy, but Josie appreciated it. It meant he was thinking critically, and also, she needed to be challenged to stay sharp. She said, "Just spit it out, Mett."

"I don't think Pax would do that. It's… stupid."

"Mett," Noah said.

Josie held up a hand, silencing him. "It is stupid, but what would also be stupid is for us not to check the most obvious places. How long will it take to have someone swing by the market and the Mitchell house? You've already got units out there."

Mettner looked at Chitwood, who shrugged. "We need to find this kid, Mett. Today. Now. Do whatever you have to do."

He sighed. "Fine. I'll send units. What about Emily? Any idea where she could be?"

"She might be with Pax," Josie pointed out.

She didn't say what they were all thinking—that the reason no one had found her yet was because she was dead.

CHAPTER THIRTY-ONE

Two hours later, an exhausted Gretchen ambled into the ICU waiting room. Everyone else had gone in and out of the room all day to eat, sleep, shower, and change clothes. Only Josie and Noah stayed. Sawyer was around somewhere, Josie knew, because she had seen him coming in and out of Lisette's room at his appointed time.

Now only Trinity and Shannon remained to keep vigil with Josie and Noah. Both of them slept on separate couches. Quietly, Gretchen walked over to where Josie and Noah sat. "How's Lisette?" she asked.

Josie said, "They had to drain some fluid from one of the wounds in her abdomen, but other than that, she's hanging on. Not awake much. We get to go in every hour for about ten minutes, but that's all."

Noah asked, "Do you have an update?"

Gretchen pulled her reading glasses from her pocket and put them on. Then she took out her notebook and flipped through some pages. She looked at the door. "The Chief should be right behind me. I just saw him at the vending machine."

They waited a few minutes until Chitwood came strolling in with a bag of potato chips and a Coke in his hands. He stood beside Gretchen, as though he was the one waiting for her and said, "Let's hear it."

Gretchen shot him a dirty look and then turned to Josie. "Mett said to tell you that you were right."

"Really?" said Noah with a slight smile on his face.

"Not you," Gretchen said. "The boss."

"I know," Noah said. "You found Pax?"

Gretchen nodded. "The second van was parked behind the produce market. He had used several pallets, empty crates and bushels to cover it up, although not very well."

"Was Emily with him?" Josie asked.

"No."

"Where was he?" Josie prodded. "With the van?"

"No. He was in the greenhouse at the Mitchell property. Curled up under one of the tables. Didn't put up a fight when patrol took him in."

Chitwood tucked the Coke can under his arm and opened his chips, the plastic crinkling. He popped a few chips into his mouth.

Josie said, "This is going to sound weird, but did you find any… buttons? Either in the van or in the greenhouse?"

Gretchen raised a brow. "You mean like the kind at the Reed Bryan murder scene? The tufted gray buttons? No. Mett told everyone to be on the lookout for those after he met with you earlier."

"Has Pax said anything?" Noah asked.

"No. He was advised of his rights. He hasn't asked for an attorney. The only thing he has asked for is to talk to Josie."

Josie's gaze snapped upward toward Gretchen's face. "What?"

"He wants to talk to you and only you."

Chitwood's fingers froze halfway between his chip bag and his mouth.

Noah said, "That's not possible."

Josie felt the pull, as she always had, toward work. Purpose. Action. Yet, her heart was in the other room with Lisette. She didn't want to leave. What if Lisette took a turn for the worse, or if she died and Josie wasn't there? On the other hand, it had been hours with little change. When the doctor came to tell them they were going to drain some fluid from her abdomen, he had said it was going to be a very long night for Lisette. Once the procedure was finished, no one would be allowed to see her for at least two hours after that. If Josie couldn't see her for two hours, then why not take some of that time to talk to Pax? The police station was only minutes away.

"What if Pax knows where Emily is?" Josie heard herself say.

Chitwood threw his chips back into the bag and rolled it up, putting it into his suit jacket pocket. Josie expected him to say something like, "You're not on the clock right now, Quinn," or "Absolutely not," but he was silent.

Noah turned to her. "You don't have to do this. It doesn't always have to be you."

Josie said, "In this case, though, it does. If we knew where Emily was, I wouldn't even consider it. But if there's even a chance that we can find her… I won't even be able to see Gram for another two hours. I'll be back before that."

"Josie," Noah said.

"There is a scared little girl out there who has just lost her entire family and probably witnessed her father's murder—although she doesn't know Reed was her father—my point is that she's lost everyone. She's deeply traumatized, and we don't know where she is right now. She has no one, Noah. No one. Even I had my—"

Josie broke off, finding it suddenly hard to force air into her lungs. She looked away from them, focusing on her breath, trying to stay calm. She felt Noah's hand slip into hers. "Your grandmother," he finished for her. "I get it."

Chitwood said, "I would not allow this if a girl's life wasn't at stake, but I can stay here while you go talk to Paxton Bryan. But you have to keep yourself together. For all we know, this kid is the one who's been running around the woods shooting at people. If you go in there, the focus has to be on Emily, not on your grandmother. You got that? If this kid ever has to go to court to be tried for what he's done, we can't have any confessions he might make thrown out because you were the one taking them."

Josie looked back at him and nodded.

Chitwood lifted his chin toward Gretchen. "Palmer, you handle this. Take Quinn over to the stationhouse. Bring her back as soon as you can. If anything happens here—if there is even a hint of a change in Mrs. Matson's condition, I'll be on the horn before you can snap your fingers. Now go."

CHAPTER THIRTY-TWO

Neither Josie nor Gretchen spoke on the drive to the stationhouse. As the large building came into view, Josie felt a release of some of the tension building inside her. Here was the place where the world made sense. Here was the place where she knew what to do and what to say. She had purpose. There were always puzzles for her mind to labor over. Always distractions from anything that her heart didn't want to dwell on. Today, most of all, she needed that feeling, if only for an hour.

Josie waited at her desk while Gretchen had Pax moved from the holding cells in the basement to one of the interrogation rooms on the second floor. Once he was in a room, Josie waited in the adjacent CCTV monitoring area while Gretchen got him a water and some crackers, which he left untouched in front of him. She read him his rights again and waited for him to request a lawyer. All he would say was, "I want to talk to Josie Quinn."

Gretchen left him at the table in the small room and met Josie in the hallway. "He's all yours."

While Gretchen disappeared into the CCTV room to monitor the interview, Josie stood in front of the door, shoring herself up. Emily. She just had to find Emily. If one good thing came out of this horrific situation, it would be locating Emily safe and alive. With a deep breath, she pushed through the door. Pax, who had been hunched over, his elbows leaning on the table, sat up. His eyes grew wide and Josie felt his palpable relief. There was a chair opposite him. Josie dragged it around to his side of the table, pushing it as close to him as she possibly could before sitting down.

He turned slightly to face her. Josie pushed her face into his personal space and said, "Where's Emily?"

His lower lip quivered. "I—I don't know."

"Pax. Someone I love is dying a mile away in the hospital. I do not have to be here. Even though you asked for me, I did not have to come. I'm here because I want to find your sister. Now where is she?"

His voice was barely audible. "I don't know. I swear to you, I don't know."

"Then why am I here, Pax?"

A single tear slid down his cheek. He didn't bother to wipe it away. His left shoulder shrugged. It was a tic, Josie realized.

"Rory killed my dad."

Josie sat back in her chair. "I'm sorry to hear that, Pax," she said. "Can you tell me about it?"

"We were in the barn. Me, Rory, Emily—"

"How did Rory and Emily end up in your barn?"

"I brought them there."

"Half the county has been looking for them for the last two days, Pax. How did you find them?"

His shoulder shrugged twice in quick succession. "When that other officer dropped me off the other day—after I was here—my dad was busy, so I grabbed my bike and I rode back up into the woods. Look, I knew Rory was in the woods, okay? I saw him that day you found me out riding around."

"Did you talk to him that day?"

"No, he was running away."

"That's a lot of woods back there," Josie said. "How could you find him when no one else could?"

"When I would come over to Miss Lorelei's house, sometimes he and I would go exploring. He said it helped him with his… creature."

"You mean his rage," Josie said.

Pax nodded. "I thought if we were friends, maybe he wouldn't have to try so hard to keep his creature from coming out. We had certain areas in the woods we always went to, and only we knew where they were. Certain trees and little gullies and stuff. So I went looking for him in those places."

Something had been bothering Josie since the day she'd been shot at in the woods. "Pax, why were you looking for Rory?"

He looked away from her. His shoulder shrugged three times, and his fingers tapped against the table.

"Pax?"

"He promised me," he said quietly.

Josie leaned in closer. "Promised you what?"

"That he wouldn't let the creature hurt them. He promised me, and he broke that promise. He killed Miss Lorelei and Holly."

"What were you going to do when you found him?" Josie asked.

Now he met her eyes. With an expression of perfect innocence, he said, "I was going to ask him why."

"That's all?"

"Hasn't anyone ever broken a promise to you?" he said. "A really important one?"

She almost said that the difference between her and him was that she would want to kill someone who broke a promise the magnitude of the one Rory had broken, but she was here to find out what happened to Emily. "You found him."

"Yeah. I was pretty high up on the mountain, almost further than we ever went, and I saw him. He had Emily with him."

Josie said, "Emily was with him. Did he say where he found her?"

"He said he went and got her. I don't know from where."

"He didn't tell you?"

"There wasn't time for that. I told him to come with me, both of them. I'd get one of my dad's vans and hide them 'cause I knew he was in big trouble, and I wanted Emily to be safe. Then we heard something in the woods."

"What did you hear?"

"Like footsteps. Like someone coming toward us. Rory shoved Emily toward me and told me to take her and go get the van. He said he'd meet us in the back of the store later. He made me take her."

"Where did you take her?" Josie asked.

"I was taking her back to the store. To hide her. I made her hide out back. A couple of hours later, I went out and Rory was there. He had walked all the way down the mountain to the market. My dad was still working in the office. Doing the books. I took one of the vans and we left."

"Pax," Josie said. "Did Rory have a gun with him?"

"No."

"Where did you take them?"

"First we just drove around. He was really upset. The creature was really bothering him. I had to find a place to stop the van so we could talk. I drove back to that old textile mill. The one that's abandoned?"

"I know it," Josie said.

"I waited for him to stop freaking out but he wouldn't. I tried to talk to him, and he said something bad happened. He said he saw a police officer and some old lady and something bad happened, and he couldn't stop it and he was sorry."

Josie's heart thudded in her chest, but she remained calm. "What else did he say?"

"That it was his fault, all his fault, that the police lady and the old lady got hurt. He kept crying and freaking out."

But the gun hadn't been found anywhere in the woods, Josie thought. "But he didn't have a gun with him? Are you sure, Pax?"

"I wouldn't let him bring a gun with us. Definitely not with Emily there. She was already upset. She kept asking what police lady, and he said he didn't know her name and it was dark. Emily asked if she had a scar and he said a big one, on the side of her face, and we knew it was you."

He looked at her then, as if looking for some kind of absolution, but Josie didn't have it to give. She swallowed. "Did he say what he did?"

"No. Just that it was very bad and that you were both probably at the hospital. Emily got really upset. She said he had to make you a doll to say he was sorry. I didn't know what the hell they were talking about, but he said if he made one could I take it to you since I knew who you were. I said if I took it to you, you would make me turn him in. So he said I could take it to the hospital and leave it on your car. I had been in your car before, so I knew which one it was. I thought what Rory was saying was bullshit, but it was important to Emily that he do it. I said I would do whatever he wanted if he would tell me why he broke his promise to me. He didn't want Emily to hear, so he asked her to look around in the woods for stuff to make this doll they kept talking about. So she said she would. I told her to stay where I could see her, though."

"What did Rory say when Emily couldn't hear him?" Josie asked.

"He said he didn't break his promise."

"What do you mean?"

"He said he hurt Holly and Miss Lorelei, but he didn't kill them. There was someone else."

CHAPTER THIRTY-THREE

Josie glanced at the CCTV camera. Gretchen was on the other side of it, listening and watching. She would take down anything Pax said so the team could track down both Rory and the other person he claimed killed his mother and sister. Josie was going back to the hospital to be with Lisette after this.

"What other person?" Josie asked.

Pax spread his hands. "I don't know. He just said he didn't kill them. The creature came out and it was bad. The creature said all these terrible things he was going to do to all of them and Miss Lorelei and Holly got scared. They told Emily to hide. That only made the creature worse. Then Miss Lorelei called someone on her cell phone."

"Who?" Josie asked.

He shrugged. "I don't know. A man. I asked him what man, and he wouldn't tell me. He just said the man showed up and when he saw that Rory was hurting Miss Lorelei, he went out to the truck, got the gun, and came in and tried to kill them all."

Josie watched Pax's face carefully for any signs of deception. Was this something he and Rory had cooked up together? Although it wasn't outside the realm of possibility that another person had been there the day Lorelei and Holly were killed, if that was true, Josie would have expected some more detail. Any detail. "Did he describe him?" she asked.

"No, but I didn't ask him to. I asked him if he knew the man and he said yes, but he wouldn't tell me who it was."

"Pax, is it possible it was your father?"

"No."

"Remember how you told us you were with him the morning that Lorelei and Holly were killed? Were you telling the truth? It's okay if you weren't, we just need to know the truth."

"He was with me. That is the truth. It couldn't have been him."

Josie said, "Do you ever remember seeing any men at their home when you were there?"

"No."

"What about Rory and Holly? Did they ever talk about their father? Do you know if he was in the picture?"

"They didn't talk about him. It was like they never had a father. When I first started going over there, Rory told me a secret. It was when Miss Lorelei wasn't listening. He said that they had a dad before Holly was born. Sometimes he would be there but not a lot. He was mean, he hated Rory, and when Holly was a baby, he went away and never came back. That's all I know."

"Did Rory ever talk about Harper's Peak?" Josie asked.

For that, she got two shoulder shrugs.

"Pax?"

"He asked me not to tell anyone."

"Can you tell me what that was?"

"You know how I told you that I have an aunt that lives in Georgia? Well, Rory claimed that his aunt lived at and ran Harper's Peak."

"Did he say whether he had ever met her?"

Pax shook his head. "No. He didn't say. I wasn't even sure if I should believe him or not, or if he was just saying it because I told him I had an aunt I never got to see."

Josie asked, "Did he say anything else about her? Anything at all?"

He shook his head. "No."

Josie moved on. "Okay, so you're at the mill. Rory denies having killed Lorelei and Holly. Emily is gathering materials for a doll. What did you do after that? Where did you spend the night?"

"In the van out by the mill. We were all tired and didn't have a plan. The next day we got up and Rory finished his doll. I didn't think leaving it for you was a good idea, but they wanted you to have it."

"Were they with you when you left it?"

He shook his head. "I took them to the farm and told them to wait in the barn. I left the doll, went back and then my dad showed up. He was furious. I tried to explain what was going on, but he didn't care. I told him what Rory told me about the man killing Lorelei and Holly, but he said it was a bunch of horseshit and that he wasn't harboring a killer. He said he was going to call the police. That's when Rory—"

He broke off, more tears leaking from his eyes. "It happened so fast. I couldn't even stop him. He was so quick."

Josie knew exactly how quick Rory was. She'd just been lucky he'd had only his fists when he attacked her, and no weapons.

"Emily was screaming and screaming and screaming. I tried to stop Rory but it was too late. By that time, my dad was already dead. I told him we had to call the police, but he said no. We were arguing. That's when Emily ran off. I went after her but I lost her. By the time I came back, Rory was gone and so was one of the vans."

"Why didn't you come to the police, Pax?" Josie asked.

He shrugged. "I wanted to. I was going to, but I was so upset. I didn't know what to do. I just wanted some time to figure out what to do. I'm sorry I hid. I know it was wrong. But now you know: Rory killed my dad."

"Where is he now?"

"I don't know."

"Where is Emily?"

"Did you not hear what I just told you?" Pax said. "I really don't know."

His chest was heaving. Josie gave him a moment to slow his breathing. There was nothing else he could offer her. It was a dead end. Still, she remembered the buttons. "Pax, Emily was placed with some people to take care of her temporarily. While she was there, she cut all the buttons from their sofa and she told the owner of the couch it was because she was afraid they were going to choke her. Do you know what that means?"

"Thought-action fusion," he said. "It's her OCD. Sometimes, in our brains, our thoughts get really mixed up so that we can't even figure out if we just thought something or if it really happened. Like she probably saw those buttons and had an intrusive thought about what if she choked on them? Then in her mind, she couldn't be sure if she had put one in her mouth or not."

"So she cut them all off?"

"To get rid of them probably, yeah," he said. "Miss Lorelei told me all about this stuff when I first started going there. I had it when I was little. Once I was counting pennies and I had a thought about eating one, and then I couldn't figure out if I had really eaten one or only thought about it. My mom took me to the hospital. Turns out I didn't eat one, only had a thought about it."

"Wouldn't Emily get rid of those all at once?" Josie asked.

He shrugged. "I don't know. She's got her own palterer, you know. I don't know what it tells her to do."

CHAPTER THIRTY-FOUR

Gretchen drove Josie back to the hospital. "What do you think of this kid?"

Josie shook her head, watching the city pass by outside her window. The sun hung low in the sky. In another hour it would be night. "I don't know what to think. The first time I met him, I thought he was living in fear of his father. Then I thought he was a sensitive soul who wanted to help us. Then I thought he was the one shooting at me. Then I thought he was a sad, lonely boy living with a father who wasn't prepared to properly support him. Now? I have no idea."

"You think there really was another man there that day, like Rory said?" Gretchen asked.

"I don't know. I really don't know. We have one set of fingerprints from the house that we haven't been able to match to anyone, which gives his story credence. But if Rory was telling the truth, wouldn't he provide more detail? Also, no one has ever actually seen Rory with the gun."

"Right," said Gretchen. "I agree. I'm going to draw up a warrant to have the entire Bryan premises searched to see if the gun turns up there. What I'm wondering is, what is Rory's end game here? He's just going to wander around the woods for the rest of his life?"

"He's fifteen," Josie pointed out. "His brain isn't fully developed. We know he doesn't want to get caught. Lorelei isolating him for so many years doesn't exactly help with his fear of people or outsiders."

"True. Then there's Emily. She can't have gotten very far on foot."

"Mett said he was sending searchers down that way and that he was going to try to get the dogs back." Josie felt as though she should say more, offer more, but all she really wanted was to get back to Lisette. Gretchen left her outside the hospital and went back to work.

Josie noticed something unusual the moment she stepped foot in the ICU waiting room. Shannon, Christian, Patrick, Trinity, Drake, Misty, Noah, and Chitwood were standing in a semicircle, talking in low whispers. For a moment, Josie stood frozen in the doorway, fearing the worst had happened. Lisette had passed on during her procedure, and they were trying to figure out how to tell her. Then she saw a bouquet of flowers on one of the tables along the wall. It lay on its side, stems bound with a white lacy ribbon.

"What is going on here?" she said.

Noah said, "Lisette is fine. She tolerated her procedure well. She's been awake. Asking for you. She, uh, won't let go of the wedding idea."

Josie walked over to the flowers and fingered the ribbon. "What is this?"

Trinity came over and took Josie's hand. "Just hear us out, okay? Remember how Lisette said she wanted to see you get married before…" Trinity trailed off, realizing what she was about to say.

Shannon picked up the thread. "You guys can always have another ceremony or reception—anything you want—some other time."

Josie looked around the room. "What are you not telling me?"

They all stared. Josie's heart sank. No one spoke. Then a voice came from the doorway. Sawyer. "She's got internal bleeding in her small bowel. They're having trouble controlling it. They can take her back to surgery, but her body's already been through so much, they're not sure she can tolerate it."

"She's going to die," Josie said softly.

Sawyer nodded.

Shannon came over and stepped between Josie and the table. "I'm so sorry, Josie."

"How long?"

Again, no one spoke. Josie looked back at Sawyer. "How long does she have?"

He shook his head, eyes glistening with unshed tears. "Hours? Maybe a day? They're going to wait till morning and if she's still with us, they'll take her back into surgery again and try to find the source. It's a slow leak, but she can't keep losing blood this way. She simply won't make it."

Josie's knees gave out. Trinity and Shannon caught her. Noah rushed over to her. The three of them guided her to a chair and sat her down. He knelt in front of her and took her hands. "We don't have to do this. It was just something we were discussing."

Misty said, "I got the flowers. It was silly, but I was so upset. I wanted to do something. It's Lisette's dying wish. I wanted to be ready in case you agreed to it. Dr. Feist said your dress is downstairs in her office. We could do it—oh, and the Chief, he can officiate, believe it or not."

Josie's eyes wandered up and over to Chitwood's face. He shrugged. "You take some online classes. You get certified to marry people in the Commonwealth. I did it for some friends a few years back."

Josie kept staring at him.

He kinked a brow. "What?" he said. "I've got friends."

Josie looked back at Sawyer. A muscle ticked in his jaw. His blue eyes, as ever, were penetrating. "I said some things," he told her. "But if this is the time we have left with her, we should give her what she wants."

Josie said, "She wants you and me not to fight, Sawyer."

"Not as much as she wants to see you get married. I don't get it, but I don't need to. I found her. At the end of her life, I had a chance to meet her and know her and learn about my father, my grandfather, her family. She could have turned me away, but she didn't. If this is what she wants, Josie, just give it to her."

Josie turned toward Noah, who still knelt before her. "This is your wedding, too," she whispered. "Your first wedding—and hopefully your only wedding—we had all those plans—"

Noah smiled. "Plans are stupid," he said. "Let's just get married."

CHAPTER THIRTY-FIVE

Someone had elevated Lisette's bed slightly and taken the time to comb out her gray curls. Josie could tell by the way the corners of her eyes crinkled and the way her upper lip curled ever so slightly, that she was in great pain. Still, she beamed as she watched Christian walk, arm-in-arm with Josie, from the doorway of her room to the bed, where Noah and Chitwood waited. Drake had gotten the rings. Josie had no idea from where. The groomsmen had been in charge of those, and she'd lost track of everything concerning their wedding the moment Holly Mitchell was found in front of the Harper's Peak church.

Misty had gone to their house and gotten Noah's tuxedo. Shannon had done her best to smooth out Josie's wedding dress and clean the dirt from the bottom of it. It was still a bit of a mess, but it would do for their purposes. Josie knew that in spite of her dress and the make-up and hair product that Misty, Shannon, and Trinity had sprayed and brushed onto her—covering the bruises left by Rory's attack quite well—she looked just as exhausted as Noah did. Still, they both smiled, and neither of them cried. The others, even Sawyer, circled the bed, all of them shifting nervously. Josie also knew that the nursing staff waited eagerly outside, ready to disperse them the moment the vows were said.

Christian kissed Josie's cheek, handed off her bouquet to Trinity, and left her facing Noah. Chitwood moved so that Lisette had full view of them both. Josie reached out a hand and placed it in Lisette's.

"You look so beautiful, dear," she said. Her voice was raspy, her breathing labored.

Chitwood cleared his throat. "We're gathered here today to join Detect—to join Josie and Noah in the bonds of matrimony. Marriage is a promise between the two of you that you will love, honor, and trust one another for the rest of your lives. Today you will commit to support, encourage, and love each other as long as you're both alive. You will dedicate yourselves to that commitment and be faithful to it and to one another. You will move forward as two unique individuals, but you'll do so together, partners in strength, joy, and also responsibilities."

Josie was surprised by Chitwood's speech. She wondered if it was from a script he had learned or if he was improvising. Either way, it was lovely. She felt Lisette squeeze her hand when he said the words 'move forward.'

"Now," said Chitwood, turning his gaze on Noah. "Noah, do you take Josie to be your wife, in the presence of these witnesses, in sickness and health, in times of both joy and sorrow, for richer or poorer, and promise to cherish her as long as you both shall live?"

Josie stared into Noah's hazel eyes, noticing the gold flecks in his irises. He smiled. His voice was husky when he said, "I do."

Josie felt tears threaten but held them back, unable to stop herself from returning his smile. Chitwood turned to her. "Josie, do you take Noah to be your husband, in the presence of these witnesses, in sickness and health, in times of both joy and sorrow, for richer or poorer, and promise to cherish him as long as you both shall live?"

Josie felt the electricity between them, like something alive, and realized she'd never felt that kind of connection to anyone before. "I do," she said.

"Now, as to the vows," Chitwood said. "I was told that you two had something prepared?"

Josie and Noah turned their heads and stared at him. "What?" Josie said.

"Didn't you prepare vows?"

"Oh," Josie said, thinking of the weeks the two of them had taken to secretly prepare vows for one another, painstakingly writing them out. They'd brought them to Harper's Peak for their wedding. She had no idea where they were now. Probably still in their luggage at the resort. Chitwood looked at her expectantly. She said, "We did, but—"

Noah silenced her by squeezing her hand. "I love you," he said. "And I promise to always run toward the danger with you."

Josie couldn't help but grin. "I love you, too," she said. "I promise to always come home to you—and never to cook, much."

Quiet laughter erupted around the room.

Josie felt Lisette's grip tighten on her hand.

"Those sound like good vows to me," Chitwood said. He looked around. "Who's got the rings?"

Drake stepped forward and deposited the rings into his open palm. He picked up the smaller one and handed it to Noah. "Place this ring on Josie's finger and repeat after me."

Josie relinquished Lisette's hand and let Noah slide her wedding band onto the ring finger of her left hand. His fingers trembled slightly as he repeated Chitwood's words. "Josie, I give you this ring as a symbol of my love and faithfulness to you."

Josie stared down at the shiny band and blinked back even more tears. Her palms were sweaty as she accepted the other ring from Chitwood. Slipping it onto Noah's ring finger, she, too repeated the words. "Noah, I give you this ring as a symbol of my love and faithfulness to you."

There was a pregnant silence in the room. Josie glanced over to see Lisette beaming. She gave a little nod and Chitwood said, "It is my pleasure and my privilege to pronounce you two married. You may kiss each other!"

Noah cupped Josie's cheeks with his palms and pulled her in, planting a long, soft kiss on her lips. Josie's hand reached for Lisette's and when she found it, Lisette's grip was firm and unyielding.

Josie kept hold of her hand while Trinity snapped some photos of them next to Lisette's bed. Then everyone lined up to offer their congratulations. Already, Josie could feel the small bit of dizzying happiness that marrying Noah had brought her slipping away, knowing that her world was going to be shattered within a matter of hours. After several minutes, a nurse entered the room and made them all leave. Except Josie. Lisette wouldn't let go.

"You have one minute," the nurse warned. "Then I have to check her over."

Josie nodded. When the nurse was gone, Lisette tugged her closer. Josie leaned in so she could better hear her words. Lisette said, "You have to learn to live with them both, dear."

"Both?" Josie said, wondering if Lisette was becoming delirious.

"The grief and the happiness." She paused, taking in a few shallow breaths. "If you can't live with them both, you'll never make it."

"Okay," Josie said.

"No, not okay." Another pause for breath. "Josie, you've never learned that some things you have to sit with and really feel before you can move past them."

She was getting tired, her breath more labored now. Josie thought of Emily and how her older sister had told her that sometimes you have to feel all the feelings until they're gone. Josie had spent her entire life pushing all the bad and terrifying feelings down as deep as she could. She didn't handle it well when they escaped from the dark place. Lisette had watched her self-destruct many times.

Josie kissed Lisette's cheek. "I understand, Gram. You rest now. I'll be back as soon as they let me."

The celebration—if it could be called that—in the waiting room was subdued. Josie could tell that both Misty and Shannon were trying not to cry. Trinity handed Drake her camera and made him take more photos. Josie wondered how they would look months from now, or on their first anniversary. Would their faces appear strained and hollow? Would they look as exhausted as Josie knew every single one of them felt? Perhaps they should have waited and married after Lisette passed; after her funeral; after an appropriate mourning period. But Josie knew the instant the thought entered her mind that there would never be an appropriate mourning period. It would have been torture planning another wedding knowing that Lisette wouldn't be there, knowing that if Josie had only stayed at Griffin Hall and walked down the aisle as planned, Lisette could have seen it. She wouldn't have been able to marry Noah after this and eventually, he would have grown tired of the grief between them forcing them apart and keeping them that way.

Lisette knew Josie better than any living person, and this wedding—bittersweet though it was—was her gift to her grand-daughter.

When enough photos had been taken, Shannon and Trinity accompanied Josie back to Dr. Feist's office to change back into her regular clothes. Back upstairs they waited. Josie and Sawyer waited to be able to see Lisette again. Josie, Noah, and Chitwood waited for news on the case. A few hours after the wedding, Mettner showed up, looking haggard, his face dark with stubble. A glance at the clock in the waiting room told Josie it was just after eleven p.m.

"We've got nothing," he told Josie, Noah, and Chitwood in the hall outside the waiting room. "Gretchen's been working on finding Rory Mitchell. I've been working the Emily angle. They're on opposite sides of the city, and our staff is stretched as thin as it can get. Even with the state police helping, we haven't found any signs of them. I can't get the dogs back till sometime tomorrow."

Josie said, "Have you found any buttons? In the search for Emily?"

"Two," he said. He took out his phone and pulled up Google Maps. After a few swipes, he turned the map toward her and used one finger to point at the screen. "Here. This is the Bryan farm, right? Here, about a mile this way…" He swiped some more, moving the map so that more of South Denton was visible. "There's a small creek. It's not even a creek. It's just a place where the water runs off at the edge of the farmland. One of the searchers found two gray buttons."

"She's walked a mile already," Chitwood said. "She can't be far, Mett. Take people off Rory Mitchell and send them over to South Denton. We already know this teenager can live out in the woods for days. Emily is an eight-year-old kid. How long is she going to last out there? She's gotta be starving, dehydrated."

Noah said, "Rory Mitchell is dangerous, Chief. He killed at least one person that we know about."

"Who's the Chief of Police, here, Fraley?" Chitwood snapped, sounding more like himself than he had all weekend. "I tell everyone else what to do, and I'm telling Mett to take three-quarters of whoever you've got on the Harper's Peak mountain and send them to South Denton. They'll start where the last buttons were found and fan out."

Josie was still staring at the screen. "May I?" she asked Mettner.

He handed it to her. To the Chief, he said, "Maybe we should get the press involved? Ask for civilians to help with the search? Amber could get something going real fast."

Josie zoomed out on the phone and turned the view to terrain, watching as the lines and asymmetrical shapes on the map turned to fields and trees.

Chitwood said, "That's a good idea, Mett. Have her talk to WYEP and see what they can whip up in a hurry, would you? It's too late for the eleven o'clock news but they can still put out a call on social media, and maybe something when they come back on air in the morning. I think they go on at four a.m. The more people we've got on this, the better."

As Josie suspected, not far from where the buttons had been found, there was a break in the forest. A small, indistinct square breaking up the unending green. "This is the old Rowland place," she said, pointing to it.

Chitwood put on his reading glasses and peered at the screen. "What's the old Rowland place?"

"Before your time," Noah said. "We used to have a billionaire living in Denton. Local celebrity, sort of. Went on to make big bucks creating security systems, but always kept a house here."

"It's been vacant for years," Josie said. "But the house is made almost entirely of glass."

"Like a greenhouse," Mettner said.

"Yes," Josie said. "It wouldn't look like a greenhouse to you or me—"

"But to an eight-year-old, it might," Mettner filled in. "We'll check it out."

Josie said, "Follow the buttons."

CHAPTER THIRTY-SIX

It was just after midnight when Dr. Justofin appeared at the door to the waiting room. Only Josie, Noah, Sawyer, and Trinity remained. Everyone else had left, gone to get rest and sustenance. Josie nudged Noah awake when she saw the doctor. Sawyer sprang out of his chair. "What is it?"

Dr. Justofin gave them a pained smile. "I'm sorry, but your grandmother is declining. We don't believe she'll be strong enough to undergo surgery in the morning."

"Is she still alive?" Trinity asked, putting a hand on Josie's back.

"Yes. She's still alive and still lucid—when she's not sleeping—but I'm not sure there's much more we can do for her. She's declined any further life-saving care."

"Can she do that?" Noah asked.

Dr. Justofin nodded. "She can. She's already signed the paperwork. We're going to move her down to a regular floor and do our best to make her comfortable. There won't be any restrictions on visitors. I'll see to it that any of you can stay with her as long as you'd like."

Josie could barely choke out a thank you. Once the doctor was gone, Trinity pulled Josie into a hug. Josie let herself sob into Trinity's shoulder for several minutes. Across from her, she could hear Sawyer weeping as well. She wanted to comfort him but couldn't bring herself to move. Did he really have no one in his life?

Noah squeezed Josie's knee. "I'll call your parents."

"And your team," said Sawyer. "This is about to be a homicide."

*

An hour later, Josie and Sawyer sent everyone home to rest, even Noah, while they kept vigil over their grandmother. They sat on either side of Lisette's bed in a new room. The floor was much quieter, with fewer alarms going off at the nurses' station. Lisette looked better without all the equipment hooked up to her. Only a single IV was left in her good arm. She smiled, first at Sawyer, then at Josie. "This is better," she said.

No, it's not, Josie wanted to shout.

"They're making me comfortable," Lisette went on. "That means they're giving me the good stuff. The really good stuff."

She closed her eyes and let out a sigh. Without opening them, she said, "I never got to say goodbye to your father, Eli. I always wished I had. Or my daughter. She was with me such a short time, and then one day, she was gone." Pausing, she took several breaths. "I never got to say goodbye to her. This is a blessing."

"How can this be a blessing?" Sawyer said, his voice breaking.

Lisette opened her eyes and looked at him lovingly. "I couldn't stay here forever, dear. We all knew that. I wish I had more time, I do…"

She drifted off, exhaustion and the drugs taking their toll once more. Josie moved her chair closer and took Lisette's hand. On the other side, her arm was in the cast, so Sawyer put her bedrail down, got as close as he could to the bed and rested his forehead on her shoulder. Josie saw his shoulders quaking.

She wasn't sure how much time went by. Her middle finger was on the inside of Lisette's wrist, counting off the faint heartbeats. Sometime later, Lisette opened her eyes again. She stared straight ahead at the foot of the bed and smiled. Then her face relaxed. Josie thought she might be going, but her pulse was still thready beneath Josie's finger. She stayed that way for several minutes.

"Sawyer," she whispered.

He lifted his head and leaned even closer, so that his ear was over her mouth. She whispered something to him that Josie couldn't hear. He went back to his position at her shoulder, weeping into the bedsheet. Lisette turned her head toward Josie.

Josie stood and folded her upper body over the bed, her face hovering just over Lisette's. Lisette whispered into her ear, kissed Josie's forehead, and squeezed her hand for the last time.

CHAPTER THIRTY-SEVEN

Josie and Sawyer waited until the medical staff made them leave the room. They stayed with Lisette until her body was cold. They waited in the hallway, standing awkwardly, until Dr. Feist arrived. She hugged them both. "I'm so sorry," she said. "I promise I'll take good care of her." She looked at Josie. "I'll give my findings to Detective Mettner."

Josie nodded. She'd never imagined that Lisette would need an autopsy after death. She had always envisioned Lisette passing away quietly in her chair while playing cards in the cafeteria at her nursing home. Or going to sleep in her room one night and simply not waking up. Dying of old age. A peaceful death. But she'd been murdered. Coldly, savagely, before Josie's eyes, and when Josie caught the person who did it, the criminal justice system would require that the extent of the injuries that killed her were documented by autopsy.

They watched as Dr. Feist wheeled Lisette's bed out of the room—her face covered with a sheet—and into one of the staff elevators at the end of the hall. Josie felt strangely numb, but she knew it was just her body clicking over to survival mode. This was how she had managed to get through a childhood of trauma, losing her father, then losing her first husband. Her mind took the unfathomable horror of her new reality and shut it away so that her body could keep doing all the things it needed to do to function and live. Sometimes, later on, there was a reckoning, if she wasn't able to keep all those bad feelings down. Most of the time, she kept them buried so far beneath the surface, she could go for long periods without any of them being triggered. It was getting more difficult with each year that passed, to not feel her feelings. She suspected that a time would come when she would pay for all those years of locking everything away.

But tonight was not that time.

She said, "Sawyer, can I call someone for you?"

"No," he said, and with that, he walked down the hall and got onto an elevator.

Josie took the steps down to the first floor and walked outside through the Emergency Department lobby. She knew she should call someone. She had a host of loved ones waiting for news, waiting to comfort her, and do all the things she could not imagine doing right now. The logistics of death. She'd always hated them. When her husband, Ray, died, his mother had done most of the funeral planning.

For now, she stood outside in the cool night air, breathing in a world without Lisette. How was that even possible?

She took out her phone and texted Noah. *She's gone.*

His reply came back immediately. *I'll be right there.*

She put her phone back into her pocket and looked toward the lobby as a police cruiser pulled up. A uniformed officer got out and opened the back door. Out stepped Mettner. He turned back toward the open door, reached into the back seat, and lifted Emily Mitchell into his arms.

Josie followed them inside.

CHAPTER THIRTY-EIGHT

Josie waited until the medical team had done their initial assessment, listening from the other side of the curtain as they determined that Emily was severely dehydrated and needed a few stitches for a cut on her arm, but that otherwise she was in fair condition. Once they left her alone with Mettner, Josie stepped into the area.

"Josie!" Emily cried. She waved her stuffed dog in the air. It looked a lot dirtier than the last time Josie had seen it.

"I'm so glad to see you," Josie said.

"You're okay," Emily said.

"Yes."

Emily lowered her voice. "Are we dead yet?"

Josie smiled. "No, we're not dead yet."

Mettner's eyes widened. "What does—you know what? I don't want to know. Emily, stay here while I talk to Detective Quinn down the hall for a few minutes."

"You mean where I can't hear you," she said pointedly.

"That's what he means," Josie said, winking at the girl.

Mettner took her arm and guided her a few cubicles away, pulling her to one side of the hall. "What are you doing here? How is Lisette?"

"She passed away," Josie said.

His face fell. "Oh my God. Boss, I'm so sorry. Do you need me to—should I—"

"Noah is on his way," she said. "Thank you."

"Okay, okay," he said, clearly flustered. "I—uh—well, you were right. Emily was at the old Rowland place. She left a little path of buttons. Hard to see in the dark, but we got some of them. She'll be okay. Social services are on the way. I already talked to Marcie. They're not going to place her at Harper's Peak, which I think is best. Gretchen had contacted Pax's aunt who lives in Georgia, told her everything that's going on, and she's expressed some interest in meeting and possibly taking Emily into her care."

"She is a blood relative," Josie noted. "Through Reed Bryan."

"Right. She was pretty upset when she heard what was going on. She confirmed what Pax had told us—that Reed wouldn't let her see him. Anyway, she's getting on the next flight. Now we just have to find Rory. But what am I saying? Your grandmother just died. You don't need to be here. I can stay with Emily."

Josie said, "Do you mind if I talk with her for a minute? You can stay. Just until Noah gets here?"

"Uh, yeah, okay, sure."

Josie walked back to Emily's cubicle. Mettner stood outside the curtain. Josie pulled a chair up to the bedside. Emily said, "Did you get your doll?"

"I did."

Emily played with the stuffed dog's ears. "He said he was sorry for the bad thing that happened."

"Who is he, Emily?" Josie asked.

She put one finger to her mouth. *Hush*. Josie reached across and pulled it away. "I know about Rory," she said. "And I know about Pax. I also know that Rory did bad things sometimes."

"You already know?"

Josie nodded.

"That bad thing that happened. Rory said someone got shot. Was it your mom?"

"My grandmother," Josie answered.

Emily lowered her voice to a whisper. "Did she die?"

"Yes," Josie said, feeling a swell of emotion in her chest and quickly pushing it down.

"I'm sorry bad things happened to you. Were you ready?"

Josie smiled. "You know what? I don't think any of us are ever ready for the bad things."

Emily nodded but didn't respond.

"Emily, did Rory tell you that he shot my grandmother? Did he say that specifically?"

She went back to playing with the dog's ears. "No. He said it was his fault."

"That's not the same thing as having actually done it. Do you understand?"

"I know."

"You were alone with Rory for a while after Pax took you to his farm. Did he tell you anything? About the things he had done?"

She shook her head.

"Did Pax tell you anything? About hurting anyone?"

"No, he didn't hurt anyone. Pax is good."

"Did he ever tell you that he hurt anyone, though?"

"No."

"Did you ever see Rory or Pax with a gun? Ever?"

"No."

"Emily, has anyone told you why we're looking for Rory?"

She hugged the dog to her chest. "Because he killed Pax's dad."

"Yes," Josie said. "But also because people think that Rory killed your mom and Holly, too. Remember the first day we talked, and I asked you a bunch of questions, and you said you couldn't tell me the answers because the bad things might happen?"

"I remember. But you know the secret now. Rory was bad. Sometimes he hurt us. Mama didn't want him to go into foster care or the 'system' so she made us all be quiet about him. She was always afraid he would go away, and we wouldn't ever get him back. She cried all the time about it."

"I'm so sorry," Josie said. "Rory told Pax that someone else was there in the house the day that your mom and Holly were killed. Do you know if that's true?"

Emily went very still. "I can't say."

"Was it Pax?"

She shook her head vehemently.

"Did you see who it was?"

Again, a vigorous shake of her head.

"Then how can you be sure there was someone else?"

"I can't tell you. Rory made me promise not to tell."

"I thought you said Rory didn't tell you anything."

Her body began to rock in the bed. She counted to six under her breath. Then she said, "I can't tell. I promised I wouldn't tell anyone. If I break a promise, another person might die. What if it's you?"

Josie reached out and touched Emily's arm. She remembered what Dr. Rosetti had said about OCD being nonsensical, about how trying to use logic was like telling a diabetic to produce more insulin. "Remember the first night we were here in the hospital and you were upset because someone had thrown away your things?"

"One, two, three. Yeah, I remember. One, two, three, four, five, six."

"Do you remember what you told me about your mom? How she said that when you feel distress, you have to 'tolerate' it."

"One, two, three, four, five, six. Yes. That's what she said."

"And Holly said that that meant you had to feel all your feelings till they're done?"

"…five, six. Yes."

"I think this is one of those times," Josie said. "The distress you're feeling about telling me? It will go away. Nothing bad will happen if you tell me what Rory said. I'm not going to die. Your brain is playing tricks on you. Lying to you."

She stopped counting, though her body continued to rock. Her fingers kneaded the fur of the dog. "Like Pax's palterer?"

Josie smiled. "Exactly like that. Did your mom talk to you about that?"

She nodded.

"Do you have a name for your… palterer?"

"I didn't have one yet. I wanted to call him LiarLiarPantsOnFire but Mama said that was too long."

Josie laughed. "I like that. What about Liar Pants for short?"

Her grip on the dog loosened. "I like that."

"I think that Liar Pants is in your brain telling you that if you tell me what Rory said, someone will die, when that's just not true. Liar Pants is making you feel that distress when you even think about telling me. Does that make sense?"

"I don't know."

"Can we try something?"

"I don't want to."

Josie leaned in closer. "I don't like feeling all my feelings either, to tell you the truth."

"You don't have a Liar Pants, though. Or a palterer."

"I don't."

"That's gotta be hard."

"It is," Josie admitted. "But I'm willing to stay here and help you, like I did before, remember? When we sat on the floor together?"

Her rocking increased. She white-knuckled the dog and counted to six three times under her breath. Josie glanced at the doorway to see Mettner, Noah, and Marcie Riebe standing there. She looked back at Emily who crossed her legs and then patted the bed in front of her. Josie climbed onto the bed with her, sitting face to face, and crossing her legs as well. Emily extended an arm and turned it so Josie could see a gash down her forearm. "I'm going to have a scar, too."

"Looks that way," Josie said.

"Do you think scars remind us of the bad things?"

Josie fingered her own scar, running her fingers from her ear to just beneath her chin. She'd always hated it. Until now. "No," she told Emily. "I think that they remind us how strong we are and how much we are able to survive—how much we can tolerate. They're... marks of badassery."

Emily giggled. "You said a bad word!"

"I did. But you know what? I think you and I have earned the right to say 'badassery.'"

Emily looked at her cut. "Mark of badassery."

"Are you ready?" Josie asked.

Emily sighed. "I'll never be ready for this. I think you were right about the being ready thing. But Mama always said it was the best thing to do, and I always felt better once we did."

Josie put her hands out and Emily placed her own hands in Josie's. She closed her eyes. "One, two, three, four, five, six. I heard a man. That's how I know. That's how I know there was someone else there. I can't—I can't—"

Josie held tight to her hands as she rocked harder. Tears spilled from the corners of her eyes. "Someone's going to die. Someone's going to die."

"It's the Liar Pants, Emily," Josie reminded her. "Don't let him boss you around. Did you hear anything the man said?"

Her eyes remained clamped shut, but her head swung back and forth. "I only heard some things. He was so loud. So mad. He said, 'enough, enough' and 'you're living in a fantasyland.'"

"Do you know who he was talking to?" Josie asked.

Her body shuddered. A sob erupted from her mouth. Josie squeezed her tiny hands. "You're doing great, Emily. I'm right here. The distress will be gone soon. Do you know who the man was talking to?"

"I don't know. I don't know. He said, 'I hate you' and he said some bad words. A lot of really bad words. He kept saying, 'No' and 'I don't care.' He said, 'this wasn't my choice.' Then I thought he was gone but he came back. I don't know all the things he said after that. It was a lot of things, and Mama was crying and Rory was shouting, 'I hate you, I hate you' and then the man yelled, 'I wish you were never born' and the boom came."

She opened her eyes finally. They were red and glassy. Tears poured down her cheeks. "I don't like this," she told Josie. "I don't like the way it feels."

"I know," said Josie. "But we're almost there. You're doing great. Had you ever seen a man before that day? At your house?"

"No. Only when Pax's dad came to get him. He was the only one. I heard a different man before though."

"You did?"

"One, two, three, four, five, six. Yes, a couple of times when Rory was trying to hurt Mama and Holly. Holly always told me to hide. That was part of the plan. I always hid until one of them told me to come out. Sometimes, I heard the man's voice. I couldn't hear what he said, but I knew it was a man's voice 'cause it didn't sound like Mama or Holly or Rory."

"But you never saw him?" Josie prodded.

"One, two, three, four, five, six. I never saw him 'cause I had to hide."

"That's very good," Josie told her, squeezing her hands. "Emily, did you ask Rory about the man the next time you saw him?"

"I didn't ask him, but he told me he didn't kill Mama and Holly. He said the man did and that he was going to make the man pay. That's why he couldn't go to the police. I told him that if he just called you, you would believe him, and you could just go get the man and put him in jail. But he said no one would ever believe him 'cause he's just a messed-up kid with 'rage issues.'"

"He was trying to find this man?"

Emily let go of one of Josie's hands long enough to swipe at her tears. "Yes. I think he was going to kill him like he killed Pax's dad."

"You have no idea who this man was?"

Emily shook her head and took a shuddering breath.

"Okay. You did great, Emily."

"I still feel it," she said, rocking.

"I'm still here," Josie told her.

They settled into a comfortable silence. Josie was in no hurry to leave. She felt a sense of peace when she was with Emily, and she knew once she left, all that waited for her was crushing grief. She was not anxious to get back to it. Once Emily let go of her hands and relaxed back into the pillow behind her, Josie climbed out of the bed. She was about to leave but had one more question. "Emily, why did you leave the house at Harper's Peak?"

"After I was there for a couple of hours, they left me alone to talk in the kitchen and Liar Pants told me if I didn't look inside every room in the house, then I might never see Mama or Holly in heaven. So I went to every room in the house and looked. I knew that lady and her husband wouldn't like it, but they didn't even notice. The lady was on the phone in the kitchen. She kept walking back and forth saying, 'Tom, Tom calm down' and 'it wasn't my choice.' Stuff like that. She never even came out to check on me! Anyway, in one of the rooms upstairs I saw a picture of her and Rory together."

Josie looked toward the opening in the curtain to make sure Mettner was still paying attention.

"What lady?"

"The lady," Emily said. "I forget her name. She got mad when I cut the buttons off her couch. I mean, I know I shouldn't have done it, but I thought I was going to choke on them."

"You saw a picture of Celeste and Rory together?" Josie clarified. "What kind of picture?"

Emily shrugged. "I don't know. They were just standing together, smiling."

"How old did Rory look in the picture? Was he a little boy?"

"No. He looked like he does now. When I saw the picture, I got scared because I knew Mama wanted Rory to be a secret. I got nervous. I was going to tell the guy—her husband—'cause he was nicer than her, but he had to go do something for work. That's when I cut the buttons off the couches. She really freaked out on me after that, so when she went back on her phone call in the kitchen, I left."

"Where were you going?"

"I just wanted to find somewhere safe. Then I saw Rory standing in the woods. I walked to him. We went into the forest, and we saw Pax and that's when everything went wrong."

CHAPTER THIRTY-NINE

"Well, shit," said Mettner as he, Josie, and Noah stood outside of the Emergency Department. "Pax was telling the truth. There's someone else."

"And Celeste Harper is a liar," Noah added. He kept looking over at Josie, and she knew he was trying to assess her. She wanted to tell him she was okay—at least, in that moment—but she didn't want to say it in front of Mettner.

"I'll get up there and see what she knows," Mettner said.

"She's not going to tell you anything," Josie said.

"But what is she hiding?" Noah asked. "Why would she be in a photo with Rory? Even if she knew about Rory, even if she had a relationship with Rory and Lorelei, why lie about it?"

Mettner said, "Maybe she didn't want her husband to know?"

"But he knew about Lorelei," Noah said.

"But not about her kids," Josie said. "Or so he said. You should bring them both in. Separate them. See what you can get out of them. Bring Tom Booth in as well. Celeste was obviously having some kind of heated discussion with him when Emily walked out."

"Yeah," Noah said. "There's a strange dynamic there between Celeste and Tom—and Adam. I'm not sure if it has any bearing on the case, but I'd definitely question Tom as well. He knew about Lorelei."

"Is this going to lead me to the killer though?" Mettner said.

"We don't know," Josie admitted. "But someone needs to talk to Celeste at the very least. She lied about not having a relationship with Lorelei. She lied about not knowing Lorelei's kids. She lied about when Emily walked off into the woods. What's she hiding? Listen, you've still got DNA evidence from the Mitchell crime scene which will take weeks to process. That could break things open but until then, you have to keep pulling at whatever loose threads you've got. Did Chitwood put the searchers back on the Harper's Peak mountain?"

Mettner nodded. "Police only, since Rory is considered possibly armed and dangerous."

Josie looked at Noah then back at Mettner. "Will you keep us updated?"

Mettner said, "Of course."

Josie leaned into Noah and he put an arm around her waist. "Take me home," she said.

Noah had brought Trout home from Misty's house, and the dog went into a frenzy when Josie walked through her front door. She'd been dreading coming home ever since the words "take me home" came out of her mouth. Lisette had spent many nights in their guest room. She was a regular visitor, and they'd had countless wonderful times with her in Josie and Noah's house. Even though she had lived full-time at the nursing home, she had been with them enough that knowing she would never return made the house feel empty and sad. Trout's frantic butt-wiggling and happy yips salved her wound a little bit. She dropped to her knees and let him lick her face. Then she rubbed his back and neck and ears, and when he flopped down and rolled over, his belly.

He followed her everywhere she went, even into the bathroom. When she went into the kitchen to eat some of a casserole that Misty had dropped off, he lay at her feet. She and Noah moved around one another silently, and she was glad that he didn't feel the need to talk or make her talk. He was simply there. They climbed into bed, Trout getting between them and pawing at the covers until Josie let him under. He pressed himself against her side. Noah rolled toward her and took her hand. When he fell asleep, she put his hand back onto his side of the bed. She picked her phone up from the nightstand and flipped it on. Her message count was in the hundreds, but there was only one person whose messages Josie cared about.

Trinity had sent her all the photos of the wedding they'd taken in the hospital. Josie scrolled through them one by one, lingering on the ones of herself and Noah standing beside Lisette's bed. The look of pure joy on Lisette's face was startling. There was one of Josie and Noah gazing at one another, that instant of happiness and delight after they'd made up their vows on the fly since the ones they'd written months ago were somewhere in a room at Harper's Peak. Behind them, Lisette grinned. There was one with Sawyer in the frame that gave Josie a jolt. He looked so much like his biological father, Eli Matson, it nearly took Josie's breath away. She'd seen the resemblance before, but it had never seemed so stark.

Why not? she wondered. She'd seen him plenty of times. She'd seen him several times before she knew who he was, and it had never crossed her mind that he resembled Eli or Lisette in any way. Of course, Lisette always said that both Eli and Sawyer looked more like her late husband than her.

Trout groaned when Josie threw off the covers and sprang out of bed. She tucked him back in and went downstairs. On a bookshelf in the living room, she and Noah had put several of their family albums. Josie found an old one that Lisette had given her years earlier. It was filled with photos of Lisette as a young woman, a wife and mother. There were photos of Eli growing up which Josie had often delighted in. She'd shared this album with Sawyer the first few times he had come over for dinner. He loved this album. She should make a copy of it. She should have done so ages ago. Josie flipped the pages until she found Lisette's wedding photo. Even then, Lisette's curls had been bouncy and unruly but brown, not gray. Her skin was unwrinkled and supple, and her smile was infectious. Her husband, Josie and Sawyer's grandfather, who had died long before either Josie or Sawyer came along, stood beside her. He had a more serious air about him. Lisette always said he was stoic. But in the photo, his lips curled into a bright smile. His face seemed to say, "Look at this incredible woman who agreed to marry me! Can you believe it?"

He looked just like Josie remembered Eli. Just like Sawyer.

"Shit," she mumbled.

She left the album out, so she'd remember to make Sawyer a copy of it and went to the kitchen. Her laptop was on the table. She turned it on and waited as it booted up. From upstairs came the sounds of dueling snores: Trout and Noah. Often, Noah would wake up if she got up in the middle of the night, but she knew the last few days had taken a toll on him. He would probably sleep through anything right about now.

Josie pulled up her internet browser and typed in the search terms. It took several minutes and four different websites to find what she was looking for: a wedding announcement and photo from eighteen years ago.

"Son of a bitch," she said, and went upstairs to get dressed.

CHAPTER FORTY

Josie tried to be as quiet as she could, but it didn't matter. As she suspected, Noah was completely passed out. After throwing on a pair of jeans, a T-shirt, and jacket, she left him a note. Trout's head popped up as she left it on Noah's nightstand, but when she assured him he was a good boy and told him to go back to sleep, he stuck his head back under the covers. Downstairs, she went into the garage and found a bin of old hunting, camping, and fishing stuff the two of them had accumulated over the years. Most of it was Noah's but when their old Chief, Wayland Harris, had died almost six years ago, his wife had given Josie a box of things from his office, including some of his hunting gear which he had found useful on occasion while on the job. Josie found one of Noah's flashlights and Chief Harris's night vision goggles. She changed the dead batteries in both and tucked them into her pockets.

In the car, she took her cell phone and quickly checked for messages from Mettner. There were several. They'd brought Celeste in for questioning. She admitted that she'd been on the phone with Tom while Emily was at the house. They'd been fighting over the fact that she and Adam had decided to take Emily in. Mettner suspected that Celeste and Tom were having an affair, but neither would confirm that. Celeste also claimed she never knew Rory existed. Couldn't pick him out of a line-up, she'd said. Claimed Emily was lying about a photo with her and Rory together. There was no such picture.

"I'll bet," Josie muttered.

Adam Long told the same story, Mettner related. Tom Booth admitted that many years ago he had spied on Lorelei after Celeste told him about her, especially given that her twenty acres stood in the way of them expanding the resort, but said he'd never officially met her and since he'd only followed her to and from the produce market once, he'd had no idea that she had had children. The three of them had given alibis for one another—they were all at the resort on Friday morning. Celeste said she had seen both Adam and Tom that morning. All three of them had been released. Back to square one.

Unless Josie could find Rory.

She was still in her driveway. She looked up at her dark house, knowing she should go back inside and get back into bed with her husband and her dog. Let someone else solve the case, get the bad guy. Sawyer's words haunted her. *The great Josie Quinn had to have the spotlight.* But that wasn't it. It wasn't that she wanted or needed the spotlight. Like Emily, she had compulsions when it came to her work. The worst case of her life was the missing girls' case from six years ago, and it hadn't even been her case. She'd been on suspension, but she'd pushed the envelope. All these years later, she was appalled at the behavior of that rash, brazen woman. Josie knew how important it was to follow all the rules and to not make things personal.

But she was still going to go get Rory.

Not as a police officer. She didn't even have her gun. She didn't need it. She would never use it on him. She was going because she had to. Because his mother had once rescued her from a snow and sleet storm. Because his mother had spent fifteen years trying to protect him, and now he was out there, alone, vulnerable, being hunted. A killer hunting a killer, she thought. It was fitting. Sad, but fitting. She was doing this as a concerned civilian, a friend of his little sister's. That's what she told herself. Once she found him, she'd deliver him safely to her team and let them do the rest. Let them arrest Lorelei and Holly's killer.

Josie knew that despite all her internal justifications, she was in the wrong. Otherwise, she wouldn't be doing this in the dark without telling anyone. She picked up her phone. Her finger lingered over Mettner's name. But she tossed it aside, popped her emergency brake and let her car roll silently out of the driveway. Once she was in the street, she turned it on and started driving.

It was five a.m. by the time Josie arrived at Harper's Peak. The sky was still an inky black. She knew she had about an hour and a half before sunrise. The grounds and parking lots were silent and still. Josie found a spot in the lot of the main building and left her car there. She was far enough from the lobby doors that no one at the front desk would notice her skulking around. Tucking her hands into her jacket pockets, she strode across the grounds like she belonged there. There was no rule against guests being outside during the night. There were several asphalt paths lit with tiny lanterns staked into the ground. She stayed off the paths but close enough to them to take advantage of their light. When she got near Griffin Hall, she veered off into the grass. Overhead, clouds covered the moon. Once she lost the light, she stopped and took out her night vision goggles, fixing them onto her head, and taking a look around. Satisfied that she wasn't going to unknowingly bump into any creatures or inanimate objects, she carried on. The walk took longer than she anticipated, but Josie wanted to approach the tiny church from the back. Once she reached the ridge, the moon emerged from the clouds, bathing everything in a silver light. She took off her goggles and pocketed them. Once her eyes adjusted, she skulked closer to the church. There was a door at the back. As she got closer to it, she saw the latch was broken.

Josie pushed the door open as slowly as possible, not wanting to make any noise. As she stepped inside, her eyes adjusted once more. The altar stone and pulpit cast large shadows against a flickering light in the center of the church. Four strides brought her to the edge of the altar. There, between the two rows of pews, on the floor, was Rory. He lay curled on his side on top of a sleeping bag. Next to him was a large duffel bag. Josie could see a piece of clothing sticking out of it. His personal belongings, she thought. He stared at a candle on the floor, its flame dancing.

"Rory," Josie whispered.

He jumped up, hands held out in front of him, searching all around. "Who is it?" he hissed.

Josie stepped closer, into the light. She held her hands out as well, to show him she was unarmed. "Josie Quinn," she said. "I talked to your sister, Emily, tonight."

Whipping around, he stared at her. His face was streaked with dirt. Locks of his thick brown hair stuck up on one side of his head. The single white forelock in the center of his forehead glowed in the candlelight. He wore a black sweatshirt and jeans streaked with dried blood. Josie guessed the blood belonged to Reed Bryan. A fetid combination of smells surrounded him—body odor, the coppery scent of blood, and something earthy. He froze in place but Josie noticed his knees were bent, the heels of his feet slightly off the floor. He was ready to pounce.

"I'm not going to hurt you," she said. "I just want to talk. Please."

"Is Emily all right?"

"Yes. She's fine."

His posture relaxed slightly. His hands dropped to his sides. "How did you find me?"

"You brought Holly here."

"Yeah, so?"

"A dead body in front of a church? No one is coming out here for at least a couple of weeks."

A hint of a smile crossed his face. "Hiding in plain sight."

"Rory, I came to ask you to come with me."

"Where?"

"To the police station."

He motioned to the altar behind her. "Are there a bunch of police outside?"

Josie shook her head. She took a step closer to him even though doing so made her heart tick faster. He was only fifteen, but he was taller than her. Although he was thin and wiry, Josie remembered well how quickly and brutally he had overcome her before. "No," she answered. "It's just me, and I'm not here as a police officer. I don't even have my gun. I'm not a threat to you—or to the creature."

"Pax told you that, didn't he?"

"Yes."

"The creature didn't kill my family. Neither did I."

"I know that," Josie said.

"How do you know?"

"I figured it out," Josie said.

"No one is going to believe me," he muttered, his voice growing small.

Josie took a step closer to him, arms still out, her shoulders aching. "I believe you."

"I brought Holly here so he would see what he had done, and so he would know that I wasn't going to let him get away with what he did, but I didn't kill that other lady. The one you were with that night. I didn't shoot at you."

"I know."

"I don't even have a gun. I never had a gun. That was my mom's. She kept it in the truck. It was for deer and bear and coyote. I was never allowed to touch it. Ever. I got real mad once and tried to get it out of the safe in the truck, but I couldn't. I didn't have the strength—even when I was most mad."

"I know," Josie said.

"But that doesn't matter," he insisted. "It doesn't matter if you don't believe me 'cause no one else will, and now I killed Pax's dad.

I didn't mean it. I didn't want to, but the creature… I got so mad. I don't even remember…"

"I don't want to talk about that," Josie said. "No matter what happens right now, tonight you're going to have to go to the police. Do you understand that?"

"I know. It's exactly what my mom didn't want."

"I'm sorry, Rory. I truly am, but right now I need you to help me. We both know who killed your mom and sister, and the first step to getting him put away is for you to come with me and tell my team everything you know."

"I don't want to turn him in," Rory said, an edge to his voice. "I want him to die. I want to kill him. I want to smash his face into a million pieces."

Josie sensed an amorphous tension around him, and she didn't want it to escalate. "I understand," she said.

He stopped talking. His dark eyes flashed in the candlelight. "Do you?"

"He killed my grandmother," Josie said. "The way you felt about your mom—that's how I felt about my grandmother. She raised me, protected me, tried to keep me out of trouble, tried to do her best for me even when it wasn't the best thing to do."

"That sounds like my mom."

Josie nodded. "I met your mom. You weren't in the house that day. She helped me. Now let me help you."

Before he could respond, there was a creaking noise. Then a gust of air blew through the small room. The candle was extinguished. Rory slammed into her, pushing her toward the altar. "We have to go," he said. He practically lifted her off her feet and threw her out the back door. She spun, disoriented, but then felt his hand in hers, tugging.

"Run," he said.

CHAPTER FORTY-ONE

Rory pulled her along as her eyes tried once more to adjust to the moonlight. The sky had lightened somewhat but it was still very dark, especially in the woods. Pretty soon, tree branches whipped across her face, and she stumbled over a gnarled root and fell. Rory lifted her to her feet and kept pulling her. "Run!" he commanded. "He'll kill us both."

As Josie stumbled through the forest behind him, she felt the sweat forming on his palm. Every so often a shaft of moonlight sliced through the trees. As they passed through one, Rory looked over his shoulder, beyond her, and she saw the fear in his wide eyes. He looked like a little boy. Gone was the monster who had attacked her in the Mitchell house. Gone was the monster who had beaten Reed Bryan with a shovel. This was the boy Lorelei saw—always—when she had looked at her son.

They ran until a stitch developed in Josie's side. Huffing, Rory stopped and leaned over, trying to catch his breath. Josie patted her pockets, looking for her night vision goggles, but they were gone. They must have fallen out. She still had her flashlight, though. When it appeared in her hand, Rory took it from her. "Don't," he said. "You'll lead him right to us."

"You already did, you little bastard."

The sound of the unfamiliar voice in the dark made them both jump. Josie moved closer to Rory and they pressed their backs together, both searching the darkness for the man.

"You ran in a circle, you idiots." The voice came again, this time from a different direction. Overhead, the trees kept much of the dusky light of the approaching dawn out, although Josie could still see some shadows. One in particular morphed into a man as it drew closer. A sliver of light revealed the face of Adam Long. A sinister smile curled his lips. His white hair was in disarray. He wore a T-shirt, and when he lifted the shotgun in his hands, Josie saw what looked like a deep, festering stab wound on the inside of his forearm.

Immediately she thought of the bloody handprint on Lorelei's truck. "Lorelei called you," Josie blurted, knowing from experience that more talking usually led to less shooting. Plus, if she could distract him, she could get the flashlight back from Rory, blind Adam with it and disarm him.

Adam said nothing, so Josie kept going. "You're their father. Rory and Holly."

"Is that what this little shit told you? I screwed my sister-in-law a few times, and he's telling you we had babies? This kid lives in a fantasyland."

"He didn't tell me," Josie said. "You've got poliosis. So did Holly, so does Rory. It's genetic. The white forelock."

Adam took one hand off the gun to tousle his hair. "My whole head is white, honey. Don't mean shit."

"I saw your wedding photo," Josie said. "It wasn't easy to find online but I did. Back then you had black hair. Except for one lock of white hair in the front. When Emily was at your house, she saw your wedding photo, but she didn't realize it was you. She thought it was Rory. She thought it was a photo of Celeste and Rory."

"So what? That kid's just as nutty as this one. All Lorelei did was screw and spit out messed-up kids."

"You're the one who's messed-up!" Rory shouted.

Josie snaked a hand behind her and grasped his arm. She didn't want him rushing Adam. He would get shot.

"Holly and Rory were yours," Josie said. "Emily was not. Lorelei tried to raise them on her own but as Rory got older and bigger, she couldn't control him. She wrote to you."

"No," Adam said.

"Yes," Josie insisted. "I have part of the letter."

"I burned that letter. I brought it back and gave it back to her. Then after—I burned it. I burned everything. Every photo. Every document. Her laptop and phone. Every shred of evidence that she could have used to claim her spawn were mine."

Josie continued, wanting to keep him distracted. "She wanted you to come clean, to tell Celeste the truth, and to help her with Rory. The day of the murders, Rory got violent, very violent, and she called you on her cell phone. You went there. I don't know why."

"I went there to tell her once and for all that I was not ever going to be her… whatever she wanted me to be. A dad. Whatever. You know I didn't even know who the hell she was when I first met her? We ran into each other at the produce market. I was checking stuff out for the menu. Here was this hippie chick with a hot ass. Lived in the woods. Would screw anytime I showed up. It was the perfect situation. I didn't find out who she was till I'd been married a year already. Found the paperwork in Celeste's things. The whole story came out. But it was okay because Lorelei didn't care. We were still going hot and heavy. Until she went and got knocked up. Even then, it wasn't so bad at first. She didn't care that I wasn't part of the kid's life. Until she got pregnant again, and this one started trying to kill his sister."

"It was perfect," Rory said. "You ruined it."

Adam gave a dry laugh. His teeth gleamed, a flash of white. The longer they stood there, the more Josie's eyes adjusted to the scant light rising in the sky. Sunrise was close. "Kid, you wouldn't know perfect if it stabbed you in the damn neck. Your mother? She was a manipulative slut. I told her that DNA or no DNA, I was not your father. She was fine with that. Till you went and got all messed-up in the head. Then all of sudden she wanted to play house. When I told her it was never going to happen, she was fine with that, too. Then all of a sudden, one day, she wants me to leave my wife."

"You could have left your wife," Josie pointed out. "There was nothing stopping you."

He shook his head, the moonlight casting shadows across his face. "I can't leave my damn wife. We have a prenup because, as you saw, Celeste is a cold, selfish, bitter, hateful bitch. If she found out about Lorelei, about the kids, I'd be out on the street with nothing. Less than nothing. And if you think I was going to go from the luxury of Harper's Peak to some shithole halfway house for messed-up kids in the woods without a penny to my name, you're crazy. Lorelei was crazy 'cause she thought I would. I went there to tell her never to call me again."

"You came to the house to kill her!" Rory shouted.

Josie felt him slip a little from her grasp. She dug her nails into his skin, and he stopped moving.

Adam said, "No, kid. I never meant to kill her. It's not my fault you got all psycho. You were going to kill her if I didn't jump in. That bullet? It was meant for you, you little shit. You stabbed me! With my own damn penknife!"

Josie thought she heard Rory sob. "What about Holly?" he cried.

"That's on you, too, kid. You were the one who tried to strangle her. How is it my fault she died? You're the one who left her up at the church."

Josie said, "Holly died from blunt force trauma to her head, not from strangulation."

Rory said, "She was trying to help me. I did strangle her. I couldn't help it. I got mad—the creature—I just, my hands were around her throat. That's when mom called him. But I didn't kill her. He came and he tried to kill me—"

"You smashed your mom's head off the counter. What did you expect?" Adam said.

"He came after me, tried to hit me," Rory explained. "Holly jumped on his back to try to stop him. He threw her off and she hit her head. That's when I grabbed his penknife from his belt and stabbed him. He went outside. Holly was okay. She got up. She was talking. Then he came back inside with the gun. He shot our mom. Holly and I ran out to the woods to get away."

"It was your shoe prints in the kitchen and out back," Josie said. "Size ten."

"Yeah," Rory said. "I went with her to get away from him. I thought she was okay, but then she fell down and… stopped breathing."

"She had a head injury," Josie said. "I'm sorry."

"I'm not," said Adam. "One down, one to go."

"Just one?" Josie asked. "You really didn't know about Emily?"

He gave a harsh laugh. "I had no idea. Never saw her. Lorelei was damn good at keeping secrets. But the kid's eight, and I stopped seeing Lorelei before she was born. I only went over there a few times after that when this monster was out of control."

"You were going to kill Emily, too!" Rory accused.

"Only if she recognized me," Adam said. "And she didn't."

"Does Celeste know?" Josie asked. "Does she know what you've done? She gave you your alibi for Friday morning."

Again, he laughed. The sound sent a chill down Josie's back. "Celeste alibied me because she thought I was at home asleep. I was, when she left to go meet Tom. They've been screwing around together for years now. They think I don't know. She left, Lorelei called, and I knew Celeste would be busy with Tom for a few hours, so I went to settle things with Lorelei once and for all. Celeste never caught on—not to any of it—and I'm keeping it that way. I've just got this last bit of clean-up to do." He lifted his chin in Rory's direction. "I've been looking for this little prick out here in the woods for days. I almost hit you that one day—hit a tree instead. You're always in the goddamn way."

"You were looking for Rory when my grandmother saw you," Josie said, trying to keep her voice from shaking.

"I couldn't exactly come out of the woods, could I? Especially not with this in my hands. I thought if I shot the two of you, I could just blame it on the kid. Then I'd find him, snap his neck, and make it look like an accident. Lots of places to fall out here."

Tears stung Josie's eyes, but she bit them back. The hand that was not holding onto Rory's arm tapped his other side, searching for the flashlight. He didn't seem to understand at first. Josie didn't want to make her movements too big and alert Adam, but their only chance of getting out of this alive was the flashlight. There was no reasoning with Adam. Unlike his son, he didn't have remorse for anything he did. Unlike his son, he didn't require rage to kill, only an opportunity. She tapped against Rory's arm again then used two fingers to walk her hand down toward his wrist. He shifted and her hand closed around the handle of the flashlight.

"Anything else you nitwits want to talk about while we're out here?" Adam asked. "Last chance. I can't wait for this to finally be over."

He lifted the shotgun and pointed it at them. Josie's finger found the button on the side of the flashlight. Out of the corner of her mouth, as quietly as she could, she said to Rory, "Run."

"What was that?" Adam asked. The gun quivered slightly. Josie swung her arm around and flicked the light on, shining it directly into his face.

One hand let go of the gun and flew up, shielding his eyes. "Bitch," he said.

Rory took off. Josie closed the distance between her and Adam at a run, leaping upward at the last moment and bringing the flashlight down on his head. He cried out but didn't drop the gun. Josie kicked where she hoped his knee was but nothing happened. She tried again. This time, he buckled slightly. Josie's hands reached out into the darkness until they found the barrel of the gun. She grabbed onto it and turned her body, hooking an elbow over the barrel of the gun so that it was beneath her armpit. Adam straightened up and pressed in behind her, his hand coming around and grabbing at her face. One of her hands let go of the shotgun and grabbed his fingers just as they dug into her chin. She twisted his fingers backward with a jerk. Bone cracked. Adam let out a high-pitched cry and fell to the ground.

Josie muscled the gun out of his grip. Choking up on the barrel like it was a baseball bat, she swung the stock at him. But in the dim light, her aim was off. The gun sailed through the air. With all her weight behind it, she was off-balance. Adam rose up behind her and tackled her. Josie went down hard but they were on a slight decline, so she used his momentum to roll him under her, and started punching. Her fists pummeled anything solid. It was too dark to choose her targets.

He muttered another curse. One of his arms flew up and backhanded her. Stars flashed across Josie's vision. Then she was on her back again but only for a second because they were rolling, rolling, and then falling.

Lots of places to fall out here.

She landed on top of him and felt the breath rush out of his body. Flailing, he tried to grab onto her but she crawled away, hands scrabbling over leaves, brush, and tree roots until the ground seemed to rise up, a slanted wall in front of her.

She had to climb. Coming to her knees, she moved side to side, trying to find a place to grab hold. It wasn't a complete vertical climb, but it was steep. A shaft of muted morning light punched through the trees overhead a few feet away. Josie lurched toward it, aware of the sounds of Adam moving now behind her. Rustling, thuds, and a few muttered curse words drew closer even though she was moving as quickly as her battered body would allow. In the faint morning light, she saw that a section of earth had fallen away to form the nearly vertical slope before her. Several large, gnarled tree roots jutted out from the dirt. If she could get a grip on one of them, she could get to higher ground and away from Adam. She had to jump up to snag the first one and pull with all her might, her shoulders and upper chest muscles protesting. She could run for miles but God save her, she couldn't do more than one pull-up.

But one was all she needed. She felt Adam's hand brush her boot as she hefted herself up and started to climb the slope. Following the light, she used her arms and legs to claw her way to the ledge they had fallen from. Twice, she felt Adam gaining on her, his hand brushing her feet. Kicking swiftly toward him sent him back down a few feet. At the top, the ledge jutted out just slightly, making the last hurdle particularly challenging. Josie used her elbows to hook her body onto it and try to pull herself over.

Then she froze, half her body above and half below. There, in the dawning morning light was a doe and two small fawns, silent and still. The doe's ears twitched, and her eyes stared into Josie's, as if surprised to see her there, but not quite sure she was a threat. This was the deer's territory, not Josie's. As Josie hung suspended, the doe's tail twitched and she sauntered off, out of the light and into the darkness of the trees beyond. Her progeny followed, moving more quickly to keep up.

Adam's heavy hand closed around Josie's calf. "You think you're getting away from me?" he snarled. "This isn't over, bitch. I'm gonna snap you in half. You hear me? I'm gonna kill you."

Josie felt him pulling on her leg and stiffened her upper body. In front of her was another knobby tree root sticking out of the ground. She grabbed on with both hands and turned her head, looking down over her shoulder.

"You can't stop it," she told him.

"Can't stop what? Death? You're right. No one is stopping me."

"No," Josie said. "Life. You can't stop life."

Then she used her free leg to kick him. His nose crunched beneath her boot tread, a solid but sickening sound. He let go and fell away, into the chasm below.

CHAPTER FORTY-TWO

She wandered the forest until she had enough bars on her cell phone to call for help. The sun was on the horizon, and Noah had already awakened to find her note and roused the cavalry. Within minutes of her call, state police searchers found her. They wanted to carry her out, but she walked under her own steam. They brought her out to the road that ran alongside Harper's Peak. Two ambulances and a half dozen police vehicles were scattered about. The troopers led her toward one of the ambulances but before they reached it, she saw Noah down the road, talking with Mettner, Chitwood, and Gretchen. When he spotted her, he started running. So did she.

They met in the middle of the scene, bodies crashing into one another. Josie let herself go limp in his arms, languishing in his warmth and his smell, the reassuring weight of him in her life.

"Hey," he whispered in her ear. "I promised to run toward the danger *with* you."

"I know," Josie said. "But I didn't know I was running toward danger. I only wanted to find Rory. Did you guys get him?"

"He's in the back of one of the ambulances," Noah said. "He took a bad spill when he was running away. They're thinking broken leg, but he'll need X-rays."

"Adam?"

Noah released her slightly from the embrace, enough to look down into her face although his arms were still wrapped around her waist, holding her upright. He shook his head.

Josie wondered if the fall had killed him. It didn't seem enough to kill him. It hadn't killed either one of them the first time, and she'd landed on top of him.

Noah said, "Looks like he hit his head on a rock."

Or, Josie thought, *someone hit him with a rock*. Rory had likely fallen off the same ledge they had, only he hadn't landed well. He was probably down there when they fell. Adam would have been disoriented on the second fall, maybe even had the wind knocked out of him. It wasn't out of the realm of possibility that Rory had summoned the strength to find a rock and put Adam out of commission permanently.

But could they prove anything? Was it even worth it to try? As things stood, Rory would be arrested and charged with Reed Bryan's murder. He would not be a threat to the public. Whether or not to investigate the manner of Adam's death wasn't up to Josie. She knew that the moment she saw the Chief striding toward her.

"Oh yeah," Noah whispered in her ear. "Chitwood's pissed."

"As opposed to what?" Josie mumbled.

Noah let go of her. Chitwood stabbed a finger in the air as he got closer. "Quinn, if your grandmother hadn't just died, I would have some nasty things to say to you. You're way out of line. This is unacceptable. You're on leave. No, suspension. You think you can do this rogue cop bullshit on my watch? What kind of department do you think I'm running? You don't get to do whatever you damn well please. You could have jeopardized the entire case—or cases—'cause there sure is a shitshow going on here today. What were you thinking? Don't tell me. You know why? 'Cause I don't want to hear a damn word out of your mouth. I don't want to see you for at least two weeks, and then, maybe—"

Josie talked over him. "Seems like you have some things to say, sir."

Chitwood went perfectly still. When he spoke again, she could still hear the wrath bubbling just beneath the surface of his words. "Get out of my sight, Quinn. You're suspended."

Josie turned away from him, walking back toward the ambulances. Strangely, she didn't feel upset. Or disappointed. Or angry. Or anything, really. She would try to keep her job, and there was a good chance that once he'd doled out appropriate punishment, Chitwood would let her back onto the force. She'd have to take what was coming to her. No question. But none of that mattered in the very near future, because she still had to lay her grandmother to rest.

She found Rory on a stretcher in the back of one of the ambulances. He sat up when he saw her, his features brightening. He tried to lift a hand in greeting, but it was handcuffed to the stretcher. "You're okay," he said. "I was worried."

Josie nodded. "You are, too. I'm glad."

"Just my leg, but they said it can be fixed. But I'm going to jail. Well, prison probably. For a long time."

"You need a lawyer," Josie said. "Make sure you ask for one. Your mental health history should be taken into account. I'm sure Dr. Buckley would be willing to testify on your behalf. Also, you're a minor. There might be special—"

"I'm not a good person," he said, cutting her off. "I'm going where I should go."

"Do you really believe that?" Josie asked.

"Don't you? Don't you think I'm a bad person? I used to hurt my mom and sisters. I didn't want to, but I did. I can't control this anger I have in me. No matter how hard I try, I think bad thoughts and do bad things. That makes me a bad person. My mom didn't understand that. But you did. That's why you came to get me. You understood my brain."

Josie climbed into the ambulance. Noah waited outside. She sat beside the stretcher. "Rory," she said.

But he didn't let her speak. "But you also believed me, about Adam. I think you were trying to help me even though you told me you had to turn me in. Why would you help me? If you knew what was in my head, why would you help me?"

Josie put her elbows on her knees and leaned toward him, feeling the full weight of her exhaustion finally. Noah was going to have to carry her to the car. "My grandmother said something to me yesterday, right before she died. She called my name, and I went to her and she whispered something in my ear."

Rory's upper body bent toward hers. "What? What did she say?"

"She said, 'You were worth it. You were worth all of it.'"

He stared at her, wide-eyed, for a long moment. Then he said, "What does it mean?"

Josie laughed. "It means that I was worth all the things she did for me—to raise me, to protect me, to help me, to keep me safe. I was worth all of that. I was worth every decision she made—the good ones and the bad ones. Rory, that's how your mother felt about you. You were worth it to her. All of it."

His head fell back into the pillow. He let out a lengthy sigh and closed his eyes. "Thank you," he said.

CHAPTER FORTY-THREE

One week later

Josie stood in the middle of the lobby of Bob's Big Party Skating Rink and looked around. Practically everyone she knew was there—even people she didn't know. The residents from Rockview sat at the long tables in front of the food counter, some in wheelchairs, others in the rink chairs with their walkers beside them. Most everyone else sat along the benches, changing from their shoes to roller skates. The skate floor was empty, but a large disco ball spun lazily, casting flecks of light everywhere. Josie watched as Bob, the rink's owner, and one of his employees, pushed a table into the center of the floor. On it, they placed two large vases of flowers, an eight-by-ten smiling photo of Lisette, and her urn. Once Bob had arranged it all, he walked back to Josie. "You ready?" he asked.

"Bob," Josie said. "My grandmother planned this with you. I had no idea. So am I ready? Not at all. But proceed anyway."

He laughed and walked off toward the DJ booth.

Trinity came flying at Josie, unsteady on a pair of skates. Josie caught her before she went face-first onto the ground. Trinity got her balance and looked down at Josie's skates. "Since when are you so good on roller skates?"

Josie shrugged. "We used to go all the time when I was in high school. Gram always felt bad because the first time I got invited to a skating party, which would have been my first time skating, I couldn't go. Because, well…"

Trinity made air quotes. "'Custody issues.' Yeah, that's what child abductors call that. Well, I have to tell you that this is the weirdest funeral service I've ever been to. Ever. And I'm practically a celebrity."

"You are a celebrity," Josie said.

"Well, yeah, okay, I am, and this is still the weirdest funeral. Although, having known Lisette for even a short time, I can't say I'm surprised."

The first strains of a disco song burst through the building. "I don't think she wanted us to call it a funeral," Josie said, shouting a little to be heard.

"Oh right," Trinity said. "A celebration of her life. But seriously, are you okay with this?"

Josie smiled. "Okay with the fact that my Gram is gone? No. Okay with this?" She waved a hand around the room as people started to fill the skating floor. "I'm pretty sure it beats every funeral and every celebration of life I've ever been to, and I've been to a lot."

Trinity hugged her. "I'm going to go find Drake."

Josie watched her go, skating up behind Drake on the floor, and grabbing his hand. He grinned at her. The disco music was bumping now, and people flew around the skate floor, kicking up a breeze that caressed Josie's face. It was hard not to smile at the whole thing. Which was exactly the point, Josie guessed.

Lisette for the win.

Two days after bringing Rory in, Josie had met with Lisette's attorney. Her will was unremarkable. She'd been living in Rockview for years and had no assets left, only a handful of personal items which she divided between Josie and Sawyer. Her funeral instructions, however, were another matter. Sawyer had watched as Josie opened the envelope, took out a single piece of paper, and smoothed out its deep creases. It had been in there for some time. It was dated the year Lisette had moved into Rockview.

"She changed her will last year," the attorney explained. "But left that. She said she didn't need to change it."

The page held two instructions: one was to cremate her, and two was to call Bob at the number below.

"Who the hell is Bob?" Josie had blurted.

As it turned out, Bob McCallum was the owner of Denton's oldest roller-skating rink. Josie hadn't even realized that skating rinks had survived into the twenty-first century, but Bob's Big Party was alive and well, just as it had been several years ago when Lisette had cooked up a crazy idea for her "funeral" and made Bob sign off on it.

"Your grandmother used to work at the jewelry store over on Campbell Street," Bob told Josie and Sawyer when they went to see him. "Remember?"

"Yes," Josie said.

"She sold me the engagement ring that I used to propose to my wife. Been married forty-seven years now. Best thing I ever did. I'd do anything for your Gram."

"That's obvious," Sawyer had said, but Bob completely missed his sarcasm, instead handing them another envelope, this one with detailed instructions in Lisette's handwriting about the party she wanted to throw to celebrate her life.

A few days after that, Bob's was full of people who had come to pay their respects to Lisette. Josie had expected resistance. Shannon suggested a compromise: a small service at a funeral home in the morning and then in the afternoon, the party at the rink. It had worked out well, and nearly everyone who had come to the funeral home was now at the rink, skating, enjoying food, or just dancing to the music.

Josie watched the crowd, finding Misty and Harris skating hand-in-hand. Shannon skated forward and back, weaving in and out of people while Christian held onto the wall that surrounded the floor. Josie's younger brother, Patrick, was there with his girl-friend. Mettner and Amber held hands as they moved in perfect harmony, swaying to the beat of the music. Gretchen turned out to be a wall-clinger, too, but she still looked like she was having the time of her life. Her adult daughter, Paula, had moved in with her that week, and Gretchen had brought her along. Paula's skating prowess was far better than her mother's, and Josie could see she was getting a giggle out of watching Gretchen find her skating legs. Even Chitwood had shown up, although he hadn't yet spoken to Josie, and he wasn't skating. He stayed in the food area with the Rockview crowd. Even Dr. Feist and several members of the ERT were out on the floor. Only Sawyer cut a solitary figure. He still hadn't apologized for anything he'd said the night Lisette was shot, but they were maintaining a truce and that was enough for Josie.

Josie couldn't help but think of Emily. She would probably love this, but she was with Pax now, and his aunt Karin. They were going to sell Reed's farm and move to Georgia for a fresh start. In the week since Adam Long's death, all the evidence had come back to corroborate his confession. His prints were the last unidentified set in the house. His blood type was O positive—matching the blood found on the truck. Lorelei's cell phone records showed that she had called him the morning of the murders. The case was closed. Josie only hoped that both Pax and Emily could find some peace in the coming months and years. Just like her, they had a lot of grieving ahead of them.

Arms wrapped around her waist. Josie looked down to see Noah lace his fingers over her stomach, his wedding band winking beneath the disco lights. He kissed her neck. "Are you fine?"

It was an inside joke. No matter how much of a mess she was on the inside, Josie always answered the question "Are you okay?" with "I'm fine." It never stopped Noah from asking.

"I don't know," Josie admitted.

He breathed into her hair. "I don't remember you promising to be honest in your vows. Is this like a bonus thing, or what?"

She laughed. *I have to start feeling all my feelings*, she thought, but didn't say it because the music faded, and Bob's voice came over the PA system. "Where are my newlyweds?" he called. "Someone told me we've got newlyweds in the house! Can I get Josie and Noah on the floor, please? Josie and Noah?"

Josie turned in Noah's arms. "My grandmother couldn't have planned this."

"No," he said. "I did."

To cheers, they skated onto the floor.

Bob announced, "Can I have everyone to the side, everyone to the side, please. Clear the floor for these newlyweds. This is their first skate as a married couple."

Noah caught her hand and she smiled at him "This is…"

She heard the first notes of their wedding song fill the air. 'Bless the Broken Road' by Rascal Flatts.

"Exactly as Lisette would have wanted it?" Noah finished for her.

Josie nodded and let him pull her in for a kiss.

A LETTER FROM LISA

Thank you so much for choosing to read *Hush Little Girl*. If you enjoyed the book and want to keep up to date with all my latest releases, just sign up at the following link. Your email address will never be shared, and you can unsubscribe at any time.

www.bookouture.com/lisa-regan

As always, it is an absolute delight to bring you another Josie Quinn book. If you're reading this, it means you didn't give up after what happened with Lisette. This was one of the hardest Josie Quinn books I've written, but I hope you know by now that if Lisette was going to go, this is how she would have wanted to do it. Also, this is going to force Josie to grow even more as a person and an investigator, and I hope you'll stick with her for the next portion of her journey.

In this book, much of the focus is on OCD and how it manifests in children. This is based not just on research but on deeply personal experience. I've lived this. OCD is something I am intimately acquainted with, and one of the things I hope you'll take away from this book is that OCD is so much more than simply liking things to be clean and orderly. It is challenging, to say the least, but the specialists who treat it are heroes. That said, any errors in my explanations or representations are entirely my own.

I adore hearing from readers. You can get in touch with me through any of the social media outlets below, including my website and Goodreads page. Also, if you are up for it, I'd really appreciate it if you'd leave a review and perhaps recommend *Hush Little Girl* to other readers. Reviews and word-of-mouth recommendations go a long way in helping readers discover my books for the first time. As always, thank you so much for your support and your enthusiasm for this series. It means the world to me. I can't wait to hear from you, and I hope to see you next time!

Thanks,
Lisa Regan

LisaReganCrimeAuthor

@LisaIRegan

www.lisaregan.com

ACKNOWLEDGMENTS

Wonderful readers! I cannot believe we are on Book 11! I hope that you'll continue this journey with me. The past year has been very difficult to write through with the state of the world, but your unwavering passion for this series has kept me going every single day. I am so grateful for you and to you! Thank you, thank you, thank you!

Thank you, as always, to my husband, Fred, and my daughter, Morgan, for all your patience and support. Thank you to my first readers: Dana Mason, Katie Mettner, Nancy S. Thompson, Maureen Downey, and Torese Hummel. Thank you to Cindy Doty. Thank you to Matty Dalrymple and Jane Kelly—my favorite Plot First Responders! You two are a gift. Thank you to my grandmothers: Helen Conlen and Marilyn House; my parents: William Regan, Donna House, Joyce Regan, Rusty House and Julie House; my brothers and sisters-in-law: Sean and Cassie House, Kevin and Christine Brock and Andy Brock; as well as my lovely sisters: Ava McKittrick and Melissia McKittrick. Thank you as well to all of the usual suspects for your spreading the word—Debbie Tralies, Jean and Dennis Regan, Tracy Dauphin, Claire Pacell, Jeanne Cassidy, Susan Sole, the Regans, the Conlens, the Houses, the McDowells, the Kays, the Funks, the Bowmans, and the Bottingers! I'd also like to thank all the amazing bloggers and reviewers who read the first ten Josie Quinn books or who have picked up the series somewhere in the middle. I really appreciate your kindness!

Thank you so very much to Sgt. Jason Jay for answering so many of my questions at every hour of the day or night. Thank you to Lee

Lofland for helping me work out some procedural issues. Thank you to Ken Fritz for helping me with my shooting scenario. Thank you to Marcie Riebe and Erin O'Brien Garcia for your help with all things related to social workers.

Thank you to Jenny Geras, Kathryn Taussig, Noelle Holten, Kim Nash, and the entire team at Bookouture, including my lovely copy editor and proofreader, for making this endeavor so smooth, so exciting and so damn much fun. Finally, thank you so much to one of my favorite people in the whole world, Jessie Botterill for always helping me work out every little thing and for virtually holding my hand during this very difficult chapter in poor Josie's life. I say it all the time but it's still true: I could not ever write a book without you now, and I would never want to! You are the most lovely, incredible, smart and savvy editor and I am so blessed to be doing this with you!